"*Ferren and the Angel* is that rare thing, a profou[...] is at the same time, funny, tender and wise. [...] – Isobelle Carmody, New York Times Best S[...]

"Captivating, dazzlingly original fantasy!"
– Ian Irvine, International Best Selling author

"Harland is a wonderful writer…he will take you to some pretty weird and wild places."
– Jack Dann, author of *The Memory Cathedral* and *Shadows in the Stone*

IFWG's Masters of Fantasy
line of titles

Ferren and the Angel

The Ferren Trilogy
Book 1

By
Richard Harland

Ferren and the Angel

All Rights Reserved

ISBN-13: 978-1-922856-29-6

Copyright ©2023 Richard Harland

V1.1 (Second Edition)

Printed in Garamond and Bricktown.

IFWG Publishing International
Gold Coast

www.ifwgpublishing.com

ACKNOWLEDGEMENTS

My heartfelt thanks to all those who have supported this book throughout its many stages: from Van Ikin, who believed in it from the earliest days, to Louise Zedda-Sampson, who propelled it into life a second time, and of course to Gerry Huntman, who made it happen.

My thanks also to Dmetri Kakmi, the very best of editors, and to Selwa Anthony, my queen of literary agents.

Next, a big thankyou to Noel Osualdini and Stephen McCracken, the team at IFWG who contributed so much care and labour to the final product. And not forgetting Elena Betti, who tolerated the demands of an interfering author and created a cover far over and above all possible demands.

Lastly—as always—a thankyou beyond thankyous to my wife Aileen for her unfailing encouragement during periods of authorial self-doubt, and for keeping my feet on the ground during periods of authorial self-absorption.

TERREN'S WORLD 3000AD

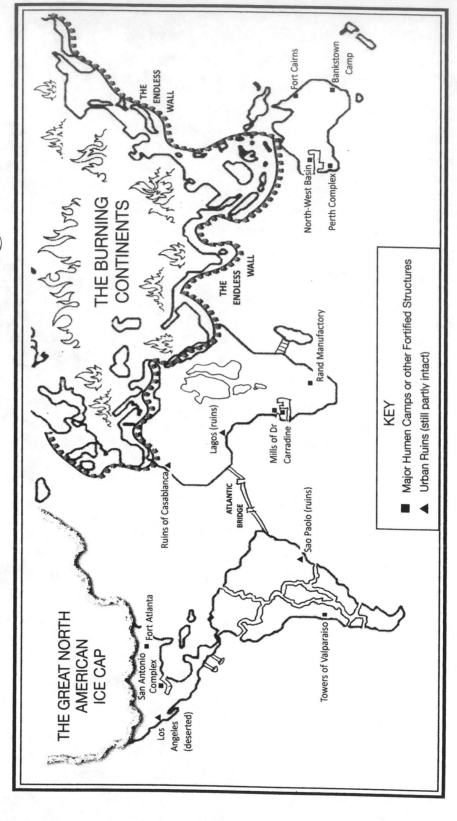

THE GREAT NORTH AMERICAN ICE CAP

THE BURNING CONTINENTS

THE ENDLESS WALL

THE ENDLESS WALL

Fort Cairns

Bankstown Camp

North-West Basin

Perth Complex

Rand Manufactory

Lagos (ruins)

Mills of Dr Carradine

Ruins of Casablanca

ATLANTIC BRIDGE

Sao Paolo (ruins)

Fort Atlanta

San Antonio Complex

Los Angeles (deserted)

Towers of Valparaiso

KEY

■ Major Humen Camps or other Fortified Structures

▲ Urban Ruins (still partly intact)

PART ONE

THE PEOPLE

1

Strange and fearful noises in the night. *Daroom! Daroom! Daroom!*—a deep-down thunder like an endless drum. Then a sharp splitting sound like the crack of a whip: *Kratt! Kratt! Kratt!* The noises throbbed through the earth and echoed across the sky.

There were voices too. *Eeeeeeyah!* A high-pitched scream passed over from horizon to horizon. Then laughter broke out in hoots and whoops. And away in the distance, grave booming words of incomprehensible giant speech:

"Fatum!"

"Excidium!"

"Mors et maleficii!"

It was the worst night in a long time. The People lay close together in their Dwelling Place. The walls of the derelict building protected them at the sides, but there was no roof overhead. They had only their blanket, a single waterproof blanket big enough to cover the whole tribe. They huddled on the floor of the Dwelling Place with the blanket over their heads.

As leader of the tribe, old Neath lay in the middle with the others around him. Closest in were the older partnered males and females. They were all wide awake, scarcely daring to breathe, staring up at the underside of the blanket. They had been through many bad nights before, but the fear never eased.

Squeezing in around them were the nursing mothers with infants. The infants whimpered pitifully at every louder *Kratt!* of the whip. When the laughter and booming voices started up, they burst into tears.

"Hush!" "Shush!" "Shush now!" their mothers whispered, and drew them in closer to the muffling warmth of their bodies.

Next around lay the unpartnered adult males and females. The males had been drinking heavily, and most of them were asleep and snoring. But still they tossed and turned and thrashed out suddenly with their arms as if to keep something at bay. Even in sleep the terrors of the night had invaded their dreams.

As for the older adolescent children, they had been pushed out to the furthest corners of the huddle. They lay curled up in small defensive balls, trying to keep away from the night air which seeped in under the edges of the blanket. They had their eyes tightly closed and their hands clamped desperately over their ears.

But still the terrors of the night intensified. Now there were lights outside too. The blanket was no protection. Unearthly illuminations pierced through the weave of the rough fibre. Flashes and flickers, colours and shadows…

The People shuddered and prayed for it all to pass.

2

Only one of the People was different. Ferren lay with the other adolescents in the outer ring of bodies under the blanket. But he was not curled up into a ball. He had lifted the edge of the blanket and was peering out into the night.

He could see movement all over the sky. Vague multitudes of shapes like wings swam slowly behind the clouds. One side of the sky was glowing bright, where distant tongues of red fire stabbed upwards from below. The tips of the tongues showed just above the wall of the Dwelling Place.

There were pale oval globes too, swarms and swarms of them. At first they were high in the sky, but as Ferren watched, they descended lower and lower. They moved with a looping, spiralling motion, in a kind of aerial dance. They seemed to be moving towards the red tongues of fire.

He knew what to expect. It wasn't the first time he had watched Heaven attacking the Earth. Suddenly the globes began to shoot forth flashes of blinding light. On—off! On—off! On—off! On—off!

He was momentarily dazzled. By the time he had blinked away the dazzle, the globes were ascending once more. They were like wafting sparks borne up on a draught of air.

But one globe wasn't ascending. It was hurtling across the sky, very low down. It seemed to be coming straight towards the Home Ground.

He stared and wriggled forward for a better look.

Still the globe came hurtling onwards. It was completely out of control. It bobbled and wobbled, struggling to rise but always losing height. The pale oval shape was rimmed with an ominous red glow.

He began to draw back under the blanket again. The thing was getting too close for comfort. Surely it wasn't going to crash on top of the Dwelling Place?

Larger and larger it loomed. Now he could see some sort of figure inside, with wings and yellow robes. Some sort of Celestial! Perhaps it was an angel? The figure twisted and turned inside its globe, and there came a sound like a thin silvery wail:

Ieeeeeee!

He pulled the blanket sharply over his head and buried his nose in the ground.

Whishhhh!

The globe whistled over the top of the Dwelling Place and hit the ground somewhere nearby.

Crump!

A dull hollow-sounding explosion. Then nothing. Silence. He breathed a sigh of relief. He lifted the edge of the blanket and peered out once more.

There was no smoke or light visible above the Dwelling Place wall. He traced the course of the globe's final plunge, trying to work out where it must have come down. Somewhere near the Beaumont Street ruins, he calculated. Probably out on the open Plain in the grass beyond the ruins.

Up above, the war in the sky continued unabated. The ascending globes had formed in a line and were streaming off on another trajectory. The strange booming voices grew louder, the red tongues of fire shifted direction.

But Ferren had something else to think about. He grinned to himself. A Celestial from Heaven's army! Crashing so close to the tribe's Home Ground! And he had watched it all! Would there be anything left to see after the crash? What an opportunity…if he dared…

3

She was Miriael the Fourteenth Angel of Observance. She lay on her side, stretched full length on the ground. Her yellow robe was in tatters, her wings were twisted beneath her, her shining golden hair was spread across the ground. The protective envelope of her globe had ruptured, and her aura drifted away, dissolving into the air like a mist of light.

She was still conscious but incapable of movement. She felt utterly, horribly exposed. As her aura dissolved, the materiality of the terrestrial world began to invade her senses.

First it was smell—the smell of the earth. Thick and heavy, with the darkness of soil and the bitterness of crushed grass. Disgustingly physical! To her, it was the very smell of corruption.

Then it was touch—the touch of cool night air on her skin. Pinprick by pinprick, it crept across her shoulders, fingered down her back, delved around her legs. The tiny sensations were agony to her pure spiritual senses. She winced as if burned by fire or stabbed by knives.

Never before had she experienced anything so gross and crude. Her enveloping globe had always kept her apart from the terrestrial atmosphere. This physical contact was too much to endure! Why hadn't she died of the shock? Why hadn't she winked instantly out of existence? Wasn't that what was supposed to happen?

She was a junior warrior angel, so not on the lofty level of the higher orders and archangels. But still, her being was immaterial spirit—it was impossible for her to survive unprotected on the Earth. She didn't *seek* extinction, some small part of her resisted. But if it had to happen, let it come quickly!

The invasion continued. Now the grass was touching her too. She could distinguish every separate blade of it, unbearably rough and rasping. And under the grass, the humps of pebbles, the gritty grainy soil. It was like a whole landscape imprinting itself on her skin.

Worst of all, the cold night air had begun to go down into her throat. She choked and coughed and gasped. Deeper and deeper it penetrated, right inside her chest. Unbelievable! She wanted to scream with the sheer intensity of it. Too much! Too much!

It was filth, it was foulness, it was degradation! She was being defiled! She prayed for unconsciousness, she prayed for it all to be over! She tried to crush the small unworthy part of her that resisted.

Yet the hours went past, and still she hadn't winked out of existence.

4

Ferren had formed his plan for tomorrow. Yes, he *did* dare! He would slip away early and investigate on his own. None of the People would come with him; they dreaded anything to do with Heaven or Celestials. In fact, they never ventured out beyond the Home Ground, certainly not as far as the Beaumont Street ruins. They would try to stop him if they knew what he was planning. But he had ways to avoid attention.

The thought of doing something so dangerous and forbidden made his heart beat faster. He still had his head out beyond the edge of the blanket, but the activity in the sky was now dying down and the flashes of light had stopped. There was only the *Daroom! Daroom!* of the drumming and the occasional *Kratt!* of the whip.

Suddenly he discovered that someone was lying up against him under the blanket. And not just lying up against him, but holding on hard and tight. Someone's arm was clasped over his legs, someone's head pressed in against his waist. He twisted round to take a look.

"Who're you?"

Two wide eyes looked back up at him. "Who're *you?*"

"Ferren."

"Thought so."

"Who're *you* then?"

There was no answer, but Ferren had already recognised her. It could only be Zonda, the daughter of Neath and the young beauty of the tribe. She had hardly seemed aware of his existence before.

"What you doing?" she demanded

"Nothing."

"Yes you are. You're sticking your head outside. What's happening?"

"It's going quieter."

"Is it nearly finished?"

"Just about. Hey, did you hear that globe go over before? Right above us."

"What's a globe?"

"Like a bubble, sort of egg-shaped. I don't know what they're made of."

"Brrr!" She shivered against him.

"I saw a Celestial inside, too. I think it was an angel."

"You look at 'em, do you?"

"I never saw one close enough to tell before."

"Your sister said she saw an angel. She used to stick her head out in the middle of the night like you."

Ferren clammed up at once. He'd spoken without thinking, but the mention of his sister reminded him what was liable to happen to anyone who acted out of the ordinary.

"Don't talk about Shanna," he muttered.

There was silence between them for a while. Then Zonda yanked on his leg. "Hey! How come you're not scared?"

"What?"

"Looking out at the war going on."

"Who says I'm not scared?"

"I says. I bet you do it every night."

"No, 'course not."

"Yes you do. You oughter be scared but you're not. You're weird."

Ferren grimaced to himself. He was really running a risk now. If Zonda reported him to her father...

He made a move to draw back under the shelter of the blanket like everyone else. But Zonda stopped him with a whisper.

"Don't move."

"Why not?"

"I like it like this. I'm comfy here."

"But I—"

"You gonna do something about it?"

"No."

"Good. 'Cos I'm gonna go to sleep."

She pressed into him again. Not so hard and tight this time, but warm and heavy. Her full plump body weighed softly against his legs.

He listened without moving, and after a while her breathing changed to a slow, regular rhythm. She had fallen asleep, still holding on to him. He didn't know what to think.

5

Early morning sunlight came streaming in over the brick walls of the Dwelling Place. The People had rolled away their blanket and now stood around blinking and bleary-eyed. Their heads were lowered, their shoulders hunched, their arms hung heavily at their sides.

They had broad, squat bodies, thick necks, small eyes and big feet. Their hair was black and matted with dirt. The males wore strips of grey woven cloth around their loins, the females wore larger pieces of cloth that also covered their breasts.

"Let us pray!"

It was Neath calling to them. The People moved across and knelt down around him. In unison they recited their morning prayer.

"Thanks be we are safe and all right,
Thanks be for the day and the light,
Thanks be that Heaven's power did not smite,
Thanks be we have come through the night."

They intoned a solemn "Amen" and whacked their foreheads with the flat of their hands. Then they turned to listen to Neath.

Neath cleared his throat. He was scarcely beyond middle age, but looked older than his years. His face was etched with lines of care, his body was bent as if under some great burden. When he spoke, his voice was slow and quavery.

"Thanks be indeed," he said. "Last night we were in deadly peril again. When Heaven makes such attacks, we could get wiped out at any time."

The People shuddered at the memory. There were moans and cries and exclamations of horror.

"Something flew over us!"

"A terrible thing in the middle of the night!"

"So close!"

Neath also shuddered, but controlled himself and continued.

"Thanks be that our allies defended the Earth and fought for us against Heaven. Remember and rejoice, that the Humen are our allies."

The People remembered, though they didn't rejoice. They bowed their heads humbly.

"Remember and rejoice," Neath repeated. "Especially you young ones. Follow the Old Ways and you'll come to no harm. Stay low, stay quiet, stay out of sight!"

The People repeated it like a chant: "Stay low, stay quiet, stay out of sight!"

"Take no chances. Don't go looking for trouble. Even when things seem bad, they can always get worse." Neath raised his arms in a gesture of blessing. "May your totems keep you safe and sound and solid through the day."

Once more the People whacked their foreheads with the flat of their hands.

6

Ferren worked with old Shuff in the Blackberry Patch. But Shuff was still taking his time over breakfast in the Dwelling Place. He wouldn't be ready to start work for a long while yet.

Ferren headed towards the Blackberry Patch as if heading off to work. Then, as soon as he was sure nobody saw him, he ducked down and turned away under cover of the High Hedge. He had his own special secret routes across the Home Ground.

There were cheeps and twitterings as he sped along. The High Hedge was home to three dozen birds, tethered and domesticated and turned into regular egg-layers. At the end of the Hedge, he peered out over a flat concrete platform with four metal poles sticking up at the corners. This was the part of the Home Ground called the Garage. In the centre of the platform was the People's fire, a perpetually smouldering pile of twigs and dry leaves. Urlish, who tended the fire, was still at her breakfast in the Dwelling Place.

Ferren crossed the Garage, then clambered over the Fence, an age-old structure of wooden posts and wire. Turning left, he followed the outside wall of a roofless ruin known as Number Forty-Two. The ruin served as a pen for blue-tongue lizards, which were an important part of the tribe's food supply. Lizards scuttled about on the other side of the wall as he passed, and he could hear someone humming a tuneless ditty. No doubt one of the lizherders had arrived for work, either Tunks or Burge.

Still moving in a crouch, he ghosted along to the Front Gardens. Unce and Dugg were the workers here, already busy among rows of carrots. He lowered himself flat to the ground and crawled along in a drainage channel between peas and beans. The green leaves of the vegetables kept him hidden from view.

He continued on across the Driveway through rows of tomatoes until he reached the stand of corn growing next to the Creek. Shielded by the tall glossy plants, he rose once more to his feet. No one had yet spotted him or called out. Another ten paces brought him to the bank of the Creek.

This was the boundary of the Home Ground. He crossed by way of a natural causeway, leaping surefooted from stone to stone. Then he plunged in among the springy head-high reeds of Rushfield on the other side. Now he was safely out of anyone's sight and could afford to walk more slowly.

The dry litter of old broken stems rustled and crunched under his feet. He kept on going to the edge of the Rushfield, parted the final screen of reeds and looked out across the open Plain. As always, the immensity of it took his breath away.

So wide and flat! The endless expanse of grass stretched away to the horizon. Everything in his upbringing told him it was alien and dangerous. Yet already he had secretly explored some distance along the course of the Creek and had visited several of the nearest ruins.

He surveyed the ruins now. Pale, scattered remnants of concrete, brick and rubble, they were smaller versions of the Home Ground itself. They rose up from the grass like lonely islands in a green ocean.

Closest of the ruins was Beaumont Street—and a tingling thrill of fear and excitement ran through him as he studied it. Where exactly had the Celestial crashed to the Earth? He calculated an approximate area to explore, then took a deep breath and dived forward in a rush.

Grass brushed around his waist with a silken hiss. It was like swimming through shimmering green water.

7

By Ferren's best guess, the area of the crash was a little to the right of Beaumont Street, and perhaps a bit beyond. His heart was in his mouth as he approached. What would remain of a Heavenly globe after it hit the ground? What would have happened to the winged figure inside?

He refused to let himself dwell on his fears. One part of him longed to look back to the security of the Home Ground, but instead he concentrated on his search and scanned before him as he walked. He didn't want to come upon danger unawares.

Five minutes of searching—and he spotted something ahead. He stopped in his tracks and stared at a strange brightness in the grass. The grass itself was different too, as he could see when he stretched up on tiptoe. Over a wide circular space, the waist-high blades had been crushed and flattened. This was the place!

He ducked his head and approached cautiously, very cautiously. Ten paces along, he paused to peer out over the top of the grass. Now he could see that the brightness came from a thousand tiny spots of glitter sprinkled across the ground.

Again he crouched, even lower, submerging completely into the grass. He advanced with infinite care, watching where he stepped, not making the slightest sound. The grass thinned out in front of him as he came towards the flattened area. Any moment now…

He was expecting to see the globe or what remained of it. Instead he saw *her*.

His jaw dropped and his eyes went wide. A long slender body, white feathered wings and shining golden hair! Never had he seen such a being in his life. This must be the yellow-robed figure inside the globe of light last night, definitely an angel such as his sister had described. But now the angel was without her globe, and her robe was in tatters.

Still, there was a faint radiance to her skin, which didn't have quite the same opacity as ordinary skin. Ferren gazed in fascination, awe and fear. Angels were supposed to have tremendous powers, and this one might do terrible things to him. At present she lay on her back, motionless, with her eyes closed. But if she sprang suddenly into life…

Yet the fascination was stronger than the fear. Hardly aware of what he was doing, he moved forward from the shelter of the grass to take a closer look.

He didn't think of her as beautiful. She was too different from the People to make comparisons. By the standards of the tribe, she was out of all proportion, abnormally long and thin. He could only think of her as a miraculous sort of oddity.

Nearer and nearer he stepped, carefully avoiding the glitter on the grass. He was as if hypnotised. He walked in a half-circle around her, observing the perfect formation of every feather in her wings, the perfect smoothness of her unblemished skin. In spite of the violence of the crash, her body bore no marks or signs of injury. Yet she appeared to be dead or dying.

Then he heard a tiny sound—what was that? He took another look at her face. Her lips surely hadn't been open before, but they were open now. As he watched, her throat moved, and a faint dry rasping came from her mouth.

She was trying to say something. Had he heard the word "water"? Of course, she wasn't addressing *him*; her eyes remained shut, and she could hardly have known he was there. But she was pleading and praying for something.

He took a step closer, and the rasping came again. This time he couldn't even guess what she was trying to say. But the sound was so dry, her throat must be parched, she *must* be thirsty.

He forgot to be afraid. "Do you want water?" he asked.

There was no reply that he could understand, just more rasping and gasping. Perhaps she hadn't even heard him. She seemed to be in a very sick state.

Every lesson he'd ever learned growing up told him to let her die. She was a soldier in Heaven's army, therefore an enemy. Yet somehow he couldn't do it.

"I'll bring you some water," he said.

The sounds from her throat grew more irregular, then stopped altogether. She was surely very close to death, but she wasn't dead yet. Although a drink of water might not help much, it was the only help he could bring.

He stepped back, straightened to his full height and surveyed the Plain. He knew where the Creek flowed not far away, and he knew a method for carrying water. He nodded to himself and set off running.

8

Five minutes later he was back. The water he brought was contained in the broad leaf of a water lily, which he held like a bowl in his cupped hands. Walking with smooth, fast strides, he had scarcely spilled a drop.

The angel still lay on her back in the middle of the flattened grass. Her arms were at her sides, her wings outspread beneath her.

"Here's some water for you," he announced.

There was no response. Balancing the cupped leaf, he came closer.

"Here!" He raised his voice. "Water!"

She opened her mouth and uttered the faintest of sounds. Whether or not she had heard him, she didn't open her eyes or turn towards him.

He had a problem, he realised. Bringing her water was the easy bit, but how to let her drink it? Obviously she couldn't sit up and take the water-lily leaf from him...and even if she could, he shrank at the thought of her hands making contact with his. In any case, she'd probably spill the water by not holding the leaf the right way.

But he couldn't give up now. The only possibility was to hold his cupped hands above her and trickle water from the leaf into her mouth. At least she was in the right position for that. Perhaps it was what she wanted, since her mouth was already open...

Hardly daring to breathe, he edged forward. He was terrified that her limbs would suddenly jerk and touch him. So far, though, she remained perfectly motionless. There was just space enough to fit his foot between her wing and arm and hair on the ground. He advanced one foot and reached forward in a half-kneeling crouch.

The feathers of her wing were immaculately white, her outspread hair was like spun gold... He forced himself to concentrate. He held his hands with the leaf six inches above her parted lips and very gently began to pour.

Water trickled down over her cheeks and chin. But some at least went into her open mouth. He continued to pour and saw the movement of her throat as she swallowed. Yes! She was drinking!

Then something extraordinary happened. Her body lit up with a weird, unearthly radiance.

SPUKKKK!

He jumped away just in time as a great flash of light exploded from her. Stumbling and falling backwards, he felt the force of it pass over him. He hit the ground, wrapped his arms over his head and buried his nose in the dirt.

In his mind, he imagined himself battered, pounded, pulverised. But, after lying quiet for a while, he discovered he wasn't actually hurt. He unwrapped his arms, lifted his head and looked round. The grass was no more flattened than before. In one wet hand, he still held the scrunched-up remnant of the water lily leaf.

I survived, he thought. *It was nothing so bad after all.*

He turned to face the angel and saw that the sudden unearthly radiance had gone from her body. Whatever she'd been doing had finished. On all fours, he approached her again.

She still had her eyes closed and her mouth open. Now, though, there was a movement he hadn't noticed before. A very gentle movement, in-out, in-out, in-out. She was breathing!

He grinned to himself. She looked more peaceful too, so perhaps he *had* helped her. Perhaps she needed the light to come out of her like that. Perhaps that was how an angel got over her sickness…

He watched for a while, but there were no further changes. He rose to his feet and spoke a farewell word to her.

"Goodbye now. I hope you're feeling better. I hope a drink was what you needed."

She gave no sign of having heard, so he turned away and started for home. By this time old Shuff would be at work in the Blackberry Patch and wondering why his assistant was missing. Ferren had already stayed far longer than he'd intended.

At the edge of the area of flattened grass, though, he couldn't resist a last lingering look. For one long moment, he gazed transfixed. Even sprawling and motionless, she had a perfect grace about her. He imagined how effortlessly she would soar through the air…

"I'll come again and check on you this afternoon," he promised, more to himself than her. Then he plunged into the tall grass and headed back to the Home Ground.

9

Ferren got into trouble with Shuff, as he'd expected. He tried his best excuses, but the old man didn't believe any of them.

"There's something different about you, boy. I don't know what it is, but I don't like it."

"I'm the same as anyone else," Ferren protested.

"No." Shuff shook his head. "You're tricksy."

The old man had a broken nose, and half of his teeth were missing.

When he spoke, his jaw worked round and round as though chewing on something.

"Bad blood in you," he said. "Bad blood in all your family."

Ferren gritted his teeth and looked away. His mother and father had been taken by the Selectors when he was too young to remember, but his sister Shanna had been taken only the year before last. He remembered *that* scene as vividly as yesterday.

"You need to sort yourself out," Shuff went on. "You're too jumpity and restless and having ideas. You need to learn the ways and leave that other stuff behind. How old are you?"

"Fifteen."

"Right. And how old was your sister when she was taken?"

"Seventeen."

"That's the age to watch out for, boy. Your sister left it too late to change."

Ferren knew what was coming next. He wished he could block his ears to Shuff's words—and block his mind to the memory, too.

"Tried to hide before the Selectors arrived, she did. She knew they'd pick her for military service. She left you with your aunt Meggen and hid herself in the Rushfield. Even had a stock of food, all planned. You maybe don't remember, boy, but the Selectors stayed two nights until she was found."

As if I could ever forget, thought Ferren. Shanna had sworn him to secrecy, and he'd played dumb for two and a half days.

"We all had to suffer because of her," Shuff went on. "And when we found her, do you know what happened? When the Selectors took her away, do you know what you did?"

"Yes," muttered Ferren. But it made no difference—Shuff intended to tell him anyway.

"You clung to her, boy. Wouldn't let go. She went off walking between them, and you kept hanging on to her and crying out. Even *she* was trying to make you let go. One of the Selectors bashed you to make you stop. And you were still trying to follow when they led her off across the Plain. Meggen and the women had to hold you back. Like you wanted to be taken too."

And I did, thought Ferren. In his eyes, Shanna had been the whole of his remaining family. The emotion rising in his throat was as sharp and painful now as it had been two years ago. But he wouldn't show it in front of Shuff.

"Yes, a bad sign," the old man continued. "We all said so. 'He'll go the same way soon enough,' we said. I'm telling you this for your own good, boy. You keep on being tricksy, there's no hope for you."

"I'll try and be more sound and solid," said Ferren, and put on his special dumb look with hanging jaw and glassy eyes. It was a look that Shanna had made him practice in the weeks before she went to hide in the Rushfield. "I'll try and be more like you."

"The sooner the better." Shuff accepted the flattery at face value. "And make sure you're here when you're meant to start working."

10

Shuff's warnings were nothing new, and their work for the day went on like any other day. The blackberry bushes were in flower, and Ferren's task was to collect insects that the lizherders would feed to the blue tongue lizards. His secondary task was to collect dry twigs for Urlish's fire. He could perform both tasks without thinking.

Yet today was not like any other day for him. Even as he crawled among the bushes, the image of the angel stayed constantly before his eyes. His discovery this morning had changed the colour of his mind.

He wondered if she was still lying as he had left her. The thought that she might fly off before he returned made his stomach lurch for a moment. But only for a moment. Hopefully she would recover, but not as quickly as that. He began planning for his afternoon visit.

A proper bowl to fill with water...yes, that was the first thing. He knew there were spare bowls kept in the Store. Then food... What kinds of food did an angel eat? He should take a variety, perhaps. There were many kinds of food also kept in the Store.

He made his preparations through the day, and was ready when Shuff came up to him late in the afternoon.

"Okay, give me what you've got, and I'll take it across."

Ferren handed over his basket filled with all the insects he'd collected, along with a bundle of twigs. Shuff emptied Ferren's basket into his own, then passed it back.

"No slacking off now. You work till dinnertime and make up for the time you missed this morning. I'll be checking."

The old man tucked Ferren's bundle of twigs under his arm and went off. He would first take the insects to the lizherders and stay watching while the lizards were fed. Then he would take the twigs to Urlish and hang around talking until dinnertime.

As soon as he'd gone, Ferren dived in under one particular bush and brought out a second bundle of twigs and second pile of insects that he'd been gathering secretly all day. He refilled his basket with the insects and left the twigs alongside. Then he set off to the Store.

Oola and Meggen were at work on the patch of ruins called the Shed, drying vegetables and strips of lizard flesh on fallen sheets of corrugated iron. He slipped past, bending almost double so they couldn't see him. Then he ducked down by the side of the Sunflower Field, where Zonda and Moya were busy plucking petals from the glorious yellow heads. The thick glossy leaves hid him from their view. A final detour around the Swimming Pool brought him to the brick walls of the Dwelling Place.

The Store was in one corner in the Dwelling Place. He launched off the ground with a mighty spring and hauled himself up on top of the wall. He would be exposed if any of the People raised their eyes in his direction, but that wasn't likely to happen. Their eyes were almost always directed down on their tasks.

He saw Neath in a different corner of the Dwelling Place, but there was no danger there. As leader of the tribe, Neath kept a tally of passing days with scratch-marks on the wall of his counting-corner. Right now, though, he was snoozing.

Picking his spot, Ferren jumped down into the Store. Bags, bowls and baskets were stacked all around, rich food aromas filled the air. A curtain separated this corner of the Dwelling Place from the area where the People slept.

He found an empty bowl for water and a bag for food. Into the bag he put fresh mushrooms, eggs, carrots, sunflower seeds, dried peas and dried beans. He doubted that an angel would eat dried strips of lizard flesh.

11

ive minutes later, he was out on the Plain and heading towards the Beaumont Street ruins. He went by way of the Creek and scooped up water in the bowl. Already the sun was low in the sky; not long until dinnertime.

He found the circular patch of flattened grass, still bright with spots of glitter. The angel hadn't flown off… In fact, she lay exactly the same as when he'd left her. She didn't look dead, but she didn't look very alive either.

Cautiously, step by step, he approached across the flattened grass. Still she remained motionless. He held out the bowl of water in one hand and the bag of food in the other.

"I'm back," he announced. "I've brought you a proper bowl of water this time. And food to eat."

She made no response, and her eyes remained closed. As he came close, though, he saw faint signs of movement and breathing.

"You should eat," he told her. "Then you'll get your strength back."

Still no response.

"I'll leave these with you, shall I? You can eat and drink when you're ready."

He placed the bowl and bag beside her, then headed back into the tall grass. But he didn't leave. Instead, he took up a position where he could watch her through a screen of green, seeing but unseen. Perhaps she would eat if she thought he wasn't around.

She didn't, however. After waiting several minutes, he frowned and gave up. What was wrong with her?

He stepped out in the open and came up close again. Unless she was wounded somewhere under her yellow robe, she didn't appear to be injured. In fact, her skin looked better than this morning, a bit more like ordinary skin.

You can't let yourself starve to death. He addressed her in his mind. *If you won't eat for yourself, I'll feed you.*

The mere idea made his heart beat faster. But once he'd thought it, he couldn't drop it. He would do the same as he'd done this morning, only this time with food instead of with water. And this time he would be prepared for her supernatural reaction. It hadn't hurt him then, so it wouldn't hurt him now.

He chose a small mushroom, broke it in halves and went down on one knee in the space between her wing, arm and hair. Her mouth, though open, wasn't quite wide enough. Very tentatively, he touched one half of mushroom against her lip—and felt a strange tingling sensation run up his arm.

He drew back and inspected his arm, but there was no visible effect. The tingle hadn't actually hurt him. Bending over her again, he discovered that her lips had parted further at the touch. Wide enough now!

He held one half of the mushroom above her mouth and dropped it in. Then, immediately afterwards, the other half. He didn't wait for her reaction, but backed away fast.

It was the same as this morning, only longer-lasting. Her body filled with a radiance, which flared to a dazzling intensity, then exploded outwards. Ferren, on his backside, retreated further and further away. But this time he didn't stop watching.

SPUKKK! SPUKK! SPUKKK! SPUKK!

The radiance came out in wave after wave. The angel's body was surrounded by a pool of flickering, crackling brightness that turned everything to shades of black and white.

SPUKKK!…SPUKK!…Spukk!…pukk!…

Gradually the brightness lost intensity. Now the waves were sputtering and spasmodic, less and less frequent. There was a final shuddering burst of light, then no more. The grass returned to its normal colour. All the radiance had spilled out of her body.

He stayed at a safe distance until he was sure it was over. The angel uttered a drawn-out moan, then rolled on her side away from him. He rose to his feet and approached once again.

With another moan, she rolled onto her back, then rolled to face him. He stopped and froze, heart pounding. Her eyes were open!

She was looking straight at him, yet her gaze was somehow unfocused.

Did she even see him? Her eyes were as blue as the bluest of skies.

"Hello." He struggled to speak. "Are you feeling better?"

Her voice was clear and musical, like a chiming of bells. "Go. Away."

"I'll come again later, shall I?"

"Go. Away."

He stood his ground, but he was still in a state of shock. After a while, she closed her eyes again.

"I'll come again tomorrow," he said, and backed away as far as the tall grass. Then he turned on his heel and started to run. He was delighted, fearful and marvelling all at the same time.

The sight of the sun now touching the horizon reminded him that it was dinnertime in the Home Ground.

12

This evening's dinner was a thick stew of carrots, corn and lizard-flesh, which the cooks served out in the usual three bowls. The biggest bowl was for the adult males, the second bowl was for adult women and their infants, while the third and smallest bowl was for younger members of the tribe neither adults nor infants. A tiny amount of stew was put aside in a special bowl for the religious ceremony.

The ceremony was performed by twilight immediately after dinner. Neath, carrying the special bowl, led the People out through the Back Door to the Sanctuary where their totems were housed. They sat in a half-circle around the miniature shelter, which was built of loose bricks with a basketwork roof. Neath lifted out the four totems and lined them up side by side on the ground.

There was a can of fly spray, a plastic cigarette lighter, a wind-up alarm clock, and a Baby Jane Ma-ma doll. They were all polished and clean and maintained in perfect condition. The People knelt in a half-circle while Neath intoned the first prayer.

> "For the day in the sun,
> For the work that is done,

O great Ancestral totems
We thank and praise thee."

He pointed to each totem in turn. "See our Fly Spray Can with holy words written upon it! See our Alarm Clock with such tiny knobs and levers! Gaze upon our Cigarette Lighter with the sacred fluid inside! And our wonderful Baby Jane, so perfect, round and shapely!"

The People responded with reverent murmurs.

"What skill!"

"What craft!"

"The work of the Ancestors!"

"Yes," said Neath. "Our Ancestors. They have departed, but they have left us these reminders of themselves. To keep and preserve in memory of the Good Times."

"Ahhhhh," the People sighed a great sigh. "The Good Times. Tell us again about the Good Times."

"It was long long ago," began Neath. "In the Good Times, our Ancestors ruled the whole Earth. Metal and glass and stone obeyed their will. They built thousands of cities, thousands and thousands of buildings. So tall and white! And streets between the buildings, where moto-cars went riding around. All the buildings and streets in our time are mere remnants of what was there in the Good Times."

The eyes of the People were wet and shining.

"All lost!"

"All gone!"

"Only the ruins remain," said Neath sadly. "Our Ancestors were very very mighty, but we are very very small. Yet still we have their precious things, to be near us and protect us through the nights."

He raised the can of fly spray aloft in both hands.

"Behold!" he cried. "The Guardian Fly Spray!"

He performed the traditional ritual, pointing the can from side to side, sweeping it high and low. The People responded with the traditional acclamations.

"O Unique New Formula!"

"O Instant Knockdown!"

"O shed thy Most Perfect Active Constituents over us!"

No one knew what the words meant, but they were very solemn and religious, handed down from generation to generation. Neath carried the can back to its place in the Sanctuary, then picked up the plastic cigarette lighter.

"Our Light in the Darkness!" he proclaimed.

He went round each member of the tribe in turn, holding the lighter in front of their faces. The People breathed deeply in and out, drawing spiritual sustenance from their totem.

"We are humble and unworthy!" they chanted. "Inspire in us the Flame of thy Spirit!"

Back into the Sanctuary went the cigarette lighter, and out came the Alarm Clock. Neath held the clock by its carrying handle and swung it solemnly from side to side.

"Ten Past Three!" he intoned, standing in front of Mell.

"Rrrring rrring!" Mell sang out at the top of her voice. She jumped up and danced around, still rrring-rrringing.

"Five to Seven!" Neath intoned, standing in front of Tunks. Up jumped Tunks, and started dancing and rrrring-rrringing too.

"Twelve Past Nine!"

"Eight Oh Six!"

"Twenty-Five to Two!"

One by one the People jumped up and joined in the singing and dancing. Soon everyone was whirling around, leaping and kicking in time to the rhythm.

"Rrrring rrring! Rrrring rrring!

Rrrring rrring! Rrrring rrring!"

The dance continued until they had whirled themselves into exhaustion. When they returned to their previous positions, Neath moved on to the fourth ritual.

He began by placing the Baby Jane Ma-ma doll in the middle of the half-circle. The doll was dressed in woollen baby-clothes and lay on her back in a basket. With elaborate religious gestures, Neath rolled up her woollen top to expose her chubby painted midriff.

Then Urlish brought him the special bowl, and he collected a morsel of stew on the index finger of his right hand. Prostrating himself before the doll, he touched his finger to her pink painted midriff. The sacrificial offering of stew lay smeared on her plastic belly button.

The People prostrated themselves too, and prayed the traditional prayer:

"O Jane of Janes and Baby of babies,
We offer our most humble food to thy belly,
For plump is thy belly and rounded upon thee;
Be near us and hear us,
Take pity upon thy People
Now and forever,
Amen."

Then they whacked their foreheads fervently with the flat of their hands. The religious ceremony was finished and complete.

13

For Miriael the Fourteenth Angel of Observance, her first day on the Earth had slipped by in a semi-conscious blur. Like a slowly guttering candle, she had resigned herself to extinction, yet she hadn't been extinguished. When her mind cleared during the second night, she realised she'd arrived at a kind of balance. The initial invasion of her spiritual senses had passed, and her body was no longer in pain.

She was conscious of her body as never before. She could feel the touch of her hip on the ground, her wing beneath her arm, her robe against her skin. No longer a simple extension of her spirit, her body sent incessant signals to her mind.

Her hearing was different too. Sound came to her with a physical vibration, almost a throbbing. Listening to the far-off maledictions of the Great Patriarchs in the sky, she heard them as dull and deep and ominous.

With the dawn, she discovered another change. When she opened her eyes on the grass around her, she saw the soft, silky surface of each individual blade rather than the essence within. Even her sight seemed to have become more tactile. And there were colours too, the green of grass and the brown of soil...such opaque colours, so thick and muddy! She shuddered at the gross materiality of the Earth.

She struggled to raise herself, but her wishes wouldn't translate into action. Instead, she felt a vague stirring and pushing in her arms and legs, yet too weak to stand or even crawl. Of course, she must have lost her power of spiritual motion when she lost her aura. Now a strange inertia weighed on her will and pinned her to the ground. She felt heavy in a way she'd never experienced before.

Why? Why? Why? She didn't understand. Her continuing existence was impossible and made no sense at all…

It was soon after dawn when she heard a rustling in the grass. Someone or something was approaching. Then the rustling stopped, followed by a long silence.

She looked and saw a shadowy figure in the tall grass nearby. A vague memory came back to her, of someone who'd been skulking around yesterday. With an effort she stretched down and spread her robe more decently over her limbs.

Then she caught a smell in the air, a strongly physical smell. She wrinkled her nose in disgust.

"Show yourself, whoever you are!"

She put a note of authority into her voice. She had no fear of anything or anyone on the Earth. She was a fighting warrior angel of the Twenty-Second Company!

"I'm Ferren of the People," said the shadow in the grass.

A Residual? She tried to recollect what she'd been taught about Residuals. She didn't know much, but she knew they were backward subhuman types dwelling in separate scattered communities on the Earth. They played no role in the great Millenary War, but hid and cowered and kept out of the way. Just as this one was hiding now.

"Show yourself!" she repeated.

After more rustling, the tall grass parted and a male figure emerged. She noted his thickset chest and shoulders, his broad grasping hands, his dirt-stained skin and dark body hair. How primitive! How coarse! Thankfully he wore a cloth around his waist, covering his lower parts.

"So you call yourself Ferren?"

"Yes. What about you?"

She frowned. He looked nervous, but not nearly as nervous as he should have been. And now he was asking questions!

25

"I am Miriael the Fourteenth Angel of Observance."

"Oh." He looked down and studied his feet. Then he looked up again. "Did you get shot down?"

Now his questions were becoming impertinent! She responded with crushing dignity. "I am here because I choose to be here."

"I thought I saw—"

"What you thought you saw is of no interest to me. I am *resting* on the Earth. Temporarily. I can return to Heaven whenever I wish."

"Oh." He sounded less than convinced. "You're not damaged, then? Your wings are still working?"

"My wings? I don't fly with my wings. My wings are simply ceremonial."

"So how do you fly?"

"By the power of my angelic aura."

"What's an aura?"

She compressed her lips and said nothing. She was annoyed with herself for getting into conversation with a Residual, and especially annoyed at having mentioned an aura that she no longer possessed.

"Where is it, your aura?" he tried again.

She didn't deign to reply. He scratched his head and looked away. Was he observing the glitter on the grass?

"You had something around you when I saw you overhead in the night," he persisted. "Like a sort of globe—"

"Be quiet!"

"All glowing and—"

"Be quiet, you stupid Residual!"

"What did you call me?"

"A Residual. Beings like you are called Residuals. Dirty smelly disgusting creatures. No better than animals."

"Hey, that's not fair! I've been helping you. I've been helping you even though you're an enemy."

"You're right, I'm an enemy. And if I hear another word from you, I'll show you how much of an enemy."

"We don't have to be enemies. I didn't mean—"

"I'll burn you up and reduce you to a cinder. Do you realise the danger you're in? I'll incinerate you!"

"Is that when you do your flash of light?"

"Not another word! If you're still here by the time I count to three…"

"I've seen your flash of light. And—"

"ONE!"

"And I don't think it's anything so much." He stood firm.

"TWO!"

He wavered. "I don't believe you can burn me up."

"THREE!"

He retreated to the edge of the flattened grass. Yet still he faced her, still he refused to run.

"Illuminatus est!" cried the angel, and willed a mighty surge of power.

There was a small crackle of sound, nothing more. The Residual who called himself Ferren continued to stare at her.

"You're not lighting up, you know," he said.

She willed again, but couldn't produce even a crackle of sound.

"I saw your flash of light once before. You're not doing it now."

She lost all self-control. "You—you—you—" She couldn't find words bad enough for cursing him.

"Maybe you're not as well as you think you are." He turned to go. "I'll come back tomorrow."

Damnation take you! she thought, and watched as he disappeared into the tall grass. She was still in a rage, but at the same time she felt slightly ridiculous.

14

It was late afternoon, and Ferren had finished his work for the day. Now he was on his way to the bottom of the Back Garden, where the Creek widened out in a shallow pool. The angel had called him dirty, smelly and disgusting, and the sneer rankled. He had decided to take a wash before dinner.

He passed Jollis and Stessa on the bank near the water, sitting with their children, Tam and Sibby. The two mothers were weaving baskets with rushes from the Rushfield, and the children were helping. Lost in his own thoughts, Ferren stood by the edge of the Creek and dipped in a foot. Then something soft and squishy hit him right between the shoulder blades.

SPLAPPP!

It was a big dollop of mud. It slid down his back and fell to the ground. There was a stifled burst of laughter.

He spun around. Zonda stood ten feet behind him… She must have been following him. Now she deliberately looked the other way, as if nothing had happened.

"Why d'you do that?"

She turned to face him again. "What?"

"You know!"

"No. What's wrong? Did someone throw some mud at you?"

"You did!"

"*Me?* Why would I want to throw mud at *you?*"

"You know you did!"

"Huh! You're not *worth* throwing mud at!"

There were giggles from nearby. The mothers and their children had been following the exchange.

He shrugged, swung away and waded out into the Creek. When the water was up around his ankles, he squatted and started to wash.

There was a splashing from behind. Zonda was wading out too. She crouched down beside him.

"Boy, you really think you're so important," she said scornfully.

"No."

"Yes you do. I know why you do."

"Why?"

"'Cos of when I came up and went to sleep next to you. You really think that meant something, don't you!"

"Doesn't mean anything to me."

"No? No? Well listen, smart-arse, it doesn't mean anything to me neither. It could've been anyone."

"Okay."

"Don't go getting ideas! I wouldn't have anything to do with *you* in a million years! Just keep away from me!"

She shuffled aside a couple of steps. She scooped up water in both hands, poured it over her shoulders, and began noisily washing herself from the waist up.

Ferren was trying not to watch. She looked back at him.

"Bet you were disappointed I didn't come up next to you last night."

He didn't answer.

"Hey, bum-features! I bet you were wondering where I was last night."

"Where were you?"

"Somewhere else, that's where. I'm not going to tell you."

"Good. I don't want to know anyway."

"You're only a little boy. I don't tell things to little boys."

"I'm fifteen. Same as you."

"But I've got more weight. I'm more solid."

She took two steps towards him and gave him a sudden push on the shoulder. Ferren lost his footing on the slippery bed of the Creek. He fell flat on his back in the shallow water. There were more giggles from the mothers and children on the bank.

"There! Not very solid are you!"

Ferren hooked his feet around Zonda's ankles and rolled over in the water, twisting her sideways. She straddled her legs and fought to keep her feet planted. But Ferren kept twisting. She was starting to slip.

"Stop it!" she cried. "Or you'll be sorry!"

"Who's gonna make me?"

"I'll tell everyone about you," she hissed.

Ferren stopped twisting. "Tell everyone what?"

"Ha!" She lowered her voice. "What you do in the middle of the night!"

Ferren stared at her in dismay. He released her legs and sat up in the water.

"Yes!" she whispered triumphantly. "Looking out at the sky when you oughter stay hidden like everyone else!"

Ferren opened his mouth to speak, then thought better of it. He rose up out of the water and walked to the bank of the Creek. Jollis and Stessa couldn't have heard Zonda's final whisper, and the children were too young to understand anyway.

Still, they were all grinning as he went past. The children clapped their hands, while Jollis gave him a knowing wink. Everyone seemed to understand *something* he didn't.

15

When he went to visit the angel next day, Ferren wasn't sure of his reception. Her anger had been real enough, even though she hadn't incinerated him. Yet nothing could have kept him away. In his whole life, she was the most amazing thing that had ever happened.

At first he hung back in the tall grass and observed from a distance. She lay on her side facing the food bag and water bowl, yet he sensed that her thoughts were far, far away. In fact, she looked rather sad.

After a minute, she observed him too. "You again. Come out where I can see you."

Her voice sounded as stern as yesterday, but with less hostility. He advanced into the area of flattened grass and stood before her. For a while, she eyed him thoughtfully as though inspecting him.

"Hmm." She concluded her examination, but didn't tell him if he'd passed.

"We don't have to be enemies," he began. "Even though you're a Celestial and I'm a—whatever you said."

"A Residual."

"Right. I don't want to be your enemy. I don't think you're bad."

"Thank you." She raised an ironic eyebrow. "I don't think you're bad either. You're of the Earth. Just different."

"We're only at war with you because of the Humen."

"You're at war with us, are you?"

"Yes, because the Humen are. We have to be, because they're our allies."

"*Allies?*"

"Didn't you know?"

"You think you're allies with the Humen?"

"We are. The armies of the Earth against the armies of Heaven."

The angel sniffed. "I think you overestimate your own importance."

"Some of us fight with the Humen against the Celestials. The ones selected for military service. My sister got selected, so she's fighting against your armies."

The angel shook her head and seemed surprised.

"What is it?" he asked.

"I've never seen any Residual fighting against us."

Now it was Ferren's turn to be surprised. "You must have!"

"No. I've flown hundreds of sorties, I've been involved in operations everywhere across this continent. No Residuals in the Humen armies."

"But the Selectors take one of us every year. My sister was the year before last. And my parents long before that…before I can even remember."

A quaver had crept into his voice, and he was aware of the angel studying him closely.

"So these Selectors *take* you for military service," she said. "You don't exactly volunteer?"

"It's our contribution to the alliance. We have to do it."

"You don't *want* to, though."

"My sister…" He gulped and couldn't continue.

"Hmm." The angel pursed her lips. "I suppose they might take Residuals to serve inside their camps. Not active duty, but civilian workers. Doing some sort of manual labour."

Ferren tried to stop thinking about Shanna. "Inside their camps? Have you seen us working there?"

"I've never seen anything inside any Humen camp. They're shielded by magnetic webs."

"Oh." He considered. "That must be it, then. Workers for manual labour."

"More likely slaves." His shocked look made her pull back. "I don't really know, I'm only guessing." She changed the subject. "When you say your sister went off with these Selectors, which way did she go?"

Ferren pointed the direction, and the angel nodded.

"They'd have taken her to the Bankstown Camp, then. As I suspected. It's the main military base for the whole continent. Probably the biggest camp in the Southern Hemisphere."

"Close to us?"

"Fifty, sixty miles along the overbridge."

"The what?"

"The Goulburn-Bankstown overbridge. Can't you see it from here?"

"No." He rose up on tiptoe and scanned in the direction. The Plain was all grass to the horizon, the same as it had always been. "What am I looking for?"

"An overbridge is a bridge across the ground. The Humen build them for sending troops along."

Ferren dropped back onto the flat of his feet. "Nothing there."

"I suppose it must be over the horizon. I've only seen the landscape looking down from above." The angel looked thoughtful. "You still miss your sister, don't you?"

"Yes."

"Why don't you go and visit her in the camp? It's only a few days' walk."

He goggled at her. The idea was so extraordinary that his mind refused to think it.

"What's the problem? Just follow the overbridge all the way."

"I couldn't."

"Why not?"

Ferren couldn't say why not. He was the only one of the People who dared venture onto the open Plain, but being completely out of sight of the Home Ground was something else again.

"Is it because of the Humen?" she asked. "You don't seem to like them much."

He had an answer for that. "I don't like them at all."

"So you don't want to go and inquire about your sister?"

"I'm scared of them. We all are."

"Yet you say you're allies with them. Very curious."

"We're scared of you too. You Celestials."

"Hmm. But *you* don't seem scared of *me*."

"Yes... I... No. I *ought* to be."

"I'm glad you're not."

She smiled at him...and all at once he realised she was beautiful, truly beautiful, beyond any conception of beauty he'd ever had before. For a moment he couldn't speak.

She changed the subject again. "Who knows about me being here? Have you told anyone?"

"No."

"Will you keep it a secret? Like a secret between friends?"

"Friends!" His heart leaped at the word.

"If you like. You say you don't want us to be enemies."

He felt that his cheeks were glowing. "I want us to be friends. Can I keep coming to see you?"

"Once a day would be appropriate."

"I can't get away much more than that anyhow."

"Then goodbye for now, Ferren. You're welcome to visit again tomorrow."

He grinned and received another gracious smile in return. He went off in a state of euphoria.

16

The leader of the tribe came across to Ferren in the Blackberry Patch.

"I need to talk to you, boy," he said. "In private."

He really did intend the talk to be private because he led Ferren all the way to the Swimming Pool, out of everyone's earshot. They stood on the broken tiles at the side, looking down at the floating sunflower petals in the fermenting ankle-deep water.

"You've been hanging around my daughter," Neath began. "You're a bad influence. I want you to stop pestering her."

"Me?" Ferren was indignant. "It's Zonda pesters me. Last time she threw mud at me. And other times—"

"Too many times. You stay away from her."

"Tell *her* that."

"I'm telling *you*. Don't answer me back. She needs a good solid male to settle her down, and you're leading her astray."

"No, she *likes* good solid males. She doesn't like me because I'm not solid enough."

"You attract her attention."

"I'm not trying to."

"But you do. You stand out. You'll end up attracting the Selectors' attention soon."

Ferren jumped at the sudden switch. Was Neath making a threat?

"I'm not old enough to be selected."

"They choose. If they don't want to wait till you're seventeen…" Neath's expression was threatening, no doubt of it. "And they might make a mistake about your age."

Or someone might tell them the wrong age, thought Ferren. He'd noticed Neath having a quiet word in one Selector's ear last year. And he'd always suspected him of encouraging them to take Shanna the year before. Why else would they have waited two nights until she was found?

Neath's thoughts must have been running along a similar track. "Your family's always been trouble," he said. "But trouble works itself out in the end."

"When the Selectors take me, you mean," Ferren muttered.

"It was a bad match, letting your parents come together." Neath went on as though he hadn't heard. "Both odd, both tricksy. They brought out the worst in each other. You don't remember them, eh?"

Ferren shook his head and said nothing.

"No, you'd have been under two when they were taken. It was a bad time, it could've had terrible consequences. When the Selectors selected your mother—"

"My father went with her," Ferren brought out between clenched teeth.

"You know, do you?"

"Shanna told me."

"Ah, your sister. Yes, your father refused to be separated from your mother. And did your sister tell you how he abused and cursed the Selectors? Putting us all at risk. So they took them as a pair, the only time it's ever happened. Lucky for us they didn't make a habit of selecting two every year."

"Lucky us," said Ferren bitterly. "Back to normal."

Neath scowled. "But *you're* still trouble, and so was your sister. We gave you every chance to grow up sound and solid, and you're still growing up tricksy. You're following right after your sister."

"She never did anything wrong."

"No? But she *was* wrong. Even as a child. Like the time I found her playing with our totems. *Playing!* With our holy totems!" Neath shuddered at the memory. "She had our Baby Jane out of the Sanctuary, and she was fussing over it and talking to it like some sort of toy. Imagining it was a child!"

You don't approve of imagining, Ferren thought but didn't say. He had said too much already.

"I knew she was lost then," Neath continued. "But you never seemed as odd as that, unless you hid it better. I had hopes you'd turn out all right." Ferren was surprised to see sorrow as well as censure in the old man's face. "Now I'm afraid the bad blood's starting to come out. The things I hear…"

For a moment Ferren feared that Zonda had informed on him to her father. "What things? Who from?"

"From Shuff especially. He doesn't trust you. Things about the way you work. And the way you talk."

Ferren breathed again. "I'll do better. I promise. And I'll keep away from your daughter. I'll never speak to her again."

Neath stared at him intently, then turned to go. "We'll see. Remember, the Selectors will be coming soon. It's nearly their time of year."

The threat remained in place. Ferren went back to work in the Blackberry Patch, vowing to do everything possible to please Shuff. But Zonda was a more difficult problem. He needed to *displease* Zonda, but in a way that would make her lose interest.

If only it was up to me to decide, he thought.

17

On his next visit to the angel, Ferren brought her fresh food and replenished her water bowl. So far as he could tell, she had hardly touched the old food. This time he spread the food bag out on the ground and arranged an inviting selection on top where she could see: mushrooms, corn and peas.

"There," he said. "It's all fresh now."

The angel barely looked at it. "Residual food and drink," she commented.

"Yes. You need to eat to get your strength back. You didn't eat much of the last lot."

"I didn't eat anything."

"Oh. Don't you like our food?"

She didn't answer.

"You must drink water, though?"

Still no reply. He shrugged and sat cross-legged in front of her. He had nothing particular to say, so he simply looked at her. Ever since he'd decided she was beautiful, he couldn't stop admiring her.

She frowned. "You shouldn't stare like that. It's not respectful."

"I didn't mean to..." he began, then blurted suddenly, "I think you're beautiful."

"Beautiful? And what kind of beauty is that? The only kind that matters to me is moral beauty."

"I don't understand."

"In Heaven, we admire moral qualities. The beauty of virtue, the beauty of wisdom, the beauty of selflessness. For myself, as a warrior angel, I aspire to the beauty of loyalty and fortitude."

"I don't... I wasn't..."

"No, I thought not. What you admire is physical beauty. I can do without being *physical*, thank you very much."

"But you have changed a bit, you know. Your skin's not so...so shimmery."

"What?"

"I didn't mean it in a bad way."

"You meant it as if I were starting to resemble your female Residuals. Don't *ever* think of me in that way."

He shook his head. "No, you're not like them. Though you are a female too."

"A female too! What a vulgar thing to say!"

"But you are."

"As an angel in the feminine mode, naturally I have the appropriate bodily form. Angels in the masculine mode have the masculine form. It's required for purely aesthetic reasons."

"Don't angels ever—"

"For purely aesthetic reasons. Not for the kind of reasons *you* imagine."

Ferren looked down at his hands, at the grass, at anything other than the angel. Whatever he said seemed to offend her. A long silence followed.

"As regards bringing me food and water…" When she spoke again, her voice remained haughty. "Please don't bother. It's not necessary."

"But what else have you got to eat?"

"The only sustenance an angel requires is the holy manna of Heaven. We don't need to *eat*, as you so crudely put it. Or *drink* either. We are beings of pure spiritual essence."

"Oh." Ferren considered. "But you ate before. And drank some water too."

"Impossible."

"It's true. When you were lying half asleep, just after you'd crashed. I fed you a mushroom."

"No."

"Yes. And I watched you swallow it."

"My spiritual essence does not absorb physical matter. I think I should know what's possible. You may imagine things in your ignorance, but that's all it is. Ignorance."

The silence this time lasted twice as long. Ferren was sure he hadn't imagined it, but he didn't want to stop being friends.

"Maybe I don't know as much as you do," he said at last.

"You don't."

"But I'm not stupid. No one ever taught me. I never had the chance to learn."

"Hmm."

"I'd *like* to learn. Will you be my teacher?"

"What good would that do you? Living among Residuals."

"I'm just curious. I'd like to learn anyway."

Her blue eyes focused upon him. "What do you want to learn?"

"About everything! The world! Everything everywhere!"

"That's a lot of teaching."

"Will you? Please?"

"I'll think about it. Perhaps next time. Come back tomorrow with something specific you'd like to ask me about."

He went off relieved that there would be a tomorrow—and hopefully more to follow. The angel had got over her haughtiness. Already he was starting to sift through the most important questions he wanted to ask.

18

Ferren was in his usual place on the outer edge of the People's blanket. He was fast asleep when someone slid up next to him and shook him by the leg.

He stirred and grimaced. It had to be Zonda. After his promise to her father, this was exactly what he didn't want.

"Pleased to see me, Ferren?"

He refused to respond. Perhaps she would go away if he kept his mouth shut.

"What's the matter? Not sticking your head out tonight?"

He breathed slowly in and out in the rhythm of sleep.

"You trying to ignore me?"

Again he felt his leg being shaken, and this time she dug in her finger-nails. He held back a yelp of pain and continued to lie inert and insensible.

"Stop it! I know what you're doing."

He shifted as if in sleep and let out a snore.

"Huh! You can't ignore *this*."

She wriggled herself half on top of him. The soft plump weight of her body pressed down on him all the way from his hip to his shoulder blade.

"Now you're getting excited," she whispered fiercely. "You know I'm here now."

He could feel the warmth of her breath on his neck and the side of his face. It was true, she *was* having an effect on him. He was completely confused. But he knew Zonda spelt trouble.

"No," he muttered, still in a sleepy voice.

"Yes." She pressed harder and tighter. "Admit it. Admit what you want to do. You're no different to any other male."

Ferren was sweating and panting. He gave up pretending. "All right. I'm awake. It was because of your father."

The pressure eased. "What about him?"

"He had a talk with me. I'm supposed to stay away from you."

"And you let that frighten you off?" She removed her weight completely, no longer touching body to body.

"He threatened me with the Selectors. He'll get them to choose me."

"Hmm." She lay quietly beside him as if reflecting. "*I* didn't tell him anything."

"Thank you. I don't look out in the nights anymore."

"Oh? But you do other things."

"No. What?"

"You go off sometimes when you should be working. I think you go exploring on the Plain."

His heart skipped a beat. "Never. I wouldn't do that. I'd have to be mad to do that."

"You *are* mad. You're not afraid of scary things." He had the impression she was staring at him in the darkness. "Except the Selectors."

"I leave work in the Blackberry Patch sometimes," he conceded. "But not to go exploring on the Plain. You *can't* have seen me."

"I've seen you slip off into the Rushfield. Where would you go from the Rushfield except out on the Plain?"

"I just sit there and think."

Zonda scoffed. "What, and play with yourself?"

He held his tongue. At least she hadn't actually seen him out on the Plain...and she certainly hadn't seen him with the angel.

"There's the place they call Beaumont Street, isn't there?" she mused. "And other ruins in the grass?"

"So they say."

"People must've explored the Plain in the past, to know about those things."

Ferren didn't like the direction of her thoughts. "But *you'd* never go out there?"

"Not by myself, no."

"You shouldn't. Too dangerous."

"Is that so?" She didn't seem convinced… In fact she seemed to be challenging him. But when she next spoke, her thoughts were on a different tack. "You should be nice to me, you know. If you think my father's going to put the Selectors onto you, you need someone to talk him out of it. I'm your only hope."

He couldn't decide how to answer, and in another moment she had wriggled away to some other place under the blanket.

19

Ferren had decided that his most important question to the angel was about Heaven itself.

"What's it like up there?" he asked.

"Well." The angel reflected for a moment, then began. "There are seven levels of Heaven. We call them Altitudes. Many different zones and halls and gardens on each Altitude, and different kinds of activities. The lower Altitudes are mainly given over to war preparations, encampments and armouries. The Twenty-Second Company—my company—has its base in the Pavilions of the Rose. The higher Altitudes are devoted to activities such as scholarship, healing, prayer, teaching… Are you taking this in?"

Ferren gulped. "I think so."

"Each kind of activity is the special province of a particular order of angels. We have a hierarchy of nine angelic orders: Seraphim, Cherubim, Ofanim or Thrones, Dominions, Powers or Potentates… You're *not* taking it in, are you?"

"It seems very complicated."

"I can't make it simple." The angel sighed. "I should've known I couldn't describe it."

"What's it like overall?" he suggested. "Does it feel different up there?"

"Of course." She sighed a longer, deeper sigh. "I'll tell you the most wonderful feeling of all. For me, anyway. In Heaven, every angel of whatever order is always aware of every other angel. Like a perpetual presence in one's mind, a perfect communion of spirits. It's a music that goes on in the background, as though we're all part of a single great choir. Whatever we do or think, we're all contributing and harmonising together. Do you understand?"

"Not really," he confessed.

"We hardly need to speak in words to communicate most of the time. We sense one another and touch spirit to spirit. Nothing like your physical sort of touch."

"Are you doing it now?"

"What?"

"Are you sensing all the other angels when you're on the Earth and they're in Heaven?"

"I'm always in contact with them. Of course I am."

"It sounds wonderful." A dismal thought crept into Ferren's mind. He struggled with it for a while, then finally had to ask. "Will you be going back up to Heaven again soon?"

"I expect so."

"How soon? Weeks? Days?"

"That depends."

"When you've finished resting?"

"Yes."

"Will your angel friends come and fetch you? Or will you fly up by yourself?" When she didn't answer immediately, he went on. "Do you have to recover your strength first?"

Her brows descended in a scowl. "Why do you assume I can't fly up already? Don't make guesses at things you don't understand."

Ferren hardly noticed the sharpness of her tone. He was sunk in depression at the thought of her leaving. The most amazing experience of his life—and it had hardly begun before it would be snatched away from him!

"You wouldn't fly back to Heaven without telling me, though?" he asked.

"Why?"

"I don't know. I'd hate to come out and just find you gone."

"Very well. I'll tell you if I can."

Another idea struck him. "Will you leave me a reminder?"

"What's a reminder?"

"Something to remember you by. So I can think about you when I look at it."

"A keepsake, you mean? A scrap of my robe, for example?"

"Yes. Or...or..."

"Or what?"

"The best thing to remind me..." The possibility took his breath away, and he couldn't find the nerve to ask.

"Say it."

It came out in a rush. "A-feather-from-your-wing."

"You think I'd pluck out one of my feathers for you?"

"No. No. Not really. It was a mad idea. I just... It would've been... Not really."

"Hmm." She appeared to consider, then avoided an answer. "Anyway, I won't be going for a while yet."

"You won't?" He brightened at once.

"I'm still resting."

"You'll keep being my teacher?"

"I don't think I can teach you much about Heaven. Too difficult."

"I had a second most important question to ask."

"Oh?"

"The war between Heaven and Earth."

"The Millenary War?"

"If that's what it's called."

"You want the whole history?"

"Yes."

"Well, I can tell you the part I know. But I'll have to think how to teach it properly."

"Tomorrow?"

"Yes, when you visit me tomorrow."

20

When night fell, Miriael rolled over on her back and looked up at the black roof of the sky. Heartache overwhelmed her. She had lied to the Residual about being in contact with other angels. She was shut out of Heaven and cut off from all angelic communication. That most wonderful sense of communion and togetherness was utterly lost to her. She could never have imagined such isolation; even if she'd imagined it, she could never have guessed the misery of it. She was irredeemably alone.

It wasn't because she lay disabled on the Earth, it was because of what she'd become in herself. When she tried to picture the divine realm on the other side of the blackness, she seemed separated from it by an infinite chasm. She didn't understand, but she felt deeply, deeply ashamed. It was out of shame that she'd lied to the Residual.

No, she wasn't supposed to survive in this half-and-half state. She remembered Shoel and Tophiel at the Battle of Albury Overbridge, when they'd been shot down and had crashed to the Earth. She had seen for herself how their auras dissipated and the light faded from their bodies, until they'd winked right out of existence. That was the way extinction was supposed to happen!

It was true she hadn't exactly welcomed extinction in the moment when her own aura dissipated. Did she carry some sort of imperfection in her nature, then? Had any angel ever been known with such imperfection before? She wished she'd paid more attention in her training studies, when the blue-robed Cherubim explained the basic principles of spirit and matter. But at the time she'd only wanted to get out into the fighting…

Several small-scale skirmishes in the night made a background to her thoughts. She was aware of the usual displays of spectral light…a singing of the *Missa Cantata* far off to the north…the rumbling wheels of the chariots of the Ofanim. Perhaps her own Twenty-Second Company was involved? She would have given anything to be with them again, touching thought to thought, sharing that special camaraderie.

She reflected on her last fateful mission. She had flown too close to the webs, of course…and had suffered that terrible numbing blow, followed by a sickening recoil that sent her spinning across the sky. What folly, what unnecessary recklessness!

She could imagine how it would have been reported back in Heaven, and how Metatron would have frowned and written it down in his brass-bound book: *Imprudence and loss of self-control by a junior warrior angel.* Concluding with her name and the words *Extinguished in action.* Then a thick black line ruled underneath.

Yes, so far as they knew, she had ceased to exist as any angel who fell to Earth should cease to exist. There would be no search sent out to find her. No one in Heaven was even thinking about her. She was reduced to talking to a Residual as her only form of company.

A trickle of wetness ran down from the corner of her eye. Miriael was crying.

21

"So, the history of the Millenary War?"

"Yes, please."

It was an overcast morning. The angel lay propped on one elbow, while Ferren sat cross-legged at a respectful distance.

"I'll need to draw a map." She pointed to the ground in front of her. "Can you clear a space?"

"What's a map?"

"Like looking down on the world from very high above. Pull out the grass here and pat the earth down flat."

Ferren set about his task. Soon there was a suitable space of patted-down earth within the angel's reach.

"Now something sharp to draw with."

He jumped up, scouted around and came back with a sharp piece of stone. The angel started to scratch lines. Sitting cross-legged again, he shuffled forward for a closer look.

"Now," she said. "This is North America here. And South America. Europe and Asia. Africa. And Australia. These are the continents."

"What's a continent?"

"A large area of land surrounded by oceans."

"What's an ocean?"

"A large area of water."

Ferren struggled to make sense of it. "Can we see the Home Ground?" he asked at last. "Can we see where we are on the Plain?"

The angel pointed with her piece of stone. "We'd be about here. On the east coast of Australia, inland from the Pacific Ocean, in the Picton area. But this whole area is only the tiniest tiniest dot on a map of the whole Earth. Each of these continents is thousands of miles across." She looked at him. "Do you understand now?"

"I'm trying," he said. "Perhaps I'll remember it now and understand it more later."

She smiled, ironically but not unkindly. "Very well. Let's start with the continent of North America."

"This one?"

"That's the one. North America is where the great Weather Wars took place over five hundred years ago. The Humen there tried to upset the equilibrium of Heaven by generating terrible electrical storms in the upper atmosphere. But we fought back by taking control of the tidal currents and prevailing winds, and turned the whole climate against them. We created the Hundred Years Blizzard. Now the continent is covered with a permanent shield of ice." She scratched a line across North America. "All the way down to here."

"What happened to the Humen?"

"They retreated into huge fortified camps like Fortress Atlanta and the San Antonio Complex. We keep them pinned down so they hardly dare come out nowadays."

"Whew!" Ferren was impressed. "They got beaten?"

"More or less. They're on the defensive. It's the same in other places. In Africa, for instance."

"This one?"

"Yes. You remember the names well. The Humen in Africa tried to go in over the Endless Wall."

She scratched a long line.

"That's a wall?"

"Yes, a tremendous fireproof wall. It runs all the way around Europe and Asia. Europe and Asia are the Burning Continents. The Endless Wall contains the fire and stops it from spreading."

"Why are they burning?"

"They've been burning ever since the Great Collapse."

"But why?"

"It happened in an earlier time, even before the Weather Wars. Please, no questions out of order, or I'll lose track."

"Sorry."

"So. In North Africa, the Humen sent special armies in over the Wall to reconquer the territory and quench the flames. For a while they succeeded, setting up colonies in Sicily and Arabia and the Ebro River basin. But we attacked their lines of communication and destroyed their tunnels and overbridges. Without supplies coming in from outside the colonies couldn't survive."

Ferren scratched his head. "I always thought the Humen side had to be winning. But they're not doing much good anywhere."

"The closest they came was in South America. Yes, there. The Humen in South America were a very grave threat a hundred years ago. Doctor Mengis and Doctor Genelle established their empire from Panama to Patagonia and turned the continent into a single vast industrial network. They mass-produced terrible new weapons, like boost-beams and force-fields and magnetic webs."

"What're they?"

"I can't explain. Too far outside your experience. The thing is, we had no answer to them. And while we were working on a counter-weapon, Doctor Mengis and Doctor Genelle boosted their Hypers up to the underside of Heaven. Hypers are one type of Humen, like Doctors and Plasmatics. Soon there were swarms and swarms of them drilling and hammering and trying to batter a way through to the First Altitude. It wasn't until the Campaign of the Five Zones that we overthrew them."

"You discovered a counter-weapon?"

"We discovered a method of counter-attack. We bypassed their armies and infiltrated their Plasmatics. Their machines on the ground went out of control, and the industrial network destroyed itself. In the end, the whole continent was torn apart." She sketched zigzag lines this way and that across South America. "South America nowadays is just a collection of broken blocks, separated by impassable fissures."

Ferren was frowning with concentration, trying to remember it all. He pointed a finger at the angel's map.

"And what about this one? Where we are?"

"Australia?"

"Yes. Aus-tra-lia. Who's winning where we are?"

"Nobody yet. There's no major fighting going on in Australia."

He stared. "But there's fighting every night! I've seen huge battles!"

"Oh, that's mostly skirmishing and manoeuvring for position. There have been some big battles in the past, but the biggest are yet to come. In fact… But I shouldn't reveal Heaven's current military information to you."

Ferren was disappointed. "I won't tell anyone. I don't know anyone to tell anyway."

"Probably not. But still no."

"Oh… Well, can I ask a question?"

The angel raised an eyebrow. "What now?"

"When did the Good Times happen?"

"The Good Times? What do you mean by the Good Times?"

"When our Ancestors ruled the world."

"*Your* ancestors?" The angel was incredulous. "The ancestors of Residuals?"

"Yes. In their cities of metal and glass and stone. Millions of tall white buildings. Moto-cars. Electrics. Film-shows. Shop-shops."

"Wherever did you hear such nonsense?"

It was Ferren's turn to be surprised. "Don't you know about the Good Times?"

"Never heard of them."

"They happened though." He considered. "Maybe a long long time ago. When did Heaven and Earth start fighting?"

"I'm not sure. I think the Millenary War has been going for a thousand years."

"The Good Times were a time of peace."

"That would have to be even earlier than the Far Past. We call the age before the Great Collapse the Far Past. I don't worry about that far back. Nobody in Heaven does, except scholars and historians."

"So the Good Times could have happened before the times you know about!" Ferren was triumphant.

"Or they could be just a dream. A primitive myth invented by story-tellers in a primitive community."

"You don't believe it?"

"Where's the evidence?"

"Everywhere. The Home Ground. Beaumont Street." Ferren waved his arms in every direction. "All the ruins. Buildings fallen down. Who were they built by?"

The angel became thoughtful. "Not by the Humen," she admitted. "I suppose they must've been built by someone." She looked at him. "Still, it could hardly have been *your* ancestors."

"Why not?"

"Well, look at you. You can't even make decent clothes for your-selves."

"But we have their things to remember them by."

"What things?"

"Our Fly Spray Can. Our Light in the Darkness. Our Alarm Clock. Our Baby Jane."

"I never heard of such things. What do they do? Are they weapons?"

"We don't know what they do. The secrets have been forgotten. But not weapons."

"Why not?"

"Everyone lived happy lives in the Good Times. The world was for pleasure and enjoyment, not fear and fighting. Not like nowadays."

There was a shining intensity in his eyes and a yearning in his voice. The angel studied him, pursing her lips.

"And you say you inherited these things?"

"We *did!* Our totems!"

"All right."

"You should ask the angels you communicate with. Ask them to tell you what happened long long ago."

"They wouldn't know. Only the scholars and historians know."

"So ask the ones you communicate with to ask *them*."

The angel shook her head and looked away. "I wouldn't want to pester them."

"Don't you think it's important?"

"I wouldn't want to pester them," she repeated. She brushed her hand across the map and obliterated the lines she'd drawn. "And now…isn't it time for you to go?"

22

There was something different about this evening's religious ceremony. Neath seemed tense and distracted, as though his mind was only half on the words he was uttering.

At the end of the Baby Jane ritual, he didn't dismiss the People with the usual blessing. Instead, he stood in front of them with a grim, foreboding look on his face. He seemed to be working himself up to some important announcement.

"Men and women of the People," he said at last. "I have been counting the days with my marks on the wall. Three hundreds. Six tens. Three ones."

The People looked across to the curtained-off counting-corner on the other side of the Dwelling Place. Puzzled and apprehensive, they turned back again to Neath.

"Men and women of the People," he said, "we are two days short of a full year since the Selectors last visited."

There was a gasp from every throat. As old dark memories returned, they looked at one another with horror-stricken eyes.

"You remember how it is," said Neath. "You remember what we have to do to contribute to the alliance."

Already the People were starting to whimper and sob. There were stifled cries from the women and children.

"Why do we have to?"

RICHARD HARLAND

"I don't want to be selected."

"They've already taken my eldest."

"There'll be none of us left."

Neath spoke firmly. "There is no help for it. The Selectors will come the day after tomorrow."

The sounds of misery rose to a crescendo. The women tore wildly at their hair, several men threw themselves forward on the ground. There were wails and shrieks and screams.

Neath lifted his quavery voice above the clamour. "I am sorry," he said. "I am sorry for us all. I wish it was different. But we are little, weak and small. Our only way is to endure."

Listening to Neath, the People fell silent. One by one the women stopped tearing at their hair and the men got up off the ground. Soon they were all kneeling again, heads bowed and shoulders hunched. The tears continued to roll down their faces.

"We must ask our totems for the strength to carry on," said Neath in a dull, flat voice. There were tears rolling down his face too. "We must prepare to suffer. We must prepare for the worst."

He looked slowly around. The People remained motionless. He raised his arms as if to give the blessing, then lowered them uselessly again.

"Tomorrow there will be no work in the fields. Tomorrow will be a day of prayers."

23

A light rain fell overnight, pattering down on the People's waterproof blanket with tiny fingertip touches. By morning it had eased to a fine drizzle. The tribe ate a dismal breakfast in the Dwelling Place.

Zonda waited until she saw her father go into his counting-corner. Today he had a three-hundred-and-sixty-fourth scratch to mark up on his wall. She finished her mouthful, followed him in through the curtain and stood watching from behind until the new scratch was made.

Then he turned. "Yes, girl?"

50

She kept her voice lowered. "Who's it going to be this year?"

He frowned. "What do you mean?"

"Who will the Selectors select?"

"They make their own decision. I don't—"

"Yes, you do. You influence them."

Neath shook his head but didn't argue.

"Are you thinking of Ferren?" she asked.

"He's the kind they like. Smart and brainy. Ideas and imagination. They could easily pick him."

"Even though he's not the proper age yet?"

Neath's only response was a shrug.

"Don't let them."

"What?"

"Don't influence them to take him early. Influence them *not* to."

"Daughter, daughter." Neath clicked his tongue. "It's my task to look after the survival of the tribe. He doesn't help us survive. The best thing he can do is get himself selected."

"I don't *want* him selected."

Fresh lines of worry appeared on Neath's lined face. "Why not? What've you been doing? Have you and him——"

"No. 'Course not."

"Do you like him?"

"No."

"Then why?"

"Just because."

Neath screwed up his eyes and scrutinised her, but discovered no answer.

"I don't understand you, girl. Why can't you settle on some sound, solid male? Someone with good blood in his veins?"

"Phuh!"

"I'm serious. Whoever you choose as a mate can be next leader of the People when I go."

"Go where?"

"When I die."

"You're not going to die. Not for years and years and years."

Neath smiled wearily. "If you say so. But I'd like to be able to train

51

the next leader before my time comes. You could have Lumb or Hulm or Tunks or Burge."

"They couldn't lead. They're just followers."

"They could lead if you were behind them pushing them on."

"They're cowards too."

"And Ferren isn't—is that it? Is that what you like about him?"

"I *don't* like him. He just interests me."

"Interests you! You have too many odd notions, girl. Always have. I can't think where you get them from. Not me, that's for sure."

Zonda held her peace.

"So how long is this interest going to last?"

She sensed a yielding. "I don't know. Maybe… Just don't let them take him this year. Please? For me?"

She knelt down in front of him and took hold of his hands.

"Father, I never ask anything from you. I'm only asking this one little thing."

"You ask for plenty. All the time. And I keep giving it to you."

He was definitely softening now. She squeezed his hands.

"I'm your only child so you *have* to love me. And I love you too. Please? Just for this year?"

"Ah, it's a weakness in me. Why can't I say no to you?" He sighed and shook his head with a sad smile. "All right. Just for this year."

"Thank you, thank you, thank you!" She jumped up and kissed him on the forehead…then went off quickly before he could change his mind.

24

The drizzle stopped later in the morning, but the sky remained overcast. Instead of going out to their separate places of work, the People stayed in and around the Dwelling Place. Some prayed before their totems in the Sanctuary, others sat talking in low voices. It was a day outside of normal days, a day of fear and waiting.

Ferren prayed to the totems too. He didn't believe they had the power to guard and protect him, yet he did believe they had *some* strange power.

It gave him a feeling of awe just to look at the fly spray can, the cigarette lighter, the alarm clock and the Ma-ma doll. At times he imagined they might start working again, as they must once have worked for the Ancestors. But he couldn't begin to imagine what sort of working it might be.

The changed conditions upset his plans for going out to visit the angel. Perhaps he could have escaped unnoticed from the People in the Dwelling Place, but he couldn't escape from Zonda. Although she didn't approach him, she was never far off, and he had the impression she was keeping an eye on him. He couldn't risk trouble on the very day before the Selectors arrived.

Lunchtime came and went, with food brought out from the Store and eaten uncooked. In the afternoon, the crowd divided: while half remained in the Dwelling Place, the other half moved across to the Swimming Pool. Ferren mingled with those who opted for the Swimming Pool, but it was no surprise when Zonda came across too. He was growing more and more frustrated.

The attraction of the Swimming Pool was the mildly alcoholic water fermenting at the bottom of the tiled basin. The older folk stretched down and scooped up the murky brown liquor in bowls. The young adult males jumped into the pool, dropped on all fours and lowered their mouths to drink. It took a great deal of drinking before the alcohol started to have its effect.

They drank to forget about the Selectors and their fear of being selected…and eventually they forgot. By late afternoon, the young adult males especially were in an uproarious mood.

"Whooo! I've drunk half a pool!"

"I'm swamped!"

"I'm sloshed in the head!"

They began a shoving contest, shoulder against shoulder. Then Lumb charged like a bull at Burge, and it turned into a head-butting contest.

GNUKKK! Lumb and Burge clashed heads, staggered and ended up sitting down suddenly in murky brown water.

CLOKKK! Tunks lunged forward at Hulm, caught him across the bridge of the nose and sent him sprawling.

Meanwhile, Burge and Lumb got back up on their feet. Tunks turned to Zonda, who stood observing from the side of the pool.

"Watch me! I'll flatten 'em all!"

"Flatten you first!" bellowed Burge.

He lowered his head and threw himself at Tunks, who braced for the collision. KNUTTT! They clashed forehead against forehead, but neither fell. In a moment, they were grappling and wrestling.

"I'm the strongest!" Burge roared.

"I'm the heaviest!" Tunks roared back.

Then Lumb slammed into the wrestling pair and knocked them both over.

"Who's the best now?" he cried, appealing to Zonda at the side of the pool. "You judge us! Who's the best?"

"You're all nongs," Zonda responded scornfully.

Still, she continued to watch as Lumb came bulldozing in for another bout. Ferren saw his opportunity. Now or never!

He backed away from the crowd round the pool, then turned on his heel and took off running. He only hoped Zonda wouldn't notice his absence for a while.

25

The sun was low in the sky and the shadows were lengthening by the time Ferren arrived at the patch of flattened grass. The angel roused up and addressed him as he approached.

"Ah! There you are!"

She looked cold and pale and somehow fragile. Her yellow robe, still damp from the overnight rain and morning drizzle, clung to her body and moulded the exact shape of her figure.

"Late for your lessons." She smiled. "What do you want to learn today?"

He stood before her, wondering how to begin. She seemed happy to see him…whereas he was saddened to think it might be for the last time.

"Bad news," he announced abruptly. "The Selectors are coming tomorrow."

"Hmm, the Selectors."

"I told you, remember. They come once a year and select one of us for military service."

"Or some other service in their camps. Yes, I remember. They're Hypers, I assume." When Ferren looked blank, she explained further. "The most common Humen type, standard troops and workers. If they're dressed all in black from top to toe, they're Hypers."

"Yes, all in black. Hypers." He nodded. "So this year it could be me selected."

"Why you?"

"I got on the wrong side of too many people. They don't like me being smart."

"They decide who the Selectors select?"

"Our leader can suggest someone. He only has to tell the Selectors I'm smart."

"It's not definite, though?"

"No-o." Ferren chewed at his lip. It was time to say what he'd come to say. "I think... I think you should go back up into Heaven. That's what I'd do if I was you."

"Why now?"

"If they take me, you'll have no one looking after you."

"Do I need looking after?"

"You'll be all on your own."

"Hmm." The angel appeared pensive. "I'd miss your visits."

Ferren's spirits lifted for a moment. He thought of asking for a reminder to take with him if he was selected, but the words wouldn't come. He couldn't even imagine her plucking a feather from her wing...

"Thank you for your advice," she said. "I'll go back to Heaven when I feel like it."

He couldn't interpret her odd tone of voice. His spirits sank again, and he began to pace gloomily back and forth. Then his gaze fell upon the water bowl...

He took another closer look, and there was no doubt about it.

"It's gone down!" he cried. "You've been drinking the water!"

"Perhaps I knocked the bowl and spilled some," she said off-handedly. But she changed her explanation when he stared straight at her. "On second thoughts, I did drink a little, I remember. But not your sort of drinking. Only to cool myself down. My body can't actually absorb water." She frowned. "Don't you believe me? Why are you looking at me like that?"

"Looking to see if your skin's different."

"Of course it isn't. I explained all of this before. My body doesn't absorb earthly food or water. It's logically and rationally impossible."

"Except you ate a mushroom."

"No."

"You swallowed it. You must've absorbed it."

"It didn't happen."

"You wouldn't remember because you were half asleep."

"I don't need to remember. I know it *couldn't* happen."

"It did. I swear. I saw it with my own eyes."

"A mushroom like this?" She reached for a mushroom that lay on top of the outspread food bag.

"Yes. I broke it in two bits."

She propped herself on one elbow, studied the mushroom and grimaced in disgust.

"Apparently you need a demonstration. Watch closely, because I'm not going to do this again."

"Break it up smaller first," he suggested.

She hardly seemed to hear. She held the mushroom between thumb and forefinger, and opened her mouth wide.

"Ready to see how my body rejects it?"

Ferren took a step backwards, remembering the previous mushroom and how she'd lit up with a flash of light. Was that rejection? But the flash had come only *after* she'd finished swallowing.

She tilted her head back and dropped the mushroom into her mouth. Perhaps she chewed… He saw her jaw move, then the swallowing in her throat.

He held his breath and waited…and waited…and waited. There was no flash, nor any other kind of reaction. Nothing. He stepped forward again.

The angel was waiting too. A look of amazement crept over her face, then a look of frustration, followed by a look of something very much like despair.

"No, no, *no*," she muttered.

"Did you absorb it?" he asked.

She seemed as if focused in on herself, unaware of Ferren or anything else in the outside world.

"It can't happen." She shook her head. "It mustn't happen. I don't want it to happen."

More and more vigorously she shook her head, so that her golden hair billowed out all around. Ferren felt sorry for her and wondered how to console her.

"You're still an angel," he said. "You're still beautiful."

There was an odd sound like a snort from somewhere behind him. He spun around and scanned the tall grass. Someone was hiding there, a darker shadow half visible through the green. Someone crouching, someone watching…

"I see you, you pervert!" Zonda rose up and showed her face above the grass. Her voice became a screech. "Found you out! You've had it now!"

26

For a moment everything froze. Ferren was stunned, deprived of willpower. He couldn't believe Zonda would have followed him so far. No other member of the tribe would have come right out across the Plain. Against every taboo!

"You filthy freak!" Her voice screeched out again. "With a Celestial! You wait till the People hear about this!"

"No! Zonda! Please!"

But already she was off and running. Her head and shoulders were visible above the grass as she sped off towards the Home Ground. And still his muscles refused to move.

The angel emerged from her own despair. "Shouldn't you stop her?"

Her words released him, and he sprang forward in pursuit. But Zonda glanced back over her shoulder and saw him coming. Immediately she accelerated.

Faster, faster, faster! He spurred himself on, he ran like the wind. He was beginning to close the gap—but still not quickly enough.

She plunged into the Rushfield twenty paces ahead of him. He crashed wildly through the reeds after her. Now she was crossing the Creek by the line of stones.

His legs were pumping and his lungs were on fire. He could hear her puffing and blowing. Only ten paces between them! He *had* to catch her, he *had* to stop her!

She swung down by the side of the Dwelling Place wall, trampling through onions and peas in the Driveway. When she came to the corner of the wall she took it wide. Ferren took it tight. There was barely a pace between them as she came up to the Back Door.

In a desperate final dive, he threw himself forward and clutched at her waist. No use! Her momentum carried her right on into the Dwelling Place. With his arms still wrapped around her waist, he was dragged in after her.

Too late he realised his mistake, too late he released his grip and tried to recover his feet. He tumbled in a heap in the middle of the floor.

The People looked up and stared at him in amazement. Then listened in even greater amazement as Zonda gasped out her accusation.

"He's been out on the Plain! He's been meeting up with a Celestial!"

There was a moment of shocked silence as the accusation sank in.

"Beat him! Smash him!" Zonda pointed a finger. "He's in love with a Celestial!"

The People converged to form a ring. As Ferren scrambled to a sitting position, he found himself hemmed in on all sides.

"You don't understand." He struggled to explain. "She's not an enemy."

Zonda spat scornfully. "He's been meeting her for days. I suspected it, now I've seen it. He thinks she's *beautiful!*"

Neath stood forward. "He's condemned himself out of his own mouth. He's betrayed our alliance and taken up with our enemies."

"Get him! Bash him!" cried Zonda.

"Yes." Neath, too, pointed an accusing finger. "He must pay."

Ferren managed to rise to his knees. "No, wait. You—"

Neath stepped round behind him, put a foot between his shoulder blades and sent him once more sprawling in the dirt.

The leader's action was like a signal to the rest of the tribe. They charged in on Ferren in a single rush. He dodged out of the way of a kick from Jossock, caught and blocked another kick from Tuller, then made a desperate dive between Unce's legs. But his attempt to wriggle a way out ended when Unce capsized and sat down on the small of his back.

Someone held his head and someone held his legs. Then they all started piling on top of him, squashing him flat. Buried under a mountain of bodies, he could no longer breathe or see. He could only hear the chant growing louder and louder.

"Get him! Bash him! Get him! Bash him! Get him! Bash him!"

Then he passed into unconsciousness.

PART TWO

THE
OVERBRIDGE

1

While the People looked down at Ferren's prostrate body, Neath called Zonda aside. His brows darkened as she reported the whole story. Zonda had observed Ferren and Miriael for many minutes before she called out; she'd heard snatches of conversation, and she'd seen the Celestial eating a mushroom.

"I don't think she can move," she told him. "She's disabled somehow."

Neath's frown grew blacker and blacker. "Revolting," he muttered. "Horrible. Unnatural."

"It made my stomach turn," Zonda agreed. "Like mated partners, they were. What'll you do?"

"I have the perfect punishment for him."

"He deserves something long and painful. What about her?"

"Her?"

"The Celestial."

"We're not going to touch her. Are you mad?"

"But she's... He's been a traitor, but she's the enemy."

"Too big an enemy for us, girl. We won't be going anywhere near her." He indicated the men and women of the tribe. "Do you think I could make them, even if I tried?"

Zonda compressed her lips in frustration. Although she wanted Ferren punished, she wanted the Celestial punished even more.

"They were both in it," she objected. "As much as each other."

But Neath was no longer listening. He clapped his hands to call the People to attention. They left Ferren lying on the ground and gathered around.

"It's all true," he told them. "One of our tribe has been consorting with the enemy."

The People glanced back at the unconscious figure and murmured among themselves.

"Always knew he was no good."

"Something wrong with him."

"Too much thinking."

Neath clapped his hands again. "He could've made trouble for us with our allies. They might've suspected we were all consorting along with him. Remember, the Selectors arrive tomorrow."

The People groaned, but Neath pressed on. "But now it can work well for us. I have decided his punishment, and his punishment is—to be handed over to the Selectors."

Zonda was taken by surprise. "No!" she cried out. "We have to punish him ourselves!"

Neath overrode her. "And we'll ask them to count him as our contribution for the year. Him instead of anyone else."

Heads began nodding on all sides. Everyone liked the idea except Zonda.

"You can't." She plucked at her father's sleeve. "Not this year, you said."

Neath pulled her close and hissed in her ear, too low for anyone else to hear. "Don't draw attention, girl. You don't want them realising what *you* did. Going out over the Plain to catch him."

The warning silenced her. She chewed at her lip and stared at the ground. Neath went on with his address to the tribe.

"All we have to us keep him prisoner till the Selectors arrive. We'll tie him up to something. Somewhere outside the Dwelling Place…"

Zonda was only half listening as they began to make arrangements. In her rage against Ferren, she'd forgotten about the Selectors. How had it all turned out so wrong? She wasn't sure what she'd expected to happen, but definitely not *this*.

2

Ferren awoke feeling battered and bruised. At first, he didn't know where he was. Night was falling, and there was no one around.

His hands were fastened behind his back, his back was propped against hard, cold metal.

Gradually he worked it out. He was sitting on the concrete platform of the Garage, facing Urlish's fire, and the hard cold metal was one of the Garage's four rusted poles. The People had tied him up as a prisoner. No doubt they were all now snug and sleeping under their blanket in the Dwelling Place.

He tugged at the rope around his wrists, but it was tightly bound in a dozen loops and secured with a knot his fingers couldn't reach. A second rope went round and round his waist and lashed him to the pole. He could see where the second rope was knotted against his midriff, but he couldn't reach that knot either.

Helpless! The ropes were far too strong to snap. The more he fought to loosen them, the tighter they seemed to cut. With his head still woozy from being knocked out, he tried to discover some means of escape.

Then a rustling from the direction of the High Hedge caught his attention. He stared at the spot, just as two birds flew out in a sudden flurry of wings. Someone was pushing through the hedge, coming towards him. A shape detached itself from the darkness.

"Who's there?"

"Shush."

A young female voice? He recognized the shape as she moved forward in the dim light.

"Zonda!"

"*Shush!*"

His first thought was that she'd come to take a secret revenge of her own on him. His second thought was that she'd ventured outside the Dwelling Place in the dark—which nobody *ever* dared do. He'd never done it himself until now. Leaving the safety of the blanket just for the sake of revenge? It didn't make sense.

It made even less sense when she came round behind the pole and knelt on the concrete edge of the platform.

"What're you doing?"

"Shut up, idiot."

He felt her fingers fumbling over the rope that bound his wrists. Then she seized on the knot and began working at it, probing and pulling.

"You're letting me go?" He couldn't believe it.

No reply. She seemed nervous; he heard her shallow, rapid breathing and felt the frantic desperation of her fumbling. She surely feared the oncoming terrors of the night, yet she'd come out anyway.

"Why?" he asked.

She cursed as the knot refused to yield. "They've done it so tight," she muttered, and tried another way of digging into it.

Fortunately, she was looking down all the time. Ferren, looking up, saw a ring of supernatural light appear and disappear on one side of the sky, even as a glow of natural twilight still lingered on the other. The fighting must be starting early tonight.

"Why are you helping me?" he asked again.

She answered as she continued working at the knot. "They want to hand you over to the Selectors tomorrow. I never meant for that to happen. You deserve more punishment, but not military service."

"Military service is the worst?"

"There's something bad about it."

"What?" Ferren thought instantly of his sister.

"I don't know. My father won't tell me. Perhaps he doesn't know. But he'll never let *me* be taken."

She was working away with her fingers—faster and faster, but less effectively.

"I won't be responsible for it happening to you," she said—then jerked sharply upright. "What's that?"

A rumble that wasn't thunder passed slowly across the sky.

"Nothing to worry about." Ferren tried to sound calm. "I've heard those sounds a hundred times. They don't do anything."

Zonda went back to the knot, but her fingers were trembling.

"Come loose, you pig of thing!" she muttered.

Ferren held his hands still, but he was growing more and more anxious. He sensed that she was about to give up any minute now.

"I can't... It won't... Oh, damnation!" She swore at the knot. "It's tighter than it was before!"

"Wait! Don't go."

Zonda was shaking her head and rising to her feet when he suddenly discovered the answer. "Use Urlish's fire!"

"What?"

"Get a burning twig from the fire! Burn through the ropes!"

Zonda caught on at once. She looked at the banked-up fire of dry twigs and leaves in the middle of the concrete platform. Then she sprang across and pulled the fire apart. She came back to Ferren carrying a twig in either hand, each tipped with glowing red.

It didn't take long. She applied the smouldering tips to the rope around his wrists, then to the rope around his waist. She broke off for a moment when a weird disembodied singing started up in the sky, but he pleaded with her.

"You've nearly done it! Please! *Please!*"

She burned through both ropes, tossed the twigs aside and unwound the rope that had bound his wrists.

"You can do the other one yourself," she told him, and jumped to her her feet. "Just clear out now. Go somewhere else. They'll never forgive you here."

The eerie singing in the sky intensified. She put her hands over her ears and ran, crouching low, back to the safety of the blanket in the Dwelling Place.

Ferren unwound the second rope from around his waist and freed himself from the pole. His bruises ached as he rose stiffly upright. Already there were blue lights sparkling and dancing above the horizon. It was going to be a fearful night for going out into the open.

But there was no alternative. Grimly, he strode across the Mushroom Beds and Sunflower Fields towards the Plain.

3

"Aaaaaah-oooooooh!
Aiii-eeeeee!
Aaaaaah-oooooooh!
Aiii-aaaaaah!"

The disembodied singing in the sky swelled to a terrifying volume. It seemed to come from some vast choir floating in the air, simultaneously near and far away. The unearthly beauty of it made Ferren's blood run cold.

Then he heard great resounding footsteps walk across the top of the sky.

Klumbb! Klumbb! Klumbb! Klumbb!

He started to run and couldn't stop running. In a numb state of fear, he fled over the Plain under the overarching sky. He had no idea of where he was or where he was heading. Every new threat started him off in a new direction. There were ruins here and there, but he didn't recognise them. He splashed across the Creek once, twice, half a dozen times. He was hopelessly lost.

And still it grew worse. Soon he heard whistles and chants and howls all around him, spreading colours and cracks of the whip! Mirages appeared in the air, shadows swept across the grass!

It was far, far worse than he could ever have imagined. He had never been so afraid in his life. This wasn't like peeping out from under the safety of the blanket—this was ultimate exposure, ultimate vulnerability. The lights and sounds were all chasing and hunting him down!

Later came words, great words, spoken in hollow, booming throats.

"POENA!"

"ULTIO!"

"ECCE IMPURITAS!"

"INTERDICTUM EST!"

Everything took place on a giant scale. He had the sense that the sky was pressing in upon him, bulging and weighing down towards the Earth. There were uncanny eyes blinking open and closed, appearing and vanishing, suspended like stars. There were bright fiery wheels, rolling overhead in twos and fours, sending out white and yellow flames. Terror upon terror upon terror!

All through the night he ran. Sometimes he raised his eyes to the sky, sometimes he wrapped his arms over his head. Several times he tripped and fell forward in the grass—then immediately hauled himself up and set off running again. He was frightened when fleeing, but he was even more frightened lying still.

Elemental dread overwhelmed him. Once again he was a child, whimpering for protection. He felt that he alone was the target towards which every terror was directed. The eyes were staring at *him,* the great words were spoken to *him,* the fiery wheels had marked *him* as their prey! *He* was the one that the sky wanted to crush! He was the one they were after!

On and on he ran, back and forth and round and round. He lost all sense of time. The hours merged and mingled together, everything repeated itself a million times over. He was unutterably weary. Sometimes he seemed to be dreaming on his feet, dreaming a nightmare that refused to end.

But it did end, finally. Gradually the whip-cracks died away and the great voices fell silent. The fiery wheels vanished, and the sky drew back from the Earth. A different kind of light crept above the horizon, the natural light of dawn. The new day was coming.

He scarcely understood the reason for his deliverance. He just pitched forward one last time in the grass, and stayed sprawling where he fell. Blessed peace, blessed calm, blessed silence!

When sunlight filtered through the green of the grass, it was the most wonderful sunlight he had ever seen. He had survived. He rolled over and curled up on his side. In one more minute he was fast asleep.

4

All through the night, Miriael had been struggling to make contact with Heaven. She had tried prayer and visioning and every form of spiritual transmission. But her spirit was dulled, and her powers of transcendental empathy seemed somehow blocked.

By the time the sun came up, she had lost all hope. She was condemned to lie down here in dirt and degradation. Miriael the Fourteenth Angel of Observance had fallen as no angel had ever fallen before. She knew there had been Fallen Angels long ago because many of them had since been allowed back up into Heaven. But none of them, so far as she knew, had ever lost their essential spiritual nature. Her case was unique.

She grimaced at the sight of her food bag and water bowl. Of course the Residual—Ferren—had meant well, only trying to help. But the fact that she could eat and drink like any creature of the Earth was the ultimate confirmation of her fallen state.

Her thoughts turned to Ferren and the young female who had screeched accusations at him. The behaviour of the young female was more what she would have expected from a Residual. An angel had been an instant enemy for *her*, but never for Ferren. Did that make Ferren unusual among his own kind? She'd been surprised by his curiosity and intelligence, but probably no other Residual shared those qualities.

We know so little about them, she thought. And it wasn't only her own ignorance. She remembered her period of training as a junior warrior angel…the long hours spent in the hushed schoolroom…the clear light of Heaven streaming in through small windowpanes…the intricate coloured maps…the serene voices of the blue-robed Cherubim. There had been so much to learn, yet when Pymander asked about the Residuals, his question had been dismissed. "No need to know about *them*." It was the same response when Eleth asked about the time before the Great Collapse. "No need to know about *that*."

She mused over her memories for a while; then her thoughts returned to the present. Now that Ferren's secret visits to her had been uncovered, she hoped he wouldn't be in more serious trouble than he already was. What about her own situation? The young female had been going to report on both of them… What would the tribe do about her? She couldn't fly, she couldn't summon help from Heaven, she had no power to destroy with a flash of light. But perhaps she could crawl to a safer spot.

When she tried, though, she couldn't do that either. She willed motion into her limbs, but the movements she produced were weak and floundering. She was like a newborn, with arms and legs that hadn't yet learned to work together. Even proper crawling was beyond her.

She gave up in frustration. Again her eye fell upon the food bag and water bowl…and a strange sensation came over her. The impulse that made her take Heavenly manna into her mouth was a spiritual need, but this was a need she'd never experienced before. A bodily craving, low down and visceral, an actual physical hunger.

She considered it for a while, but it didn't go away. The hollowness inside her demanded satisfaction. Obscene, but undeniable… When she looked at the items of food laid out on the bag beside her, she could almost taste them.

What does it matter anyway? she told herself. She'd already eaten at least one mushroom. She reached out and scooped up half a dozen sunflower seeds, dropped them into her mouth and began chewing.

5

"It can't be!"
"He couldn't have!"
"What do we do?"

The People stared in amazement at the cast-off ropes lying around the pole on the Garage platform. Then Neath examined the burnt ends of the ropes and worked out how it had been done. "Twigs from the fire. He must've reached out to the fire somehow."

To the People, the prisoner's escape still seemed almost supernatural. They were more worried about the consequences than how it had been done.

"Now we've got no one to hand over to the Selectors!"
"They'll take one of us instead!"
"What do we do?"

Neath raised and flapped his arms for attention. "We search the Home Ground for him. He could be trying to hide somewhere. Doing the same as his sister did."

The People spread out to search: in the Sunflower Field, the High Hedge, the Rushfield, the Blackberry Patch. Only Zonda didn't participate.

She was sure Ferren would have followed her suggestion and gone out beyond the Home Ground altogether. Everyone seemed to have forgotten he'd been on the open Plain many times already. She stood with her hands on her hips, reflecting.

Then an idea came to her—as a way of checking on his escape. It was something she would never even have thought of before. But after what she'd done yesterday, she dared.

She wandered across to the roofless ruins of Number Forty-Two, where the blue-tongue lizards were kept in pens. The walls were low in some places, high in others. She mounted a section of wall that came down to the level of her hip, then advanced along the top with her arms spread wide for balance. As the wall rose, she climbed higher and higher, step by step and stone by stone. Concentrating on where to place her feet, she refused to let her gaze stray until she reached the very highest point of the walls.

Finally she looked—and almost fell. Her head swam. The world was so big all around!

Beyond the familiar structures of the Home Ground, a sea of grass stretched out endlessly in all directions. Green, green, endless green! A breeze blew against her cheek, the sun beating down seemed almost on top of her.

Then she planted her feet more firmly, and the giddiness passed. She shielded her eyes with one hand and scanned around in search of Ferren.

Pale scattered bits of ruin...the winding watercourse of the Creek... but no Ferren. Had he gone to see that Celestial again? Was he lying beside her in the grass? The thought left a bitter taste in her mouth.

She shifted the position of her feet on the wall to look out on the other side. She knew there was a glitter on the grass where the Celestial lay. Before she could locate it, though, she saw something else.

Approaching across the Plain were two black figures. Selectors! Brutal and sinister, they ploughed forward through the grass. Their black rubbery suits covered them from head to toe, fitting tight over their bodies like black rubbery skin. So close already!

A shadow gripped her heart, and she shivered in spite of the sun. For a moment she was paralysed. Then a voice called out behind her, below in the Front Gardens.

"Daughter! Come down!"

It was her father, and he was both frightened and angry. "What're you doing?" he shouted. "Keep low, keep small, keep out of sight!"

She responded with a shout of her own, loud enough for the whole tribe to hear.

"It's the Selectors! They're nearly here! The Selectors are coming!"

She took one last glance at the two figures before jumping down. Now they were staring straight at her, and she could see the eyeslits in their black rubbery suits. Behind the slits gleamed a bright, uncanny light not like ordinary eyes at all.

She jumped down so fast that she missed her landing and fell sprawling on the ground.

6

By the time the Selectors came into the Dwelling Place, Neath had the People all lined up against one wall. The women were sobbing, the children were blubbering, the men were trembling with fear.

The Selectors were much taller than any of the tribe. Their feet were shod in heavy boots with metal spikes, and they had slits for mouths as well as for eyes. One carried a bulky canvas pack on his back.

Close up, their black rubbery suits displayed individual decorations. The one without the pack had SELECTOR No.1 printed across his shoulders, while various parts of his suit were painted with pictures. On the back of his head, whorls of light brown colour imitated human hair; the sides of his head were illustrated with human ears; and pink-painted fingernails adorned the tips of his black-gloved fingers.

The second Selector was labelled SELECTOR No.2. Other words in red and white were scribbled everywhere over his suit:

HYPER-POWER!
WE COLLECT!
NO MESSING!
WIPE OUT!!!

He also wore a cage of steel wire over his head like a helmet.

The two black figures cast a spell of instant horror. They stood for a moment in the Back Door, then marched across to the centre of the Dwelling Place. The crying and blubbering died away, replaced by a numb sort of silence.

Neath went up to them, faced Selector No.1 and bowed. His whole posture expressed fawning humility. Zonda felt embarrassed for him.

"You the chief of this lot, old man?" The mouth opened like a trap, disclosing two rows of metallic teeth. The voice was dry and sneering.

"I am, fellow-allies, I am."

"Okay. We're gonna select one of you lot for military service."

"I know, fellow-allies. Every year."

"Very good, *fellow-ally*. Smart sucker ain't you? Hope you got some other smart suckers here for us to look at."

Neath was apologetic. "We had one just like you want. We were going to hand him over to you."

"So?"

"He escaped."

Selector No.1 laughed with a sound like metal being scraped. He turned to his companion. "Ain't they something?"

"Full of excuses!" Selector No.2 had the same dry, sneering voice. "Trying to get out of their contribution!"

"No, no." Neath was almost cringing now. "We want to do it. The same as every year."

Zonda listened with growing frustration. Why didn't her father mention the Celestial? Couldn't he see the opportunity?

She stepped forward from the line. "We can do a different contribution," she said.

"Huh?"

"We made a discovery. You'll be interested."

Neath made hushing gestures and tried to stand in front of her. "Not us. It was that one who escaped. We disown him. Nothing to do with us."

"Shut it." Selector No.1 dismissed him and beckoned Zonda closer. "What discovery?"

Still Neath tried to interpose. "She doesn't mean anything. My daughter. We're not involved with—"

"*Shut it!*" Selector No.1 gave him a prod in the chest that sent him stumbling backwards, then turned again to Zonda. "Explain."

"There's a Celestial lying out on the Plain. I saw her yesterday."

The Selectors *were* interested. "What sort of Celestial?"

"I don't know. Long golden hair. Blue eyes."

"What colour robes?"

"Yellow."

The Selectors exchanged glances. "A junior warrior angel?" Selector No.2 couldn't believe it.

"These dummies ain't lying," said Selector No.1. "They don't have the brains."

"She was on the ground like she couldn't move," said Zonda.

"What about her aura?" asked Selector No.1.

"Her what?"

"A globe of light around her. Shape of an egg."

"No. Didn't see that."

The Selectors shook their heads in amazement. An iridescent sort of spittle was visible inside their mouths, moving and gleaming in the narrow slits. Selector No.1 turned to Selector No.2.

"This has to be investigated."

"She can take us to the place." Selector No.2 nodded towards Zonda.

"Yes, and grandpa too." Selector No.1 pointed a black finger at Neath. "Get moving, both of you."

"She's an enemy, right?" Zonda suggested. "You have to punish her."

The Selectors didn't bother to answer. Zonda started forward before they could give her a push, and Neath followed her out the Back Door.

7

Zonda remembered the route and found the place again. The junior warrior angel lay as before in the centre of her patch of flattened grass.

"There she is!" Zonda stopped at the edge of the tall grass and looked out ahead.

The others stopped too. Neath uttered a groan, but the Selectors were excited.

"It's true!" Selector No.2 whistled. "Who'd have believed it?"

"And no aura," Selector No.1 agreed. "I thought they couldn't survive in our atmosphere."

The angel must have heard their voices. She changed her position on the ground to lie facing them.

"Barely surviving, by the looks of it," said Selector No.2.

"But does she have the charge for a flash?" Selector No.1 turned to Zonda. "How close did you go before?"

"I didn't, but Ferren did. Right next to her, he was." Zonda sniffed. "You oughter…"

The Selector was no longer listening. "I'm thinking, she could've blasted us already if she was going to do it."

"If she still had the power." Selector No.2 nodded.

"Hmm."

Neath spoke up suddenly. "Can we go now?" he asked, wringing his hands.

"No," said Selector No.1. "We have a use for you."

He seized the old man suddenly by the shoulders and propelled him out onto the patch of flattened grass.

"Walk up close to her!" he ordered.

Neath advanced another three tottering paces, then collapsed in a heap on the ground.

"Closer!"

Neath struggled to rise, but his face was grey with fear.

"I'll do it," said Zonda, and marched out from the shelter of the tall grass. She was afraid, but not nearly so terrified as her father.

The angel looked up at her and frowned—but nothing else.

"No flash!" cried Selector No.1. "Keep walking!" he ordered. "Close enough to touch!"

The angel seemed to have decided on silence. Zonda continued to walk forward, in smaller and smaller steps.

"Now touch!"

Zonda shook her head. "You do it!" she retorted. "If you're so—"

There was a hiss behind her—then a rush of movement—then a thump on her back that sent her pitching forward, headlong to the ground. Her forearm fell across the angel's outspread hair.

"Aiieee!" she shrieked as she realised what she was touching. She scrambled away, expecting to be seared or scorched or something horrible. But when she inspected her arm—

"Nothing!" Selector No.1 roared in triumph.

In the next moment, Selector No.2 came charging up beside him. "Yarooo! We caught us an angel!"

They stood over the angel and brandished their fists. Neath had already retreated into the tall grass again, and Zonda shuffled a little further away.

"First live capture ever," said Selector No.1. "They'll be knocked out when they hear this back at base."

"Contact 'em now."

"Okay. Hold still."

While his colleague held still, Selector No.1 unbuckled a flap of the pack on his back. Digging inside, he brought out a small black box with a silvery spike. Then he walked a short distance away, extended the spike, raised the box to his mouthslit and spoke into it. All Zonda could hear was a burring, crackling sound.

Meanwhile, Selector No.2 had decided to have some fun with their victim. He took a step forward to stand straddling her waist.

"You airy fairy fart!" he jeered. "We gotcha now, ain't we?"

The angel remained silent, passive and unmoving.

"*Ain't we?*" he repeated, and gave her a kick. The angel tried to roll away, but was trapped between his boots.

"Won't do you no good being beautiful now! I spit on beautiful! I hate it! I'll show you what I do to beautiful!"

He raised one foot and stamped down hard on the angel's wings. Zonda gasped. The angel's mouth opened in an O of shock and pain, but she made no sound. The lack of reaction only enraged the Selector even more.

"Pretty little feathers! Pretty-pretty-pretty! They won't be so white by the time I've finished! You won't be so pure and perfect then!"

He stamped again and again. The angel flailed feebly in a flurry of feathers.

"Defile and desecrate!" There was a hot, mad glare in his eyeslits. "Defile and desecrate! Defile and—"

"Stop that!" Selector No.1's harsh voice cut across his bellowing.

"What? Why?"

"Leave her be."

"I'm sick of angels being pure and perfect."

Selector No.1 indicated the black box he held in his hand. "I've been talking to base, and they want her kept prisoner. Kept in good condition for the Doctors. You damage her, and they'll empty you out."

Selector No.2 snarled, but he was beaten. He stepped away from the angel.

"I'd have plucked her like a chicken," he muttered. "I'd've defiled her good."

"Shut up and let me think." Selector No.1 was clearly the one in charge. "They're sending transport, but it'll take a few days to arrive. We can't leave her out here."

He stroked his black rubber chin with a black rubber finger, then nodded towards Zonda and her father. "I reckon we'll chain her to a wall in their dump of a place. It's not like she's got much strength anyway. And we'll round up some dummies to carry her." He swung to Selector No.2. "Right. You go back, round 'em up and march 'em out here."

"Why me?" Selector No.2 was still in an ugly mood. "Why not you?"

"'Cos I don't trust you. I'm not leaving you with her on your own."

So Selector No.2 went off to the Home Ground, and Neath went after him. Zonda sat quietly at the side of the flattened grass and waited to watch the next stage of proceedings.

8

For the People it was like a long evil dream. First the horror of being driven out into the open over the Plain; then the shock of seeing a real live Celestial; then, worst of all, the terror of being forced to touch her, lift her up and carry her. They flinched and quailed and whimpered. But Zonda assured them they wouldn't get hurt, and their fear of the Selectors was greater than any other fear.

So they carried her on their shoulders back to the Home Ground. Their minds had gone completely blank and numb. They didn't want to think and they didn't want to understand.

But when the Selectors had the angel transported right into the Dwelling Place, Zonda understood—and protested.

"You can't put her here. This is where we sleep at night. We can't sleep if she's here in the middle of us."

"So don't sleep," growled Selector No.2.

Zonda directed her appeal to Selector No.1. "Can't you put her somewhere else in the Home Ground?"

He shook his head. "These are the strongest walls."

"What about the Store, then?" Zonda pointed. "Over there, in the corner behind the curtain. Same wall, but she'll be out of our way. 'Least, we won't have to see her."

Selector No.1 crossed to the Store and looked in through the curtain. The inspection proved satisfactory. He signalled to Selector No.2, who drove the bearers forward into the Store. All had their eyes half shut and shrank from the angel even as they balanced her on their shoulders. When Selector No.1 gave the order, they slid her roughly to the floor and scurried out in a hurry.

Zonda kept the curtain parted and peered in. The angel lay unmoving between high-piled stacks of bags, bowls and baskets. Selector No.1 delved into the pack on Selector No.2's back and brought out a length of chain, a padlock and an assortment of tools.

Then the two of them knelt and set about securing their prisoner. They wound an end of the chain around the angel's left ankle and fastened it tight it with the padlock. Selector No.1 turned a key in the lock and put the key in his pocket. Selector No.2 picked up a tool with a long metal point and tapped a spot on the wall.

"Bolt here?" he suggested.

Selector No.1 nodded. "Yeah, solid as anywhere." Then he caught sight of Zonda. "What're you staring at?"

"Nothing. You know she needs feeding?"

Selector No.2 uttered a harsh laugh. "Angels don't eat terrestrial food, dummy."

Zonda stood her ground. "*She* does. I saw her, she put a mushroom in her mouth."

"Phah!" Selector No.2 waved her away, but Selector No.1 looked thoughtful.

"Hold on." He turned to Selector No.2. "You remember, the water bowl and bag of food on the grass? You saw them."

"The mushroom came from that bag," Zonda piped up. "Ferren must've taken—"

Selector No.1 continued to address his colleague. "*Nothing* about this makes sense. If an angel can survive in our atmosphere, who knows what else she can do?" He scowled at the angel's prostrate body. "We just gotta keep her surviving. If she *does* want food and water…" He swung suddenly to Zonda. "You feed her if she needs feeding."

"Me?"

"You. What's your name?"

"Zonda."

"Okay, Zonda. You're responsible for her. If she snuffs out, I'll snuff *you* out. Got it?"

Zonda gulped and said nothing. Selector No.1 snapped his fingers.

"Start drilling," he ordered Selector No.2. "I'm going to tell these dummies what's what."

Zonda backed away as he rose to his feet. In the main area of the Dwelling Place, the People sat huddled in a state of mute misery. Some had their arms wrapped over their heads, others were moaning quietly to themselves. None dared look at the Selector when he emerged through the curtain.

"Listen up!" He clapped his hands. "This is what's going to happen. That junior warrior angel"—he jerked a thumb towards the Store— "she stays chained up until transport arrives. Nobody to go in there except you." His eyeslits swivelled to focus on Zonda. "And nobody to talk to her *including* you."

A vibrating drone came from behind the curtain. Selector No.2 had begun drilling into the wall.

Selector No.1 raised his voice above the drone. "We won't be staying in your pigsty dump, we'll be camping outside. But very close. And we'll come in to check on her every day."

Neath made an effort to sit up straight, recovering his leadership role at last. "How long until she goes, fellow-ally?"

"Three, four days. Depends if the transport starts out straightaway."

"What if Heaven tries to rescue her?"

"Nah. Heaven doesn't know, or they'd have rescued her already. We'll be close by if they try anything."

"But if they send a really big force?" Neath's voice was shaky but persistent. "They could kill us all."

"They wouldn't do that to you, old man." Selector No.1 sneered. "They have ethical principles they're supposed to follow. Like not slaughtering the innocent."

"But—"

"They have ethical principles, but *I* don't. You want to stay alive, it's *me* you have to worry about." He grinned a savage grin, showing the metallic teeth in his mouthslit. "On the other hand, if you do well looking after this angel, maybe we'll let you off your military service contribution this year. Hey?"

"Thank you." Neath lowered his head in gratitude. Then he looked around for support from the rest of the tribe. "Thank you," he prompted.

"Thank you," they echoed. "Thank you, thank you, thank you."

"*If* you do well," said Selector No.1. "Now quit blathering. No need for you all hanging around. Go off and do whatever you do."

9

Ferren slept through until late. When he opened his eyes, the sun was high in the sky, already past noon.

He felt battered and bruised. Fleeing from the terrors of the night, he'd forgotten the beating he'd been given, but the aches and soreness came back to him now. He remembered Zonda encouraging the People to beat him up, then Zonda freeing him to escape afterwards. Why? It was a total mystery...

He levered himself stiffly from the ground and rose head and shoulders above the level of the grass. Endless green stretched out in all directions. After running so far through the night, he had no idea where he'd ended up. There were ruins here and there, but he didn't know any of them.

Then he saw the line of a watercourse like a long parting through the grass. Could it be a different stretch of the Creek? Feeling thirsty, he headed towards it.

The water ran clear over pebbles and silt, the low banks were thick with weeds. He waded into the shallows and scooped up handfuls of water to drink. Then he washed himself all over. Although he had plenty of bruises, he had few cuts or abrasions, and none of them deep.

Remembering the People's treatment for wounds, he collected leaves from several weeds: dock leaves, mallow leaves and sorrel leaves. He rolled and crushed the leaves between his hands, then rubbed the juice onto his bruises and abrasions. The cooling, soothing effect gave him immediate relief.

Meanwhile, he was thinking… When he stood up again, he paid closer attention to the ruins he hadn't recognised before. And yes, that *could* be Beaumont Street—only seen from an entirely unfamiliar angle. And if that *was* Beaumont Street, then that ruin further off had to be the Home Ground. Suddenly he felt certain of it. For all the great distances he'd covered through the night, he'd been running around in circles!

He focused again on Beaumont Street and remembered the angel Miriael. Would she still be lying out in the grass, or would she have taken his advice and returned to Heaven? So much had happened since that last unfinished conversation…

He set off at once at a fast jog through the grass. The angel had said they could be friends, and now he had no one else in the world. He skirted close by tumbledown concrete slabs of the Beaumont Street ruins, and came to the place of flattened grass.

But she wasn't there. The food bag and water bowl remained, and the same sprinkling of glitter. But no Miriael.

Then he spotted something—two somethings—very pure and white against the green of the grass. Could it be? He darted across and knelt to inspect. Two white feathers from her wings!

His heart swelled with conflicting emotions. He felt sad and sorry that she'd gone, but he felt proud and elated that she'd left him this reminder of herself. Even though she'd returned to Heaven, she hadn't forgotten him when she went off. And not just one feather as he'd suggested, but two! She must have really liked him!

He gathered them up with care. They were quite small, obviously not the largest feathers from her wings, but perfectly formed as if sculpted with infinite delicacy. And so very very white! He vowed to treasure them as long as he lived, and think of her every time he looked at them.

He unwrapped his loincloth a little from his waist and threaded the quills in and out through the weave of the cloth. When he was sure the feathers were secure, he rewrapped the cloth and rolled it over at the top. Now his treasures were snug against his hip, yet completely hidden from view.

He walked away from the circle of flattened grass feeling like a very special person indeed.

10

Ferren's good mood didn't last long. He was happy for the angel to have gone back up to Heaven, but he was miserable for himself. Now more than ever he was alone. He could have stood and howled to the universe.

They'll never forgive you here. Zonda's words echoed and re echoed in his mind—and he knew they were true. Still, he couldn't resist going to take another look at the Home Ground.

He came up on the Blackberry Patch side and peered forward over the grass. The top of old Shuff's head was just visible above the blackberry bushes; further back, he caught a glimpse of one of the women crossing from the Shed in the direction of the Swimming Pool. Were the People all working the same as usual?

Yet today was the day of the Selectors. Had they come and gone already? But if they'd taken somebody off for military service, the People should have been weeping and wailing. At the very least there should have been a ritual of consolation with the totems.

He couldn't understand it—and he couldn't ask anyone for answers. His exclusion came home to him more sharply than ever. Events in the Home Ground were going on without him, while he'd been cut out of the story.

He turned away and wandered over the Plain for a time. In one place he found a redcurrant bush and gorged himself on the small round fruits. In another place he found a sweet potato root, which he dug up and ate uncooked. But he wasn't searching for food, just walking for the sake of walking.

He knew he ought to go off elsewhere and start some new sort of life of his own. But he had no idea what sort of life it could be. His tribe was his whole existence, and he couldn't imagine another world.

In the end, he had to come back for another look. Crossing the Creek, he circled around and approached the Home Ground from the other side. He crept right into the Rushfield and looked out at the basket-weavers on the muddy bank.

They were both there, Jollis and Stessa with their children, Tam and Sibby. The women weren't actually working, only sitting in silence with doleful expressions. The children were strangely quiet too. So things *weren't* back to normal—but what were they?

He was close enough to call out, and for a moment he nearly did. But Zonda's words discouraged him: *They'll never forgive you here.* He could ask questions, but Jollis and Stessa wouldn't reply. They'd probably pretend they couldn't see or hear him.

It was hopeless. He felt like a ghost haunting the scenes of his past. He swung around and headed back out into the grass of the Plain. Then, twenty paces away, an aroma came to his nostrils. The smell of dinner cooking!

He stopped and sniffed again. Perhaps a shift in the breeze had just wafted the savoury aroma in his direction. It smelled like bean stew with meat, onions and tomatoes…his very favourite. He could almost taste the flavours in his mouth.

How long until the People in the fields were called in for dinner? Then everyone would gather in the Dwelling Place…the stew would be served in the usual three bowls…the usual jostling for position…the glorious satisfaction of a full belly! And afterwards, the evening rituals and the comfort and warmth of snuggling under the blanket…

There was a wetness on his cheeks, and he realised he was crying. He couldn't help it, he wanted his home back and his life back. He didn't want to wander out over the Plain with no company except small creatures in the grass and birds in the sky. He would do anything to be a part of his tribe again!

They'll never forgive you here, Zonda had said. But might they forget if he hung around for weeks…or months…or perhaps a year?

He jumped at a glimpse of movement and ducked his head down just in time. Someone was walking out from the Home Ground!

But none of the People *ever* walked out from the Home Ground… Cautiously, he raised his head high enough to take a look. Two black figures were striding forward through the grass. Selectors!

He shuddered. He'd seen Selectors before—some years the same ones and some years different—but their menacing appearance was always a shock. They must have been inside the Home Ground all this time, and now were they leaving…

Except they weren't leaving. They stopped a mere thirty or so paces away from the ruins and began stamping down the grass. Then one unslung a big pack from his back, and the two of them dug into it. They brought out a pole, ropes and a tightly rolled bundle of canvas.

Ferren continued to watch as one extended the pole and planted it in the ground. Then they unfurled the canvas and spread it out over the pole. They were erecting some kind of pyramid-shaped tent for themselves. The canvas was as black and ominous as their own rubbery suits.

Clearly they intended to stay. Ferren remembered how Selectors had stayed and waited for his sister when she'd hidden away two years ago. Were they staying to wait for *him* now?

He didn't know, he couldn't find out and it didn't matter anyway. He only knew he couldn't stay hanging around the Home Ground—not for a year or a month or a week, not even for a minute longer. He kept his head down low and crept away through the grass. The decision had been made for him.

11

Ferren walked in a straight line away from the Selectors and the Home Ground. But his straight line wasn't a straight line to anywhere. He only knew what he was leaving behind; every other direction was the same to him.

He passed beyond the limit of all previous explorations, yet the Plain remained unchanged, endless grass with scattered rubble and ruin.

Cocooned in his own misery, he watched his feet moving one in front of the other, mechanically covering ground. Time passed, but time had no meaning for him.

But it had a meaning when he realised the day was coming to an end. He raised his eyes and saw that the sun was already touching the horizon. Soon it would be dark, soon he would be pursued by the terrors of the night. And he would be once more out in the open…

He was starting to panic when something odd drew his attention. The horizon ahead of him was perfectly, unnaturally level. Although the Plain was generally flat, it couldn't be *that* flat.

He had no notion of what he was looking at, but he set off jogging towards it. He was hoping against hope for some sort of shelter for the night.

Coming closer, he squinted and shaded his eyes. Now he could see an artificial structure built up off the ground on stilts. It seemed to run in either direction like a black line drawn across the bottom of the sky.

He nodded as the explanation jumped into his mind. Of course! This must be the overbridge that the angel had told him about. She had said it wasn't far in this direction. An overbridge leading to the biggest Humen camp on the continent, an overbridge along which members of his tribe had to march when selected for military service…

Would it provide shelter, though? The light was now fading fast, with only a small portion of sun still showing. He picked up his pace and kept jogging.

Soon he could make out all the details. The stilts were immense pylons arranged in pairs and spaced at regular intervals. Both the pylons and the deck they supported were made of some dull black metal.

Then the vegetation changed. A short distance away from the over-bridge, the grass of the Plain gave way to weeds. He slowed and advanced more warily through the weeds, scanning from side to side. The vast structure was silent and deserted.

Eventually he came right up to the pylons, which were bedded in pairs of square concrete blocks. Now the ground was bare, where even the weeds didn't grow. Continuing forward, he passed in under the deck, which was as wide as a roof. It was dim and shadowy here, with hollow sounds and echoes.

With the deck as a roof, he was at least partially sheltered from the sky. He craned his neck to look up and saw a crisscross underframe of diagonal struts beneath the girders and plates of the deck itself. So this was the kind of thing the Humen built: massive, angular, ugly.

He looked again at the ground and concrete blocks—and decided he could do better than just a roof high overhead. Between each pair of blocks was a narrow channel. Wide enough to lie in, snug enough to protect him at the sides.

Then he thought of an extra cover. He could pile up weeds in the channel, then burrow in underneath! Like being under the blanket in the Dwelling Place! He set to work immediately.

Heading to the nearest patch of weeds, he tore them up by handfuls and carried them across to deposit in the channel. By now, the sun had gone down, and a light wind had sprung up. The wind's eerie whistling through the struts of the overbridge was like a prelude to the supernatural sounds of the night.

Back and forth he went, building his pile of weeds to a satisfactory height. He flung on one last armful, then wriggled his way underneath. Covered above and walled in at the sides, he felt warm and safe and secure.

It wasn't like being in his proper place in his proper home. But it would do. He had found a way to survive…and he intended to keep on surviving.

12

That night, Ferren dreamed a vivid dream. It started from the real memory of his sister Shanna when the Selectors took her away. But in the dream, he wasn't crying and hopelessly hanging on to her— he actually went with her, and nobody held him back. The two of them marched out over the Creek and across the Plain, with the Selectors following. They were doing military service together.

In the next part of the dream, they were striding along on top of the overbridge. Faster and faster their feet pounded the metal deck, faster and faster they swung their arms. Ferren could hardly keep up with his sister, and the Selectors could hardly keep up with either of them. The overbridge stretched out straight ahead all the way to the horizon.

"We're going to see what's there to see, we're going to see what's there to see!" they sang as they marched. It was military service, but it was also a great adventure…

When Ferren awoke, he had no idea where he was. His nostrils inhaled the dank, acrid smell of weeds, his eyes registered weak daylight coming in through tiny chinks. There should have been People breathing and snoring and stirring around him, but there was only a soundless hush.

Then gradually it all came back…his solitude and exile. For the first time in his life, he had slept alone. But he still felt as if Shanna was with him.

He pushed aside his cover of weeds and sat upright. While the overbridge remained a great shadow over his head, low beams of early morning sunlight lit up the ground all around. He rose to his feet and brushed off remnants of weed still clinging to him.

Time to begin a new day! Time to begin a new life!

He walked to the side of the overbridge and the edge of the bare ground. Endless and featureless, the Plain spread out before him. Though he stared in the direction of the Home Ground, he knew he wouldn't be able to see it. Nor Beaumont Street either…

He remembered the angel and the two white feathers he'd found yesterday. She'd gone back up to Heaven, but she'd left him the best of reminders. On impulse, he unrolled the top of the cloth around his waist. Yes, her feathers were in place exactly where he'd threaded them, not crushed or crumpled in any way. He grinned to himself.

Thinking of the angel, a conversation they'd had some days ago came back to him. He'd told her about his sister, and she'd said he ought to go and visit her. All he had to do was follow the overbridge to the Humen camp, she'd said. *All he had to do!* At the time, it had seemed impossible.

Yet somehow the impossible wasn't impossible anymore. Since yesterday, the thousand reasons why he couldn't even think of such a journey had ceased to exist. What else did he have to do now? He was condemned to leave everything behind anyway, so he needed some purpose for living.

And *this*, at least, would be an excellent purpose.

He stepped out further to take a look along the overbridge. Pylon after pylon marched away in regular succession, diminishing into the distance. The overbridge really did stretch straight to the horizon, as it had done in his dream. It was also as deserted as yesterday evening.

How long would it take to walk to the Humen camp? But time didn't matter, since he had nothing to come back to. Perhaps, if he found Shanna there, he could volunteer to stay and work alongside her? Even if military service meant working as a slave, or something as bad as Zonda imagined...he'd still rather be a slave with his sister than remain on his own forever.

He set off at once. Later he could look out for a stream in which to wash, later he could forage for nuts and seeds and berries. He walked past concrete blocks and pylons at the edge of the bare ground. No one travelling along the overbridge could see him unless they were right at the side; in any case, he expected to hear them long before they saw him.

He touched the rolled-over top of his loincloth and the feathers through the cloth.

"Wish me luck," he murmured. "I'm following your advice."

13

The Selectors were indeed Hypers, as Miriael had already guessed from Ferren's account. In the past, she had fought massed units of Hypers and destroyed some of them with the power of her flash. But never before had she encountered any close up.

While the Selectors chained her to the wall, she had pretended weakness and fatigue so they wouldn't start questioning her. The weakness was hardly a pretence anyway. Afterwards, she had examined their handiwork: one end of the chain padlocked right around her ankle, the other fastened to a bolt drilled into solid brick. There was no way she could break free.

The Residual Zonda put out a bowl for food and a bowl for water, but made it very plain she was acting under orders. When Miriael tried to ask what had happened to Ferren, the girl only scowled and muttered under her breath.

She continued to mutter as she moved about collecting food for the food bowl from various bags and baskets. "Phh! Long streak of nothing." "Skinny as a snake." "Thinks she's beautiful."

Apart from Ferren, Miriael had never encountered Residuals close up either. But seeing Zonda now, one thing struck her that she'd noticed in Ferren without thinking about it. Was it a characteristic of all Residuals? In contrast to all Hypers?

On the second day of her captivity, she attempted a friendly overture. "You're Zonda, aren't you? I heard you say your name yesterday. I'm Miriael."

Zonda dropped her eyes and mumbled from the side of her mouth. "Not allowed to talk to you."

It was her eyes that Miriael needed to look into. She gave up on friendliness and went for the direct approach.

"Raise your eyes!" she commanded. "Look at me now!"

Zonda did as she was told, though not out of obedience. Her mouth fell open, and she stared at the angel in surprise. Miriael probed deep into her eyes...and had her answer before Zonda could turn away again.

"Just as I thought."

"You can't order me around!" Zonda still mumbled from the side of her mouth as though that didn't count as talking.

"It's all right. I needed to check. Did you know you have a soul?"

Zonda responded with a grunt—but a quizzical sort of grunt.

"A spark of the divine in you," Miriael explained. "Your soul is what your mind and thinking grows from. It makes you alive as a human—"

Miriael broke off as a sound came from the Dwelling Place: an ominous crunch of heavy spiked boots across the floor. In the next moment the curtain was thrown back, and the Selectors appeared.

"What's this?" Selector No.1 looked at the way Zonda and Miriael faced one another. "Not talking, are you?"

Zonda moved back against the wall, making space for the Selectors to enter the Store.

"It wasn't me talking to *her*," she retorted. "I can't stop her talking to *me*."

"Hah! She's found her voice, then?"

"Yes," said Miriael in a loud, sharp voice. She now wanted to make them look at her "When I know who I'm talking to."

Two pairs of eyeslits swivelled towards her. She focused on Selector No.2 and probed into the light behind the slits. A spectral sort of light, restless and active... Deeper and deeper she probed.

"Stop that!" he roared suddenly. "Stop looking at me!"

Still she continued to stare, and the eyeslits continued to stare back.

"What is it?" asked Selector No.1.

"She's...she's trying to search into me. And sneering! She *despises* me! Nobody does that to me!"

Too late Miriael adjusted the downward curve of her mouth. Selector No.1 lunged forward with his boot upraised. But Selector No.2 pulled him back before he could stamp down.

"No, she's afraid of you. See, she's shaking!"

"That's not fear, that's scorn. She thinks she's so much better than us."

Everyone's so much better, thought Miriael. *Residuals are so much better.*

"Forget her," said Selector No.1. "She has no idea what we are."

"She does. She despises us for being Hypers."

"Like I despise all fairy fluff. Let her be."

Selector No.2 allowed his colleague to lead him out through the curtain. Still, he managed one last threat before he left. "I'll finish her good, I swear. She gives me that look again, I'll finish her."

They continued talking on the other side of the curtain. Then Selector No.1 called Zonda outside to question her about the angel's eating habits. Miriael heard their voices, but hardly listened to their words.

She couldn't get over the shock of looking into a Hyper's eyes. Even though she had guessed in advance, it was another thing to actually confront a being without a soul. Such terrible lifeless emptiness! She shivered at the recollection. The Selectors moved and spoke and functioned, yet they were mere shells of human beings. There was thinking and intelligence in the light behind those eyeslits, but there was no originating spark. Whatever animated them was unnatural and unholy. How could such beings exist? How could they *dare* to exist?

14

All morning, Ferren walked along in the shadow of the overbridge. He was ready to hide at the first hint of danger, but there was never anyone travelling along on the top. At the start of his journey, he went past a ramp sloping down to the ground from the deck, labelled on large signs as **D223**. Later he went past other ramps labelled **D222**, **D221**, **D220** and **D219**.

He had no problem finding food or water. In one place, a stream flowed across under the overbridge; in another place, a vine with orange fruits grew twining around one of the pylons. The vine was of a kind he'd never seen before, but he sniffed and tested the fruit, then bit into one. It was sweet and delicious, more sweet and delicious than anything he'd ever tasted.

I'm learning about the world, he thought. *There must be so many wonderful things in it!*

The landscape changed as he journeyed on. The level Plain gave way to low rolling hills, and the grass gave way to thornbushes. Sometimes the thornbushes came right in under the overbridge, and he had to zigzag around them or force a passage between them.

There were new sights in the distance too. He saw ruined buildings far larger than the Home Ground or any of the neighbouring ruins. One structure looked like a bridge, a decrepit stone version of the overbridge itself. Also in the distance stood three metal drums, not old or decrepit but shiny and silvery. He might have been tempted to explore except for his more important purpose.

The sun was high in the sky when he became aware of something bigger than low hills ahead. A ridge as steep as a cliff stretched all the way across the horizon. A fine haze lay over it like a veil of drifting smoke.

Then the thornbushes thinned out and gave way to barren ground. Instead of soft soil underfoot, now there was grit and sand and gravel, with occasional bits of half-buried brick and tile. Ferren continued to walk by the side of the pylons.

By and by, jagged fissures opened up in the ground. Like cuts or wounds, they split the bare stony surface, running in every direction. Many were dressed as wounds too, closed up with stitches of wire or held fast with metal staples. Sometimes he saw caps of metal soldered over the ground like sticking plasters.

What strange events had happened here? he wondered. Probably something to do with the war…

The ridge ahead loomed larger and higher; the overbridge cut through it in a V-shaped cleft. On the brow of the ridge, he saw a line of giant steel letters erected on upright frames, spelling out huge mysterious words:

THE RAZORBACK THROUGHPASS
STAGE 4 OF THE GOULBURN TO BANKSTOWN PROJECT
LANDSCAPING BY DR. VERRIL STAINES

Meanwhile, the air was growing hot with a heat that was more than the warmth of the sun. He wiped the sweat from his forehead and kept his eyes on the cleft ahead. A smell of burning came to his nostrils, seemingly wafted from the ridge itself.

At close quarters, the ridge was wrapped in a mesh of woven wire, as though its steep slopes needed holding in. The surface under the wire was black and charred, with a sprinkling of white ash. Nothing burned there at present—but he received a shock when he looked ahead to where the cleft cut through. The whole interior of the ridge was smouldering with a dull red light!

He came right up to the mouth of the cleft and stopped. Now he could see the layers within: a thick, tarry substance under the outer surface of rock and ash, then a glowing molten core under the tar.

He tried to go on, but it was like being in an oven. With every pace, the heat under his feet grew more intense. The walls on either side seemed to rise and bear down on him in sweltering waves. Impossible to walk through at the bottom of the cleft!

Yet he couldn't give up now. It was surely possible to pass through on the overbridge itself, or why would the bridge have been built? If that was the way to do it, that was what he would have to do.

He stepped up to the nearest pylon and mounted the concrete block at its base. Wrapping his arms around the metal, he began to work his way higher and higher. There were plenty of projecting bolt-heads for handholds and footholds. Soon he was swarming up over the outer struts of the crisscross underframe.

The final obstacle was a cordon of cables strung on stanchions and running all the way along the edge of the deck. The cables were sheathed in red and white plastic and gave off a low, continuous hum. He didn't like the sound or the look of them. Still, he took a deep breath and slid forward under the lowest cable. His skin shrunk and tingled as he passed underneath, but he made no contact.

Safely through to the roadway, he jumped to his feet and scanned ahead. The overbridge ran through the cleft with a thirty-foot space on either side. It would be hot, but not unbearable—and not for long. He could see where the molten core of the ridge came to an end and the cleft opened out onto another landscape.

Hopefully, the overbridge would remain as deserted as it had been all morning. He fixed his eyes on the triangle of daylight ahead and strode forward. The slatted metal plates of the roadway resonated in tiny vibrations under his feet.

15

Zonda bustled about in the Store, gathering food from various bags and loading it into a couple of baskets. Miriael watched with curiosity. The food wasn't for her; Zonda carried the first basket out through the curtain, then returned a minute later to take out the second. Returning after another minute, she began collecting bowls, a pot, a mortar and pestle.

"What's all of that for?" Miriael asked.

Zonda didn't answer the question, but she did answer. "Huh! One more job I have to do because of you," she snorted, and went out for the third time.

At least she's not refusing to talk to me today, thought Miriael. When the girl next returned, she tried to open up a conversation.

"What job do you have to do because of me?"

Zonda planted her hands on her hips and scowled. "I have to carry everything out to the cooks making dinner. They won't come into the Store as long as you're here."

"Because the Selectors ordered them not to?"

"They wouldn't anyway. They're scared of you."

"Oh." Miriael considered. "But you're not. Nor was Ferren."

"Phuh! *Him!*"

"What's happened to him?"

"He got what he deserved."

"You told on him?"

"'Course I told on him. Making out with a Celestial. He's not normal."

"Where is he?"

"He escaped and ran off." Zonda dropped her voice to a whisper. "I let him go."

"You did? Why?"

"Shush, not so loud. They were going to hand him over to the Selectors."

Miriael was pleased and relieved by the news on Ferren. "He was worried about being selected anyway," she commented.

"Yeah, he was always liable to end up selected. Too clever."

"The Selectors select for intelligence?" Miriael remembered that Ferren had said something similar.

Zonda nodded. "He thought for himself too much. Same as the rest of his family. They all got taken for military service, and he was the only one left."

"Why do they select for intelligence?"

"Who knows? Always have. Maybe the clever ones are better at fighting."

"Except they don't do any fighting," Miriael murmured thoughtfully. "There must be another reason."

Zonda shrugged, and seemed to have lost interest. Miriael reserved the mystery for another time.

"You're a lot like Ferren yourself, you know," she said.

"Me?" Zonda was indignant. "Am not!"

"You're not scared of me. And you think for yourself too. I'm sure you do."

Zonda shook her head. "Nah, never. I'm not clever. I'm good and sound and solid."

She twirled on the spot, showing off her physical attributes. It was true she was sturdily built, with wide hips and very full breasts.

"You don't want to be compared to Ferren?"

"He's a freak."

"But do you dislike him?"

Zonda's only answer was a loud sniff. She stopped twirling and strutted from the Store as though she'd been insulted. But Miriael wasn't convinced.

There's more to you than meets the eye, she thought.

16

The overbridge went on and on. Always straight and level, always the same black, slatted surface, always the same red and white cables at the sides.

Ferren had decided to continue walking along the top. Scanning constantly ahead, he expected to spot any Humen before they spotted him; then he could slide over the side of the deck and hide in the underframe. He made far faster progress than walking on the ground.

The cleft through the ridge was now far behind him. The new landscape was a great concave basin filled with dark red dust and no vegetation of any kind. A strong breeze had sprung up, and long grey clouds covered the face of the sun. The dust stirred and swirled in thin curling wisps.

Though there were no weeds to make a cover for himself, he still hoped to find a snug channel between paired concrete blocks under the overbridge. When the sun sank close to the horizon, it was time to seek out shelter for the night.

A ramp labelled **D202** saved him the trouble of climbing down a pylon. He descended by an easy slope and stepped out into gentle, billowy dunes of red dust. At once he sank in up to his calves. The dust had an unpleasant smell, heavy and rich and sickly. He lifted his legs high and headed towards the nearest concrete blocks, kicking up dark red clouds as he went.

The channel between the blocks was similar to his last night's shelter. Looking down at it, he had the idea of digging a deeper hollow to make up for the lack of cover. The soft, loose dust should be easy to shift.

He dropped to his knees and began scooping out dust in great handfuls. The smell, even stronger now, made him wrinkle his nose in disgust. He couldn't think what it reminded him of…

Then he felt something under his hands. Something cold and smooth and buried in the dust. Instinctively he recoiled. Then he got a grip on himself and dug down again. He took hold of the thing and pulled it out into the fading light.

It was a bone. Long, slightly curved and yellowy-white. He stared at it, frowning and puzzled.

He plunged both arms back into the dust and started groping around. Immediately he came upon another bone, and another, and another. Soon he was finding them everywhere.

Then he discovered a skull. He lifted it out with a shudder. There was no mistaking the high domed shape: a *human* skull. The place was a graveyard of skeletons!

He jumped to his feet—and made a further discovery. Where he had been kneeling, his knees were the colour of blood. A bright red smear all over them! He went to wipe it off with his hands and found that the palms of his hands were blood-red too. For a moment he was on the verge of panic.

Then he realised. The blood was coming from the dust itself. Moistened by the sweat on his skin, it had changed back to its original state. The dark red dust was old, dried blood! *That* was what the sickly-sweet smell reminded him of!

He gazed around in amazement. The entire landscape was a basin of red dust—a basin of old dried blood. What a stupendous slaughter must once have taken place here! What a bloodbath! It defied imagination.

He grimaced and shook his head. One thing was for sure: he wasn't going to spend the night sleeping on top of dried blood and bones.

He considered the possibilities. If he couldn't sleep on the ground, the only alternative was the overbridge. But he had to have somewhere protected. He raised his eyes and surveyed the underframe. Perhaps he could wedge himself in there?

He clambered up the nearest pylon and swung across under the deck. Crawling and squeezing his way among crisscross struts and braces, he was soon encompassed in a forest of metal, with a solid black roof overhead. Here it was dark, and the wind scarcely penetrated.

He selected a big horizontal girder for sleeping on. But how to stop himself rolling off in his sleep? The answer came to him in a flash of inspiration.

He lay flat along the girder directly below a suitable strut. Then he unfastened the ends of the cloth around his waist, where the angel's feathers were still threaded. He unwrapped sufficient material, passed the ends around the strut and knotted them tight.

Now he was safe in a kind of sling. Even fast asleep, he wouldn't be able to fall. He turned on his side and brought a hand round to cushion his cheek against the hard metal.

17

"Why do we choose the smartest suckers? What's it to you?"
"Just curious."

"Is that so?"

The Selectors had come to check up on Miriael. While Zonda waited and Selector No.1 watched, Selector No.2 inspected Miriael's chain and the bolt that fixed it to the wall. Clouds advanced across the sky, foreboding rain.

"See, they're more interesting when they've got some brains." Selector No. 1 was in a conversational mood. "More fun, eh, No.2?"

He glanced across to his colleague, who frowned and said nothing.

"Yeah, that's how we like 'em," he went on. "Minds with a bit of imagination. Not that we get much from dummies like these."

Selector No.2 looked up from his inspection. "You shouldn't talk to her."

"Oh? Says who?"

"She's trying to dig out information."

"Won't do her much good. She's off to the Doctors in a couple of days."

"She wants to know too much," Selector No.2 persisted. "Sticking her nose into things."

"What don't you want me to know?" Miriael asked.

Selector No.2 turned on her with a snarl. "Shut yer face!"

"Is there some secret—"

"*Shut it!*"

He still held the chain in his black-gloved hands. In the next moment, he wrapped a loop around Miriael's throat and pulled hard. She felt a sharp cutting pain and struggled for breath.

"Don't!" cried Zonda.

"Stop!" ordered Selector No.1.

But violence seemed to release Selector No.2's pent up rage. He pulled the loop tighter and tighter—until Zonda jumped across and tried to wrestle the chain from him.

His rage found a new target. He drew back a hand and gave the girl an almighty swipe across the side of her head. She went flying across the Store and smashed into stacks of bowls and bags and baskets.

Miriael felt the chain loosen around her neck and managed to catch her breath. The stacks continued to tumble down over Zonda as she lay sprawling. Dried food and preserves spilled out everywhere.

"Leave her alone!" cried Miriael.

Selector No.2 only laughed nastily.

"Why do you care?" asked Selector No.1. "She's nothing."

"*You're* nothing! At least she's got a soul!"

There was a moment of absolute silence. Then Selector No.1 sprang forward across the Store and stood over Miriael clenching his fists. He was obviously itching to lay into her.

"Now you see!" crowed Selector No.2. "Told you she despised us!"

Selector No.1 unclenched his fists and took a backwards step as though to avoid temptation. "No, we can't damage her," he muttered regretfully. "The Doctors wouldn't like it."

"Let's give her a good kicking."

"*No.*" Selector No.1 shook his head. "But I've got another idea."

He turned to Zonda, who had been pushing her way out from all the fallen bowls, bags and baskets. "You! Dummy! Call in the rest of your lot." He jerked a thumb towards the main Dwelling Place area. "I want 'em gathered out there."

Zonda fingered the ugly red welt in her left cheek. "That's my father's job," she responded sullenly.

"*Then get him to do it!*" the Selector roared.

18

Miriael lay on the ground in the middle of the Dwelling Place. Selector No.2 had unlocked the padlock fastening the chain to her ankle and had dragged her out from the Store. As the People came in from the fields, Selector No.1 directed them to form up in a ring around her. Overhead, the sky was now covered by heavy black cloud.

"Okay." Selector No.1 surveyed the assembly. "You're our allies, right? Fighting on the side of the Earth? *Right?*"

He waited, and Neath led the response. "We are. We contribute as we can." Others muttered agreement and humbly bowed their heads.

"And here's our enemy." The Selector flicked a boot towards the outstretched angel. "My enemy and yours. So what do we do to our enemies?"

The People looked at one another in fearful confusion. They didn't know what to say.

"Hah! I'll show you what *I* do!"

Selector No.1 bent low and spat. Hot, wet saliva showered Miriael's face and trickled down over her skin. It felt thick and glutinous, like slime.

"Now watch me!" yelled Selector No.2, stepping up. "Get a load of this, pretty-pretty!"

Miriael tried to turn her face to the ground, but he grabbed her by the hair and lifted her head. Pain shot through her scalp, while another kind of agony came from the angle of her neck. She could see the spittle rolling around and building up in his mouthslit. She closed her eyes in the instant before he spat.

It was the most disgusting thing she'd ever experienced. Spittle slid down over her forehead, eyelids and cheeks. It felt like poison burning into her skin.

Then Selector No.1 raised his voice. "Now you lot! Time to show your loyalty! Time to show what you think of our enemies!"

So began a slow circuit of the whole ring of the People. Selector No.2 dragged Miriael along by the hair and made her crawl on her hands and knees. No member of the tribe was allowed to hold back.

"Go on, spit on her!" bellowed Selector No.1. "Don't let her despise you! Give it to her good!"

"All you've got!" added Selector No.2.

The People were afraid of the Celestial—but even more afraid of the Selectors. When they were forced to it, they darted forward, spat quickly, then backed away in a hurry. But Selector No.1 wouldn't let them off so easily.

"More spit! Do it properly! Do it again!"

They had to keep spitting until the Selectors were satisfied. Soon Miriael was dripping with spittle—not only her face but her hair, robe, wings and shoulders. She closed her eyes, closed her mind and crawled where Selector No.2 dragged her.

Halfway round, Selector No.1 had a further idea. "Tell her what she is!" he ordered Cress, who had just managed a satisfactory spit. "Tell her she's scum!"

"Scum," Cress echoed faintly.

"And a namby-pamby weakling!"

"Weakling. Namby. Pamby."

Cress hardly addressed the words to Miriael, but Selector No.1 improved the procedure as they went around.

"Shout it in her face," he told Hodd. "Scream it. She's an airy-fairy fart and a waste of space."

One after another, the People spat and yelled insults. Zonda was last at the end of the circuit.

"Better make this good," Selector No.1 warned her. "We already have doubts whose side you're on."

"I'm on Earth's side!" Zonda protested, and spat volubly. She also showered Miriael with new terms of abuse: "wingless wonder" and "flightless flop".

"Okay." Selector No.1 pointed to the curtain that covered the Store. "Now go bring out some stuff from in there."

"Food?"

"Yeah, food. And plenty of it."

Zonda went off through the curtain. Selector No.2 pulled Miriael by the hair to the centre of the ring, then released her.

Selector No.1 addressed the People. "Now you get a chance to show what you can do. Target practice. If anyone doesn't try and aim straight… I'll be watching you."

When Zonda brought out various kinds of food, he checked the contents of the bags and baskets.

"Nothing too hard," he said. "We want soft and squishy."

Then he and his colleague stepped back to watch. "Okay, let's mess her up. Start chucking!"

Missiles bombarded Miriael from all sides: tomatoes, fruit, birds' eggs and lizard meat. The Selectors laughed and jeered as tomatoes and eggs burst and splattered all over her.

"Don't forget her wings!" they yelled. "Who's gonna get her wings?"

Soon Miriael's white wings were as smeared and filthy as the rest of her. She tried to crawl from the centre of the ring, looking for a way of escape. But the Selectors wouldn't let her break out.

"Drive her back!" they yelled at the People. "Use yer feet!"

The People raised their feet to push her back, yet still shrank from actual contact. Miriael saw a gap between them and pressed on towards it. But her movements were slow, and Selector No.2 came round at the back of the ring to block her off. He stooped to the ground.

"Bit of dirt'll do her good!" he shouted—and scooped up dirt and flung it in her face.

For a moment she couldn't see, blinking and spluttering. She backed away, and Selector No.2 came after her. He kept hurling dirt until the air around her was a thick, choking cloud.

"Not so pure and perfect now!" he jeered.

He stopped only when she retreated back into the centre of the ring. She was now coated and caked with dirt that stuck to the glutinous slop already covering her. He left her there for the next bombardment.

But Selector No.1 had a different idea. "It needs rubbing in!" He scanned the People and pointed to Neath. "You! Old man! Go and rub it into her hair and skin!"

Neath changed colour. "But I can't...I..."

"Use yer hands, *fellow-ally*. Get rubbing!"

Neath took a step towards the angel, then faltered to a halt. Selector No.1 marched across to push him forward—then stopped. A big drop of rain had just landed on his shoulder.

He brushed it away, but a second drop followed the first, then another, and another. The black cloud overhead had finally decided to discharge its load. He snorted and shook himself against the wet.

The raindrops continued to multiply, heavier and heavier. Selector No.1 turned to Selector No.2.

"Okay, that'll do for now. Put her back in her corner. Fun's over."

Selector No.2 seized Miriael by the hair and dragged her back to the Store. Selector No.1 clapped his hands to disperse the gathering.

"Clear off! Quick smart! The lot of you!"

The People were happy to obey.

19

The rain that had begun in the afternoon fell on Ferren walking along the overbridge. But the cold and wet didn't bother him. He trudged on like an automaton.

He had left the red basin behind and was now crossing a region of dense forest. The tops of the trees rose up level with the roadway, lapping all around in masses of dark green foliage. It was impossible to see through to the ground beneath. In the grey, obscuring rain, the overbridge seemed to be floating on a surface of dim rolling waves. Looking out over the cordon at the side was like looking out over the side of a ship.

But Ferren had long since stopped looking. He walked with lowered head, closed off in a world of his own. He was thinking about the People and the Home Ground…

What would they be doing right now? He pictured Shuff at work in the Blackberry Patch, gathering insects for the lizards and twigs for Urlish's fire. Would Neath have nominated someone else to assist him? He pictured Neath in his counting-corner…and Mell, Vitch and Lillam cooking dinner…

He had forgotten to keep a lookout ahead, but now he felt a vibration in the metal roadway under his feet. He emerged instantly from his reverie and tried to catch some sound through the drumming of the rain.

Yes, there it was: a tramp of marching feet and a rumble of iron wheels. Humen soldiers! They were approaching along the overbridge—and already close!

He didn't have time to think twice. Only the screen of the rain had hidden them from his view—and him from theirs. He crossed to the side of the bridge, intending to slide under the cordon of cables, then lower himself down into the underframe.

But now he could see a dozen dim shadows looming through the rain. They marched side by side in a line across the roadway, and they were almost upon him. He had left it too late!

He made an instant decision, took two steps running and hurled himself clean over the top of the cordon.

For a moment he was as if suspended in the grey, rainy air. Then he plummeted earthwards.

WHOOOSH! He smashed down into the treetop foliage, descending through densely packed twigs and leaves. PROING! He slammed into a springy branch and bounced off sideways. GNUTT! He collided with a massive tree trunk. He grabbed hold of it, then slipped off and started falling again. THUBBB! He made a bone-jarring landing on solid ground.

He was winded and shaken but otherwise unhurt. He twisted around to look back up. There was a gap in the foliage like a window overhead, and the soldiers marched past as he watched.

He could see the ones closest to the cordon, heads down in the rain.

They were clad in black from head to toe and looked like Selectors. He remembered the angel's name for soldiers of the type—*Hypers*, she called them. He couldn't see the rumbling thing on wheels that accompanied them, but no doubt it was some sort of transport machine.

At least he hadn't been spotted. He continued to stare up through the gap in the foliage long after the Hypers had gone by. Gradually the sounds of boots and wheels faded into the distance.

With a sigh of relief, he sat up and considered his surroundings. Down here the daylight scarcely penetrated, and his eyes took a while to adjust.

It was utterly hushed, utterly becalmed. The only sound was the sound of raindrops pattering on the leaves far above. All around, the trunks of the trees were massive and black, furred with age and blotched with lichen. Trailing fibrous growths and creepers hung from the branches.

He had regained his breath after the shock of his fall. But the air he inhaled was stale and stagnant, smelling of decay. The whole place was like a tomb.

Still, he wasn't in a hurry to go back up on top of the overbridge. Perhaps he could find food in this forest? He decided to explore further.

20

There were many forms of plant life that might have been edible, but not many that Ferren dared eat. He picked and chewed only familiar-looking nuts and berries. Fungi grew everywhere on dead wood and fallen branches, but not like the mushrooms of the People's Mushroom Beds. These were mottled in bright colours, yellow and pink and purple, with a bloated toadlike appearance. When he kicked at their domes, they revealed a spongy cellular flesh and oozed a milky juice.

Deeper and deeper he advanced. He couldn't keep track of his path through the trees, but took care to move always in the same general direction. So long as the overbridge was at his back, he could be sure of returning to some point along its length.

Gradually the forest grew more dense and tangled. Again and again, he had to step over twisting, intricate roots that covered the ground. The carpet of dead mouldered leaves was soft underfoot; the trunks of the trees squeezed closer and closer together.

He stopped at one particular tree laden with hanging clusters of nuts. Very tempting, tasty-looking nuts… He looked around for something with which to knock them down. Even the lowest-hanging clusters were beyond his reach without a stick.

The answer lay nearby: a much smaller tree with long, thin branches. He could break off a branch to use as a stick. He reached down with both hands and prepared to snap the wood at its weakest point.

"Oo-ooh!"

What was that? He looked around but there was nothing to see. Had he imagined it? So faint and fleeting, like a tiny wail in the air. Perhaps his ears were playing tricks on him.

He reached down a second time—and again the strange sounds started up. There were more of them now, and louder than before.

"Oo-ooo-oh!"

"No-ooo!"

"Please!"

"Do-ooon't!"

No doubt about it! A whole host of tiny voices were all piping and fluting in long, woeful tones.

"Hey! Where are you? What are you?"

He swivelled in every direction and swished his arms this way and that. The voices seemed to come from among the leaves and twigs and roots, both overhead and on the ground. But he couldn't locate the source.

"Stop!"

"No mo-ore!"

"I'll tell!"

"And me-eee!"

"We'll all tell!"

"Just be still!"

He stopped his swishing. "Be still?"

"Plee-eease! You're disturbing us."

"You're dislodging us."

He peered down. He could swear some of the voices were coming from right beside his feet.

"Why can't I see you?" he demanded.

"Because you don't look in the right way."

"You have to learn how to look."

Still he didn't understand. "Are you *inside* the leaves?"

"Nooo-oo. We're *between* the leaves."

"And the twigs and roots and things."

"We're in the *patterns* between."

"Don't touch!" There was a sudden sharp shriek as Ferren bent down and stretched out an exploratory hand. "That's my bit of bark!"

"Your bit of bark?"

"The bit of bark by your foot. And the two dead leaves on the left. And that piece of moss at the side. Join up the corners! Connect the points! Can't you see the pattern?"

Ferren traced mental lines between the corners and points, from the leaves to the bark to the moss. "Mmmm. I sort of see it."

"Well, that's me-eee! That's how I exist!"

"That's how we all exist!"

"In the patterns."

"So you mustn't ever break the patterns."

"We get dislodged when you knock things out of position."

"Then we drift around in the air."

"For days and days."

"All we want is a place to settle."

"All we want is rest and pee-eace."

Ferren almost felt like crying, they sounded so sad and hopeless. But instead he asked, "Are you everywhere in this forest?"

"Yes. The Forest of the Morphs."

"We are the Morphs."

"Thousands and thousands of us."

"Souls of the dead with nowhere to go-ooo."

"I get it." Ferren scratched his head. "And where do you want to go?"

"To Heaven."

"But they won't let us in."

"The Gates of Heaven are locked and shut. I went up there."

"And me!"

"And me-ee!"

"We had to come back down to Earth again."

"Oh! Oh! We don't want to live like this!"

"But we haven't got a home!"

"No home!"

"No home!"

"No ho-ooo-ome!"

They were all wailing and grieving pitifully now. From near and far, more and more voices joined in.

"No ho-ooo-ooo-ome!"

Ferren couldn't stand it. It reminded him that he, too, didn't have a home. He turned away and started to run back in the direction of the overbridge. Tears were streaming down his face.

"Noo-ooo-OOO! Hoo-ooo-OOOME!"

Still the lament spread and swelled. He clapped his hands over his ears and kept running. At last he came to the pylons of the overbridge, black metal and white concrete blocks appearing through the gloom. He made for the nearest one.

Soon he was shinning up the vertical struts and back to the roadway.

21

"Zonda!" Miriael called out. She heard people eating an early morning meal on the other side of the curtain and hoped Zonda was among them. She hadn't seen the girl since yesterday's scene of humiliation. "Zonda!"

Her call caused a rustle of movement followed by a murmur of low voices. Then the curtain drew back, and Zonda stepped forward into the Store.

"Sorry about yesterday," she said. "I didn't *want* to spit on you."

"I know."

"Or throw stuff at you. The Selectors would've turned on me if I hadn't."

"I understand. Nobody wanted to do it. And you defended me, too."

"I did?"

"When the Selector was strangling me with my chain. You took a nasty blow trying to stop him."

"Umm." Zonda fingered the welt across her cheek. "This, you mean."

"You were very brave. Thank you."

Zonda accepted the gratitude with a grin. "Yeah, I was kind of brave."

"And thank you for coming in now when I called."

"I couldn't come before. My father didn't want me to clean you up. He thought the Selectors would prefer you to stay dirty."

"I already cleaned myself." Miriael displayed her improved appearance. "The rain washed a lot of it off. I used water from my drinking bowl for the rest."

"I'll get you fresh water. And food." Zonda's gaze travelled over Miriael's hair, wings and limbs. "You did a good job of it."

"I think I'm growing stronger every day. In fact, I'm sure I am."

While Zonda gathered a selection of food for the food bowl, Miriael mused on the paradox of yesterday's events. Although she'd been utterly shamed and degraded, yet she'd also managed an unexpected success. For the first time since falling to Earth, she could crawl. She now knew she could move around by herself without an aura.

Zonda finished filling the food bowl, then sat down facing her.

"Your father is the leader of the tribe, isn't he?" Miriael asked.

"Yes. He doesn't like to upset the Selectors. We had a ceremony of salvation last night because we obeyed the Selectors and didn't get punished. He said our totems protected us."

"He seems very humble, the way he tries to please the Selectors."

"Oh, we're all very humble." A sour expression twisted Zonda's mouth as she launched into a singsong chant.

> "O we are little, weak and small
> We do not matter much at all
> O grant that we may not offend
> And live our lives through to the end.

"That's one of our prayers," she explained.

"But do *you* really believe it?"

Zonda shrugged. 'It's the way we live. If you call it living.'

You're so similar to Ferren, Miriael thought to herself. Aloud, she said, "Tell me about your totems."

The sour expression vanished. "Our totems?"

"Ferren told me about them once. But he didn't really describe them. He said you inherited them from your Ancestors."

She must have sounded sceptical because Zonda fired up at once. "We did! It's true! Don't you believe it?"

"I'd like to hear about them first."

"We have our Baby Jane. Our Alarm Clock. Our Light in the Darkness. And our Guardian Fly Spray."

"Describe them."

"Well, um… Our Baby Jane is like a baby. She wears special clothes and lies in a basket. Our Alarm Clock is sort of round-shaped. All metal except some glass at the front. And lots of fiddly bits."

"How do you mean, fiddly?"

"Bits that stick out. Some like little wheels…and some…I don't know…" Zonda spread her hands in despair. "I *can't* describe them. We inherited them from our Ancestors," she concluded lamely.

"All right. Tell me about your Ancestors, then."

Zonda's eyes lit up with pride and excitement. "They ruled the Earth and did all sorts of things a long time ago. There were millions and millions of them. They lived in great cities like Syd-nee and Mel-born and Briz-ban. Tall white cities full of buildings and moto-cars and things we can't even imagine…"

Faster and faster she rattled on. Although the names and words she used had no definite meaning for her, yet they were charged with emotion. Miriael observed the yearning look on her face and remembered a similar look on Ferren's face when speaking of the Ancestors.

"They were free to make their lives whatever they wanted. All sorts of things to do. They could *choose!* Every day was new and different. And when…"

Miriael listened to the tone of Zonda's voice rather than her words. She hadn't exactly believed or disbelieved Ferren, but Zonda's conviction was beginning to sway her doubts. Perhaps the Ancestors were partly a myth, but there was surely *some* reality behind it. Present-day Residuals lived very primitive lives, but perhaps there were reasons why they had lost the skills and powers of a past civilisation. Miriael glimpsed a possible explanation and wished she could talk to some of the scholars in Heaven about it…

Still Zonda rattled on, hardly pausing to draw breath as her account became more and more scattered and repetitive. Then suddenly she stopped. "Aren't you listening?"

"I was considering and deciding," Miriael excused herself. "I still don't know what to believe. I'd believe if I saw definite evidence."

"What, like our totems?"

Miriael hadn't been thinking about the totems, but she thought about them now. "They *would* be evidence, if I could see them."

Zonda screwed up her face. "They're supposed to stay in the Sanctuary, except for ceremonies. Maybe I could smuggle one out."

"Then I could tell if they come from some ancient civilisation."

"You'd have to promise not to touch. Only looking."

"I promise."

"Well…" Zonda crossed to the curtain and peeked out. "Nobody around," she muttered to herself.

She returned to collect a basket from a stack of empty baskets, then a bag from a pile of empty bags.

"I'll start with our Guardian Fly Spray," she told Miriael. "I'll hide it under a bag in this basket."

The angel repressed a smile on hearing her say "start". If this particular totem was the *start*, then hopefully the rest would follow.

22

All day, Ferren had been crossing a new kind of landscape. After the Forest of the Morphs, he had arrived at an endless flat field of yellowy-brown clay. The field was ploughed in parallel furrows, and there were rows of small conical mounds set alongside the furrows. Every mound was the same size, shape and rusty red colour as every other mound. The arrangement was as symmetrical as a chessboard.

Then he noticed something away to his right: a straight black line running along above the ground. It had to be a second overbridge—and heading in the same direction as his own. Although far off in the distance at first, it came gradually closer as he went on. Presumably, the overbridges were converging towards the Humen camp.

The second overbridge seemed as deserted as his own, yet he began to feel more and more exposed up on top. In the end, he decided to climb down. It would be slower but safer walking along on the clay. He slid under the cables and descended by handholds and footholds to the ground below. Advancing under the middle of the overbridge, he was able to look out between pylons on either side while remaining less visible himself.

He was thankful to be less visible when another overbridge appeared soon afterwards on his left. It too was converging towards the Humen camp—and it was *not* deserted. Three figures marched along the top, silhouetted against the light of the sky. They were some way behind him, but progressing much faster.

As he continued on at his limited pace, little by little the distance between the overbridges narrowed. At the same time, the three figures were gaining on him. He could now see that one of the three was being led on a chain.

He stopped, shielding himself behind a pylon, and waited and watched. The chained figure trudged along with lowered head and hunched shoulders, whereas the other two marched with a swagger. The swaggerers looked very much like Selectors—the type of Humen called Hypers. But who or what was the third figure? Ferren had a bad feeling in the pit of his stomach as they came up parallel with him.

The third figure was a woman. Her hair hung loose, and she wore a cloth around her waist, another around her breasts. She was exactly like a woman of the People except for the different greenish colour of the cloth. Ferren remembered the angel talking about people like the People… Residuals, she'd called them, as though there were many more living on the Earth. This must be a woman from another tribe.

But why she was being led on a chain? Was she a prisoner because she'd done something wrong? Or was she a prisoner simply because she'd been selected for military service?

He reflected. Shanna hadn't been led away on a chain, and nor had any of the others selected from the People. But what if the Selectors did the chaining only when they were out of sight from the Home Ground? Was this the "something bad" that Zonda had suspected about military service?

He trusted the Humen even less than before. So far, he hadn't made up his mind what to do when he arrived at the Humen camp, but he made up his mind now. No, he would *not* present himself at the gates or apply for entry. He would find a way to enter secretly and look around before he spoke to anyone.

He waited until the three figures had marched on well ahead, then resumed his advance between the pylons. He saw no further travellers on the overbridges.

Sunset was only an hour away when he became aware of a strange vibration in the air. Hardly a sound, it was more a dull throbbing pulse of huge machinery. Surely the Humen camp! He must be coming close now!

He couldn't resist going up for a look. Shinning to the top of a pylon, he scanned his own overbridge and the overbridges left and right. All deserted. He crawled onto the roadway and rose cautiously upright.

The source of the throbbing sound was a looming shape like a nest of shadows. It was several miles ahead, yet so vast it seemed to fill up half the sky. He couldn't make out the details, and the shadows kept shifting in a way he didn't understand. Still, the sense of power that emanated from the place was overwhelming.

He laughed a little crazily and brandished a fist. At last his journey was nearly over. One more night sleeping in the underframe, then tomorrow he would find a secret way in. He had made it!

23

Miriael hadn't seen the Selectors all day, until they turned up just before nightfall. The People, who had been unrolling their blanket for sleep, cowered out of the way in the Dwelling Place. Zonda followed the Selectors into the Store.

"Big day for you tomorrow, pretty-pretty." Selector No.1 opened his mouthslit in a mockery of a grin. "Your transport arrives."

"Off to the Doctors," added Selector No.2. "They'll dig out everything you know."

What do I know? Miriael asked herself. She didn't know Heaven's specific strategies, but she knew they were building up forces to counter a major Humen offensive to be launched from Australia. Heaven knew what the Humen were planning, but the Humen didn't know they knew. Could the Doctors force her to reveal that?

"I'm only a junior warrior angel," she told the Selectors. "No one tells me anything."

"It's not what you know, it's what you *are*," said Selector No.1.

"They'll take you apart," said Selector No.2.

Selector No.1 laughed. "Tiny slice by slice! They'll analyse everything about you and work out how angels function. That's the best information of all. Then they can develop weapons to use against you. Special weapons to wipe out every angel everywhere."

Miriael tried not to show her shock and horror. Here was something she hadn't anticipated! She'd survived on the Earth as angels weren't supposed to survive—but this would be her ultimate act of betrayal. She would give away invaluable secrets even if she never uttered a word!

"I'm not a proper angel," she protested. "No proper angel could survive in Earth's atmosphere without an aura."

"Yeah, you're a freak," Selector No.1 agreed. "Our Doctors will work on that too. They'll analyse what you were and what you've become. Maybe it's a weak point in all you airy-fairy lot."

"They're very clever, our Doctors," Selector No.2 put in. "You wouldn't believe the things they can do with their science and surgery."

Miriael didn't know much about the Doctors except that they were the leaders of Humen forces on every inhabited continent.

"Not so clever, or they'd have won this war long ago," she sniffed.

"It'll happen sooner than you think," Selector No.1 replied. "You lot stay the same, but our technology gets better and better. See, our Doctors keep learning 'cos they live for centuries."

"And we have ten of 'em here in the Bankstown Camp," added Selector No.2. "Some that came across from South America. And there's more on the—"

"Enough." Selector No.1 cut him off short. "All she needs to know is what they'll do to her. When they cut into their first live specimen with their surgical instruments...hah! Then she'll wish she'd never survived a moment down here!"

He turned his back and walked out of the Store. Selector No.2 snorted with vicious laughter and went after him.

Miriael had always known this time would come, but it had never seemed so urgent and important. Now she understood what would be done to her, she was desperate.

24

All night, the angel tossed and turned. If only she could make contact with Heaven, if only she could warn them! But such communication was blocked to her.

Towards dawn, she fell into a light sleep and dreamed in a way she'd never experienced before. In the dream, she was back up in Heaven in the Gardens of Liriam on the Third Altitude. The light was wonderfully clear, the eternal early morning light of Heaven. She lay on emerald green grass dotted with small yellow flowers like stars.

Everything was very calm and peaceful, far removed from the military activities of the First and Second Altitudes. The Third Altitude was the Altitude for Training and Education. High in the air a faint echo of singing drifted down from the hymning choirs of the Fourth Altitude.

But she couldn't be calm or peaceful herself. Her desperation when awake was still with her in her dream. She had a warning to pass on. Who to tell?

Then she observed three angels on the other side of the Gardens. They had the furled double wings and wore the maroon robes of the Order of Dominions. Their auras glowed as they glided over the grass. She waved an arm to attract their attention.

"Please!" she called out. "I have something urgent to tell you! Please!"

But the three angels didn't hear or notice her. Perhaps they were too far away. She raised her voice and waved more vigorously. But they disappeared down the slope, out of sight.

She shook her head in frustration. If only she wasn't fastened by this chain around her ankle! She looked down at it—and discovered that it was no longer there.

Free! She rose to her feet. At the very same moment a peal of bells rang out. It came from Gebron, Holy City of the Third Altitude.

She turned to survey the city, lying in the distance. Its roofs were tiled with silver and gold, its walls were washed in tints of ochre and cream. There were parapets and belfries, gables and cupolas. Everything had a soft, mellow, ageless appearance...

Without transition, she found herself walking in the Holy City. She passed along familiar streets and alleys, with their rounded cobblestones, their archways and balconies, their windows of small glass panes. She stood on the Bridge of Clare, one of the famous bridges of Gebron, and looked down over the railings into the bottomless abyss of radiant light below.

Then she saw Harahel approaching the bridge—Harahel the old Assistant Librarian, with his venerable curling beard. Only now he wore the green sash of a Chief Librarian. He must have been recently promoted, she thought to herself.

She smiled as he came up the steps onto the bridge. His head was bowed, and he was deep in thought.

"Harahel," she said. "I'm so glad to see you."

But Harahel didn't respond, didn't even look at her. He walked right past as though she wasn't there.

She frowned in puzzled surprise. Why was he ignoring her?

She hurried away from the Bridge of Clare, passed under the Arch of the Holy Rood, and emerged into Prosica Lane. Halfway down Prosica Lane was her old training school.

The lane stirred a thousand memories, but even as she walked, she noticed how things had changed. A different insignia mounted over a doorway...an old bell-pull taken down...and in the Court of the Observatory, three new window boxes overflowing with red geraniums...

She came up to the window of her old schoolroom and peered

inside. Six bright-haired student angels sat at their desks, heads lowered, busily writing with long quill pens. Unfamiliar faces—but the rest of the room was the same. She looked at the brass-topped benches, the wooden stools, the stacks of leather-bound books in the corners. Then she saw her old teacher, Eiael, sitting in his huge carved chair at the front.

She cried out and knocked on the window. "Eiael! Sir! Eiael!"

But no one turned towards her. The Seraph continued to gaze out over his pupils. The six student angels continued to write.

She hammered furiously on the glass. "It's me! Miriael! The Fourteenth Angel of Observance! Listen to me!"

But it was as though she produced no sound at all. She felt a rising wave of panic. What was happening? Was this her dream or wasn't it? If it was her dream, why couldn't she be in it? How could she be less real than her own dream? It didn't make sense!

She fled down Prosica Lane to the intersection with the Street of Scrolls. Here were many fine buildings decorated in gold leaf and fluted crystal. The polished paving was of gleaming white marble.

A formal procession of junior angels came trooping along the Street of Scrolls. Side by side they advanced towards her, with their ceremonial silver helmets and ceremonial silver spears. They looked like cadets marching to a Field Parade, just as she had once marched herself.

She ran straight at them with outspread arms. They wouldn't be able to ignore her when she banged right into them!

"Look at me!" she screamed at the top of her voice. "I'm here! Here! Here!"

But the bodies of the angels passed clean through her. No collision, no contact. The procession never faltered, their eyes never wavered. They passed clean through her as though she were made of thin air.

She stood in the street staring after them, stunned and shaking. So it was true! She didn't exist up here! Her body was chained to a wall down below on the Earth! Tears sprang into her eyes, and she fled weeping, weeping, weeping...

25

Still in her dream, still weeping, she found herself in a small open square. She didn't remember the place, but there were many such squares on the Third Altitude, with sanded paths between triangles of grass. A delicate fountain with a green copper bowl sprayed water into the air and cast a shimmering multi-coloured rainbow.

She felt utterly hopeless and forlorn. She was lying on wet grass at the foot of the fountain and never wanted to move again. But then she heard two voices approaching. She rubbed her eyes and looked up.

They were two very important angels talking on very serious matters. One she recognised as Baruch, the Chancellor of all the schools on this Altitude. The other was a tall Aeon from a higher Altitude, completely unfamiliar to her. Since he carried a Staff of Glory, she guessed he must be an archistratege from the Conclave of the Hebdomad.

They came and stood beside the fountain, their sandaled feet just inches from where she lay. The Aeon was describing some new weapon to be used in the war.

"It'll take them by surprise. We have to choose the best moment for maximum impact."

Baruch looked thoughtful. "But a Celestial Sun! Can't you trial it first?"

"How could we? It'll only work once."

Miriael realised she shouldn't be listening. Here was even more information that the Doctors would be able to extract from her! She rolled over on the grass and put up her hands to cover her ears.

"What's that?" cried Baruch, breaking in on the Aeon's explanations. "Where?"

"Near your foot! Like a moving strand of gold!"

Baruch went down on one knee, pointing. The angel held her breath. She moved her head just a little to the side.

"Ah! There it is again!"

The Aeon knelt down next to Baruch. His aura was like soft warm sunshine.

"I see it now," he said. "I believe it's a strand of hair."

He bent over the angel's invisible form and reached down with thumb and forefinger. Very carefully he lifted up a single strand of the angel's hair.

"Oh, it's attached!" he exclaimed. "But I can't see how!"

"A presence?"

Baruch searched and felt around with outstretched hands. His brows were furrowed in deep concentration.

"Yes, I've found it. I'm touching a faint presence here. Someone lying on the ground."

He encircled the angel's waist approximately with his arms.

"Who are you? Speak to us!"

The angel made a mighty effort to stay calm.

"I'm Miriael! The Fourteenth Angel of Observance!"

Baruch looked across triumphantly at the Aeon, who nodded.

"Go on!" cried the old Chancellor. "We're hearing you!"

"I'm still alive on the Earth!"

But even as she spoke, she had a sense that the world of the Third Altitude was starting to blur around her. The grass and the fountain, the robes and faces of the two angels—everything seemed to be slipping away.

"She's falling back!" Baruch exclaimed. "I can't keep a grip!"

"Stay with us!" cried the Aeon. "Where on the Earth?"

"Picton sector!"

"Yes, yes! Speak up!"

"Near the Goulburn to Bankstown overbridge! Residual community!"

But she felt herself growing heavier and heavier. She was dropping down, falling through the grass. Baruch and the Aeon dropped down too, trying to stay with her. Baruch was trying to maintain his hold, but she was no longer within the circle of his arms.

"Humen coming tomorrow!" she cried. "Doctors…extract…information!"

She plummeted past the Fifteen Stars of the Second Altitude. Faster and faster and faster. There was a glimpse of snowy peaks and green hills. Vainly the two angels beat around in the air. They had lost contact entirely.

"He-e-e-e-e-lp!"

The First Altitude came and went in a rush of crimson and gold, banners and pavilions. She was falling right out of Heaven, back down to the Earth. With a sudden jarring bump, she returned to her own body on the hard ground.

What had happened? Was it some kind of vision? Had she really communicated in a dream? Would they be able to find her again if she had?

She blinked and shook herself, returning slowly to her senses. On the Earth a new day had dawned. She inhaled the food smells of the Store and observed the chain that fastened her to the wall.

Outside in the Dwelling Place, some sort of disturbance had broken out. Many voices were shouting one over another; the only word she could clearly hear was "Selectors".

26

Zonda was eating her breakfast when Losh, Stax and Cholly came running into the Dwelling Place. The youngsters bubbled with excitement.

"Selectors gone! No tent! Gone and left us!"

Zonda didn't believe it. Yesterday evening, the Selectors had been saying that transport for the angel would arrive today—why would they disappear now? She went with her father and half a dozen others to the bank of the Creek, where the youngsters had been looking out over the Plain.

"See! Tent's gone!" cried Losh, pointing to the spot. Then his face fell. "Oh."

Everyone saw what he'd seen. Further in the distance, a line of black-clad figures had just come into view. They advanced alongside their transport machine, which was a flat-topped, self-propelled trolley on wheels.

Neath tried to calm everyone down. "It's what they told us, they're here to collect that Celestial. Just stay quiet and low. It'll soon be over for good."

More and more People came up to stand on the bank and observe. Now they could hear the menacing rumble of iron wheels and the harsh voice of the leader shouting orders. Selector No.1 was no longer in charge, but he was there in the line with his painted-on hair and ears. Selector No.2 marched beside him, distinguished by the wire cage over his head. Other figures had white words scribbled across their black rubbery suits, many wore studs or chains or metal plates.

The leader himself was a great hulking Hyper whose suit was painted with pictures of open wounds dripping blood. A steel collar encircled his neck and a black spike stuck out from the top of his skull.

Zonda turned to her father. "What do we do? They can't bring that machine into our Home Ground. They'll flatten the walls and fields and everything."

Neath shook his head. "Keep out of their way. Don't provoke them."

"No, we have to explain. Let them stop their machine on the other side of the Creek. They can carry the Celestial out there."

Neath remained reluctant. Zonda grabbed him by the hand.

"Come on, we can talk to them, can't we? You and me. You're always calling them fellow-allies."

"Yes, but—"

"Come *on!*"

Still protesting, Neath went with her. They waded across the Creek and came up into the grass on the other side.

Zonda didn't like the openness of the Plain, but her misgivings were nothing compared to her father's. She could feel his hand trembling in hers as she pulled him along. She was afraid to let go in case he turned tail and headed for home.

The Hypers and their transport machine were much closer now. The leader barked instructions to the machine as though it could understand and obey. But the language he used was strangely mathematical, a string of numbers rather than ordinary language. In response, the sound from the machine changed to a low *gruk-gruk-gruk-gruk*, as if scolding and muttering to itself. Zonda could see the cylinders and rods that drove

119

the six heavy wheels, but she couldn't see any driver.

She led her father up to the leader. "Speak to him," she urged.

"Greetings, fellow-ally," said Neath.

Not for an instant did the leader break stride. Zonda and Neath were forced to hurry along beside him.

"We can show you the best place to wait with your machine." Zonda took over the explanation. "Then we'll lead a couple of your men to collect the Celestial."

The leader looked across to Selector No.1. "Who are these suckers?" he asked.

"Residual crud," answered Selector No.1. "They belong to this dump."

"We just want to help," said Zonda.

The leader dismissed her without a glance. "Rack off."

"But you don't know—"

Selector No.1 pointed a black-gloved hand. "Head for that brick wall over there."

The leader barked another string of numbers at the transport machine. Immediately the wheels veered to the right, and the muttering sound accelerated. Now the machine was aiming straight at the Dwelling Place, and the Creek was no more than twenty paces ahead.

On the other side of the Creek, the People stared in horror. They seemed paralysed, incapable of moving out of the way.

"No! Please! Stop!" Zonda appealed to the leader. "You can't do this!"

For the first time, he turned and paid attention to her. He laughed and showed his pointed metal teeth.

"We can do *anything*," he said.

Zonda's eyes filled with tears of rage and frustration, but she didn't know what else to say.

Instead there came a different kind of answer. From high overhead, a mighty flourish of trumpets rang out, long and deep and golden.

What now? Had the transport arrived so early?

27

BRRRAAAARRRRRRHHHHHHHH!!!!

As the sonorous echoing note died away, the Hypers halted in their tracks and looked up.

"Slag it!" The leader pounded his fist into the palm of his hand. "A flock of scummy angels!"

Slowly descending from above were thirty bright, clear globes. They came down in a V formation, chanting a triumphant battle cry.

"*Hallelujah! Hallelujah! Hallelujah!*"

The Hypers turned to their leader.

"What now?"

"We can't fight all that lot!"

The leader was like a baffled beast. "Orderly retreat!" he snarled.

He rattled out another sequence of numbers, and the transport machine reversed direction and accelerated. It sped across the Plain with the Hypers racing beside it.

Only the leader didn't move. He seemed rooted to the spot by sheer intensity of hatred. His mouth was working and his eyes glaring. He sprayed out a shower of iridescent spittle in the direction of the descending globes.

The three leading angels dived down over the transport machine. One after the other they exploded three blinding flashes of light.

SPAKKK! SPAKKK! SPAKKK!

The dazzle was unbelievable. Even at a distance it struck like a blow. The leader of the Hypers was flung over backwards and knocked Neath and Zonda flat in his fall.

For a moment the world was sheer black and white; then gradually the colour returned. Zonda moved away, but her father remained sprawling under the leader. Somehow their limbs had got tangled up together.

"I'm sorry," Neath bleated pathetically. "Sorry, fellow-ally. Not my fault."

As he tried to extricate himself, the leader sat up. His face was a black savage mask. He took hold of Neath's left arm and snapped it in one swift movement like a piece of rotten wood.

"You stupid nobhead," he said.

He reached out for Neath's right arm and snapped it in the same way. "Stupid," he said.

He caught hold of Neath's thin legs, where they stuck out at an angle under his own. This time there was a double crack.

"Nobhead," he said.

The transport machine was still rolling on across the Plain, but most of the Hypers had been left behind. They crawled around like worms, rubbing at their eyes with desperate hands.

"Blinded!" they cried. "I'm blinded!"

Kicking Neath aside like a limp rag doll, the leader rose to his feet and surveyed the scene. Then he sprinted across to his blinded men. One by one, he grabbed them by the scruffs of their necks, yanked them upright and started them off running in the right direction.

"Quit moaning! Get moving!"

They moved at a shambling trot. The leader kicked and cuffed at them from behind.

"Faster! Faster!"

Soon they were catching up to the transport machine again. The leader barked a mathematical command and brought the machine to a halt. He picked up the blinded Hypers and deposited them like sacks of potatoes on the flat trolley-top.

Then another command, and the machine accelerated forward once more. Now it was travelling at top speed: *grukker-grukker-grukker-grukker-grukker!*

High overhead, the angels had assembled for another attack. Bright and terrible they descended. They hovered all together directly above the machine.

SPAKKAKKAKKAKKAKKAKKAKKAKK!!!!!

This time the flashes were simultaneous. It was like the eruption of a thousand suns. Hypers screamed out in agony from the middle of the light.

When the dazzle finally cleared, there was a huge patch of whitened withered grass. The transport machine was motionless, slewed round at an angle with its rods and cylinders bent and twisted. On top of the machine lay bodies reduced to bleached stiff corpses. Around the machine other Hypers were squirming as though trying to wrestle with themselves. One seemed to be digging a hole in the earth with his head. They were all in their death-throes.

But there were two survivors, who had managed to dive in under the transport machine before the light hit. One was the leader with his collar and spike and blood-painted suit. The other wore a wire cage over his head—Selector No.2. They crawled out blinking and squinting.

The leader took a brief look at the scene, then wrapped his arms protectively over his head and set off running in the direction of the overbridge. Selector No.2 ran after him. Their course across the Plain was an erratic zigzag as they kept twisting around to stare up at the sky.

The angels circled high above, making no further move to attack. They seemed to have decided that sufficient destruction had been done. The two survivors carried out their retreat unopposed, diminishing into the distance.

Zonda knelt beside the broken body of her father and wept.

PART THREE

THE HUMEN

1

Two oval globes of glowing light flew low over the Home Ground. Within each globe was the figure of a winged angel. They halted and hung motionless directly above the Store, then started to descend.

Miriael propped herself up against the wall and sat watching. Both angels wore robes of the same yellow colour as her own.

Slowly lower and lower, floating and bobbling. Taking care to avoid contact with bags, bowls and baskets, they came to rest just a hand-breadth above the ground.

One angel was male, with golden-tawny hair. The other was female, with golden-blonde hair. Miriael recognised them at once.

"Chrymos! Neriah!" she cried, delighted. "It's you!"

"Junior Angel Chrymos," said Chrymos formally.

"Junior Angel Neriah," said Neriah.

"It was such a relief when I heard your trumpet-call!" Miriael rushed on. She didn't notice they were staring at her in amazement. "You've rescued me from the Humen! I couldn't believe I'd really communicated a message to Heaven!"

"Yes."

"You blasted them with the Light, didn't you?"

"Yes."

"I saw the flashes from here. I bet they—"

She broke off, suddenly aware of being stared at. They were looking her up and down, examining her all over. She shrank with embarrassment.

"Why are you looking at me like that?"

There was a strange expression in their eyes.

"You've changed," said Neriah at last.

"Unbelievable," said Chrymos. "So—*solid!*"

Miriael had a cold sinking feeling in the pit of her stomach. But she put on a brave face.

"You couldn't imagine the things I've endured. I've had my wings stamped on by Hypers. I've had to eat Residual food to survive. I've been chained up and spat at and dragged by the hair and…"

She faltered to a halt. There was no mistaking the expression in their eyes now. It was an expression of utter revulsion.

"You had to *eat?*"

"*Residual* food?"

"How *shameful!*"

Miriael was mortified. Tears began to gather under her eyelids, and she couldn't bring herself to speak. Chrymos and Neriah turned away and began talking between themselves.

"What ever will they say in Heaven?"

"It's never happened before!"

"Why didn't she give herself up to extinction?"

"No decent angel would stoop to *that!*"

The tears spilled out and rolled down Miriael's face. She felt like some kind of monster. The disgrace, the dishonour of what she'd done…

They turned back to her again.

"We shall return to Heaven and make a full report."

"You can expect a further inspection later. The authorities will want to deal with this."

Through her tears, Miriael saw that the auras of the two angels were pulsing with a brighter radiance. They must be going away already, she realised with surprise.

"Can't you help me?" she cried.

"I don't think there's much help for you," said Chrymos coldly.

"Don't go! Not yet!"

But it was no use. Chrymos and Neriah floated slowly upwards above the Store. Then with a sudden change of speed, they shot off high into the sky. In a moment they were out of sight.

2

Zonda dragged her father through the grass back to the Home Ground. She gripped him under the armpits and pulled backwards as gently as possible. Though he moaned and made noises in his throat, he seemed scarcely conscious. But broken arms and legs weren't enough to kill him.

The People still stood like mindless cattle on the bank of the Creek. Some of them must surely have seen what had happened to Neath, yet no one came to help until Zonda arrived on the opposite bank. Then Jossock, Lumb, Burge and Tunks came across to lift him up and carry him over the water.

"No jolting!" cried Zonda. "Carry him to his counting-corner."

The rest of the tribe trailed behind as they made their way to the Dwelling Place and the counting-corner. Many looked fearfully towards the other curtained-off corner where the angel lay still chained up in the Store.

"Two of them came down visiting her," they muttered among themselves.

"Celestials in our Dwelling Place..."

"Horrible lit-up globes..."

Zonda paid no attention. She held up the curtain while Jossock, Lumb, Burge and Tunks carried Neath into the corner, then directed the lowering of his body to the floor.

"Now go away," she told them. "He needs rest and quiet."

The curtain fell back as the adult males retreated outside. Zonda arranged her father in a more comfortable position, then brought her ear up close to his lips. He was no longer making noises in his throat, but his breathing was faint and fluttery.

"You'll get better," she whispered. "Your bones will knit back together, and you'll—"

She spun around. The curtain had opened again, and half a dozen faces peered in.

"What?"

"When will he wake up?"

"We need his wisdom."

"We don't know what to do."

"Go bite your bums," Zonda told them.

"But we have to ask him."

"He said it would be all over after today."

"He said that Celestial would be gone."

"But she isn't."

"How do we get rid of her now?"

"How do we go back to our normal lives?"

"He always said we had to keep to the Old Ways."

"But we can't when she's—"

Zonda jumped to her feet in a temper. "Old Ways, Old Ways, Old Ways! I'm sick of the Old Ways!" She pointed to her father. "What have the Old Ways done for *him?*"

They began once more to gripe and grumble—until Zonda made a rush at them, hands raised to slap at their faces. They withdrew in a hurry, and the curtain dropped back into place.

"Go away, stay away!" she shouted, then knelt by her father again.

3

Ferren stood between the pylons under the overbridge. He understood now why the shape of the Humen camp appeared to keep shifting. The impression came from great mobile canopies of wire which cycled and scanned in constant rotation. Vibrating like the multiple wings of some enormous insect, they overlapped to shield the camp under an impenetrable defensive net.

Behind the canopies, the interior of the camp remained mostly hidden. Sometimes there were glimpses of yellowish vapour clouds and tall plumes of steam; at other times patches of fiery red incandescence came and went. But Ferren could never see the source of the vapour or steam or incandescence.

Below the canopies, a more solid barrier blocked his view. The entire camp was walled off behind a kind of scarp or embankment. The only gaps were where overbridges cut through—no doubt guarded by gates and sentries. He had already decided to steer clear of such entry points.

As well as the embankment, there was an encircling lake like a moat. The furrowed clay of the landscape ran right up to the edge of the water, which looked very black and brooding. Ferren approached the lake under the overbridge, then spied out left and right.

He was in luck. At the base of the embankment were several large concrete pipes opening out onto the water. It made sense: the Humen expected any assault to come from Heaven above, not from a single small Residual creeping in below. If he crossed the lake under cover of the overbridge, he could paddle or swim to the nearest outlet.

First, he set about camouflaging himself. Scooping up handfuls of clay, he added water from the lake and smeared the muddy mixture over his face, arms and torso. Darkened and dirtied, he would be harder to spot from a distance.

Next, he advanced into the lake between the pylons. The black water looked noxious, but didn't seem to sting or hurt the skin. Further and further he waded in. There were no sounds from the overbridge over his head, nor any signs of movement on other converging overbridges.

He kept going until the embankment loomed in front of him. Even here, the water reached only hip-high. He bent at the knees, crouching low, and waded out into the open.

Nobody shouted a threat or a challenge. Shadows passed over him and made him jump—but they were only cast by the camp's rotating wire canopies. Hidden underwater with only his head showing, he continued close to the embankment towards the nearest concrete pipe.

He was twenty paces away when the lake suddenly deepened. He stood up straight, but the water rose past his waist, then his chest, then his chin. With a last deep breath, he struck out in a wild doggy paddle.

Swimming was entirely new to him. He spluttered and splashed and could hardly keep the water out of his nostrils. But he didn't have far to go. Soon he reached the pipe and was able to cling onto the rim of it. Then he hauled himself up and inside the concrete mouth.

No one could see him now. He squatted for a moment, coughing and spitting and recovering his breath. The inside of the pipe was smooth and cylindrical with a trickle of green sludge at the bottom. He looked to the other end and, yes, there was a circle of daylight. The pipe tunnelled all the way through to the interior of the camp.

When he clambered to his feet, he discovered he could stand nearly straight. He straddled the sludge with a foot on either side and advanced up a gentle slope. A foul stagnant smell made him hold his nose closed. In the darkest middle part of the tunnel, he had to fight against closing his eyes as well.

Although he moved quietly, every sound turned into a thousand echoes. His breath and his footsteps seemed like thunder in his ears. But the echoes were drowned out by the noises of the camp as he approached the far end of the tunnel. He could hear clanging and hammering…an on-off hissing…sometimes a high-pitched whistle…

Beyond the circle of daylight, an open channel fed into the pipe—also of concrete, but wider and shoulder-high. If he crouched down low, he could continue unobserved towards the centre of the camp.

He stuck out his head for a quick peek, and his eyes took in an expanse of black cinders and a forest of metal chimneys. Hundreds of chimneys rose like trees out of the ground, varying in height, all painted in yellow and grey stripes. There were no Humen close by, which was good, but he saw no Residuals on military service either.

Wraaaahhh! Wraaaahhh! Wraaaahhh!

An ear-splitting blare of sirens made him duck his head back in a hurry. The sound came from a dozen directions all at once. Had he been spotted?

But the sound had nothing to do with him. After the sirens, a booming, crackling amplified voice took over.

"ATTENTION ALL PERSONNEL! THIS IS AN ANNOUNCE-MENT FROM YOUR DOCTORS! PHASE RED STATUS IN THE SOUTH-WEST SECTOR! PREPARE FOR GENERAL MOBIL-ISATION! MAJOR OFFENSIVE IMPENDING! FURTHER ANNOUNCEMENTS TO FOLLOW!"

The voice clicked off, and for a moment the camp seemed suspended in silence. Then came a growing murmur of activity. Shouts, orders, marching feet, machines cranking into life. Everywhere was a stirring, swelling wave of movement and busyness.

Ferren shrank back further inside the pipe. Whatever was happening made exploration too risky right now. He calculated the hours until nightfall, when he could creep about under cover of darkness. Yes, better to postpone his search for Shanna and the other Residuals until then.

He settled himself down in the pipe to wait.

4

They were four great Seraphim: Nathanael, Cedrion, Bethor and Adonael. Inside their globes, they wore the purple robes of their Order and carried silver swords in scabbards at their sides. The swords indicated that they were mighty princes in Heaven, each in charge of a myriad of lesser angels. They lit up the twilight with the radiance of their auras.

Miriael felt an instinctive humility. She was painfully aware of her own missing aura and lightless body. She sat upright on the floor of the Store as they hovered before her, inspecting her all over with stern, cold eyes.

Finally she could stand it no longer. "Excuse me," she said. "What are you going to do with me?"

The silent inspection continued for another long minute. Then they looked at one another, communicating spirit to spirit.

Miriael tried again. "Are you going to lift me back up into Heaven?"

"Lift you?" Nathanael's voice was deep and resonant. "How could we do that?"

"You would only fall back down under your own weight," said Bethor.

"You lack the aura of a proper angel," said Adonael.

Miriael swallowed hard. "I just thought there might be a way…"

Nathanael looked down at her. "Possibly there is. But it depends on you."

"You have lost your true nature by eating Residual food," said Cedrion. "You must never touch such food again."

"Oh." Miriael considered. "Then I'll recover my true nature?"

"We believe so," said Bethor.

Their expressions conveyed the same disgust that Miriael had seen on the faces of Chrymos and Neriah.

"Your body has become a thing of the Earth," Nathanael told her. "You must aspire to a better higher state."

"I will," Miriael promised. "I *want* to return to Heaven."

"As it may be," said Cedrion.

"And you have very little time to achieve it," added Adonael. "The Humen will be coming back, probably with a whole army."

"For me? Do I matter so much?"

"You're a source of information to them," said Adonael. "You know about the overall strategic situation, of course?"

Miriael nodded. "The Humen are building up their forces in Australia, and we're building up a counter-force. But they don't know we'll be ready for them."

"Precisely."

Miriael didn't mention the other form of information that could be extracted from her—about the functioning of angels in general. She pointed to the chain that fixed her to the wall.

"Will you set me free now? Then I can move away from here before the Humen come back."

Stern frowns appeared on their brows.

"How would you move without your aura?" asked Cedrion.

"I can crawl."

"Crawl!" They looked at her with horrified revulsion.

"How low!"

"How shameful!"

"An angel crawling!"

"No!" Nathanael raised his voice. "You must move by the power of spiritual volition alone. Improve yourself. Forget about any other form of locomotion."

"But if the Humen come back while I'm still improving…"

"That is Heaven's concern," said Nathanael.

"We don't wish for added complications." Bethor curled his lip. "Such as not knowing where you might have crawled off to."

Of course they were right, Miriael told herself. They *had* to be right. They were great princes in Heaven, far wiser than any junior warrior angel...

"No more earthly food or drink, I promise." She made a solemn vow. "I'll work on improving my spiritual state. Anything to get back up to Heaven."

"As you were and should have been," said Adonael.

They folded their hands in prayer and raised their eyes to Heaven, preparing to ascend. But Cedrion lowered his gaze for a final word.

"Also, no more visionary dreaming," he said.

"You mean, like my dream with Baruch and the Aeon?"

"Yes. You must *not* come up to Heaven in that way."

"But how else can I communicate? I've lost the power to—"

"Do not communicate. We shall return to you here to observe your progress."

The discussion was closed, and Miriael fell silent. With a tremendous pulsing radiance, the Seraphim ascended out of the Store, higher and higher into the darkening sky.

5

When night fell, Ferren expected the activity in the Humen camp to die down. Instead, powerful arc-lights switched on, casting wide beams of blue-white illumination. Still, there were plenty of shadows for creeping about in.

Already he had peered out several times from his concrete pipe, scanning for Residual workers—or Residual slaves. He had seen several teams of Hypers marching purposefully this way or that, but so far, not a single Residual. Perhaps they worked only indoors, out of sight in workshops and factories...

He waited a while after nightfall, planning a route for his search. He intended to begin by following the open channel towards the centre of the camp.

Finally, he flexed his cramped limbs and set off. Ducking his head down low in the channel, he passed straight through the forest of painted chimneys. On one side, he heard a rhythmical *thump-thump-thump* of machinery; on the other side, the harsh voice of a Hyper calling out what sounded like a string of numbers.

"48 + 95 x 3.88!"

He continued further into the camp, where the channel took a right-angled turn to the left, then another to the right. Now he heard other mechanical sounds: grindings and creakings, clatterings and rattlings. What made such sounds he couldn't begin to guess. He kept on going until he came to a relatively quiet spot that was also in shadow. Then he clambered out from the channel.

He had come to an area of huts, half-cylindrical in shape with corrugated iron roofs. He darted from row to row, pausing at every corner to scout ahead. There were windows at both ends of the half-cylinders, and he stopped repeatedly to peer inside. But he saw no workers or slaves, only racks of shelves and big square cartons. The huts weren't workshops or factories or even dormitories.

The area of huts ended with a deep trench. He climbed down and out again on the other side. Now he was in an area of wooden pallets stacked high with drums, crates, giant spools of wire and boxes wrapped in silver foil. Still there was nobody around, neither Hypers nor Residuals.

There *was* movement, though. When he looked up, he saw cables overhead, and wheeled contraptions that ran on them, dangling down hooks. Sometimes the hooks carried crates, drums, spools or boxes. All movement seemed to radiate out from a central hub, where something nested on top of a pole encased in a dome of glass.

At first he feared that the thing might have spotted him, and dived back under cover. After watching for a while, though, he decided that the thing was just another kind of machine, unable to see or hear. Still, he didn't like the blobby grey look of it, nor the fine glistening fibres that connected it to the contraptions with the hooks.

He was thankful to leave that area behind. He crossed an empty space of gratings set into the ground and arrived at an area of tall, rounded shapes like upright urns. Coated with chalky sediment, they were like an army of pale ghosts. Every now and then, one let out a great *whoosh!* and shot a gush of white vapour high in the air. Ferren flinched and jumped.

There were no Hypers or Residuals in the area of the urns, nor in the next area either. Now he walked between pyramids of coal, sand, lime and slag. He had long since lost all sense of direction—but he wasn't aiming to return to his concrete pipe anyway.

After the pyramids came a roadway of grey ash and grit, then an area of long, low brick buildings. His hopes rose as he approached.

Maybe this is what a factory looks like? he thought.

The whole area was black with soot and half hidden in clouds of smoke. The brick buildings were set out in a complicated pattern like a maze. In fact, they lacked the windows of ordinary buildings, and their roofs came up only shoulder high. Still, their inside rooms might go down below the ground.

Entering the maze, he searched for some sort of door or opening. The interiors of the buildings seemed to be lit up with orange-red light, which showed through tiny chinks under the metal roofs.

Ussh-gaah! Ussh-gaah! Ussh-gaah! Ussh-gaah!

The sound brought him to a halt. He thought at first that it came from the buildings—then realised it came from a dense cloud of smoke up ahead. As he stood puzzled, the sound grew louder and the smoke rolled closer. There were mechanical clanks and rumbles too.

Then a shape loomed through the smoke: a huge gantry moving on caterpillar tracks. Although it was coming straight towards him, its advance was very slow, repeatedly stopping and starting. He resisted the urge to flee and stayed watching.

Each time it stopped, the machine lowered an arm and lifted the roof clean off one of the buildings. The metal roofs, he now saw, were really metal lids. With another arm, the machine then probed down deep inside the building, which simultaneously released great billows of smoke. Then the second arm withdrew, the first arm replaced the lid, and the machine lumbered forward to the next building.

It was another automatic process, another machine with no driver or operator. He wasn't afraid of being observed, but he was very curious about the orange-red glow when the lids were lifted. Was that *fire* that filled the buildings?

The mobile gantry was twenty paces away when he stepped across to investigate the nearest building. He expected the metal roof to be hot—

but not for the intensity of heat that burned his fingertips. He jumped back so fast he lost his footing and went sprawling on the ground.

In the same moment, the gantry made another advance on its caterpillar tracks. Ferren saw it bearing down on him and scuttled aside. But he need not have worried; the machine came to another stop five paces away.

Ussh-gaah! Yugh-gaah! Yugh-gaah!

The sound was even more startling at close quarters. It was exactly like somebody straining and grunting with effort, and it changed as the machine went through different functions. Stopping, extending an arm, lifting a lid, extending a second arm, probing into the fire… The sound when probing into the fire was almost like gasping: *Ah-gnah-gnuff! Ah-gnah-gnuff!*

Yet there was no living creature involved. Looking in through the caterpillar tracks, Ferren saw only cylinders and chambers, levers and pistons. Every mechanical action happened all by itself.

A dispiriting thought came to him: why would the Humen even need slaves or workers if machines could perform every task for them? And yet he *had* seen Selectors leading chained Residuals to the camp…

He left the area of low brick buildings to continue his explorations elsewhere. But what if the angel was wrong, and Residuals were sent out from the camp as soldiers to the fighting? He felt sure that Shanna would sooner become a soldier than a slave. But in that case, he would never meet up with her again.

6

Moving from area to area of the camp, Ferren came across many more machines and sometimes teams of Hypers, but never any Residuals. He grew accustomed to ignoring the machines and staying clear of the Hypers.

One time, though, he didn't stay clear enough. He had been investigating a circular concrete cistern full of caustic-smelling liquid when a train of buckets on wheels came suddenly round a corner. The buckets were hauled by a snub-nosed machine, but there were also four Hypers marching beside it. He dropped down out of sight behind the cistern.

The Hypers wore the usual all-encompassing black suits, ornamented with the usual studs and chains. Slogans were scribbled across their chests and backs:

BE MY VICTIM!
THE MINCING MACHINE!
CORPSES INCORPORATED!
GETCHA DEATH WARRANT SIGNED HERE!

Ferren remained crouching with only his eyes looking out. The bucket-train and Hypers passed by on the other side of the cistern. Then one Hyper barked an order:

"22 – 5.75 x 42!" barked a harsh Hyper's voice.

Ferren had heard that kind of mathematical command before. But who was the Hyper addressing? The snub-nosed machine? But which part of the machine?

"84 x 8 + 91.2%."

Since all four Hypers now had their backs to him, Ferren rose to his full height for a better view. The one giving commands was leaning towards the hood that covered the engine of the machine. But it was another who, for no obvious reason, suddenly looked back over his shoulder.

"Who's that?"

It was too late to duck. All four Hypers had now turned around and spotted him.

"The saboteur! Must be the saboteur!"

"Get him!"

"Grab him!"

They abandoned the bucket-train and charged around on both sides of the cistern. Ferren ran for his life—past tanks and bins, then domes and scaffolding, then wheels and cogs and pulleys.

The Hypers couldn't catch him up, but they didn't stop chasing. They kicked up such a racket with their boots and shouting, they could hardly be following the sound of his footsteps. He swerved round a row of tall metal cabinets—and for a moment he was out of their sight. In the next moment he came to a triangular glass building with an open doorway.

He flung himself inside and pulled the door shut behind him.

The glass building was filled with fruit-bearing plants growing in troughs. The foliage hid him, and so did the mistiness of the air. He dropped flat on his belly and wriggled further away from the door.

The Hypers ran right past outside. Glancing back, Ferren saw them as mere shadows through the glass. He had shaken off the pursuit! With a sigh of relief, he hurried on to a second door at the other end of the building.

Slipping out through the door, he came to an area of insulation-padded pipes running over the ground. He crossed them by means of a rubber-coated walkway and arrived on the edge of a wide tarmac compound.

Huge, strange shapes were drawn up on the compound like a mighty congregation of prehistoric monsters. There were about fifty of them, some long, some squat, some projecting in lumps and bulges. Whatever they were, they were all hidden under green tarpaulins. The compound seemed quiet and deserted.

He made his way forward between the monsters. Now he could see the rims of wheels peeping out below the tarpaulins. The air was heavy with smells of oil and grease.

He hadn't gone far when a trickle of liquid crossed his path. It leaked out from one particular monster and formed a puddle on the tarmac. Although it looked as clear as water, it smelled sweet and fruity. He remembered the fruit growing in the triangular glass building, and realised all at once how hungry he was. Why hadn't he thought to pick some on the way through? But perhaps this liquid would satisfy thirst *and* hunger.

He got down on his hands and knees, dabbed a finger into the liquid and raised it to his mouth. The taste was delicious, like fruity syrup. If he could trace the trickle to its source…

He lifted the edge of the tarpaulin and crawled in under the belly of the monster. All he could see was a chassis of metal ribs over his head. But he could hear a sound: *plop! plop! plop!* The syrup was dripping down somewhere very close

He rolled onto his back, felt around overhead and made contact with a plastic hose connected to a metal tank. The leak came from the join between the tank and the hose.

He shifted to lie directly under the leak, opened his mouth and let the drops fall onto his tongue. The syrup was somehow filling as well as thirst-quenching. But it was a very slow process, one drop at a time.

He was still lying there when he became aware of a faint brightening of the light. The first signs of dawn were creeping in under the tarpaulin.

By and by, the belly of the monster came more clearly into view. Beyond the ribs of the chassis were complicated shafts and drivebelts; and beyond the shafts and drivebelts, odd metal parts like perforated funnels and steel cylinders. It was all completely incomprehensible.

What interested him most was what he could see higher up again. There were hollow, empty spaces in the very belly of the monster. One large cavity at the side particularly drew his attention—recessed above a metal flap that arched over a huge wheel. He could easily climb up there between the ribs and shafts and drivebelts...and it was just the right size for curling up in...

He considered. He hadn't slept for a day and a night, and he was very, very tired. Here he could stay snug and safe, with the convenience of the syrup for food and drink when he wanted.

He decided to make the cavity his hiding place. He would sleep through the day and go back to his searching after nightfall.

7

*Z*onda explained her absence. "I've been looking after my father." She eyed Miriael's food bowl and drinking bowl, which still contained water, sunflower seeds and tomatoes from the day before. "Seems you had enough to eat, anyway."

"I've stopped eating," Miriael told her.

"Why?"

"I want to return to Heaven, and terrestrial substance weighs me down."

Zonda shrugged. "Funny thing to do, stop eating. Won't you starve to death?"

"I'm working to recover my true spiritual nature."

"All right," Zonda shrugged again. "Makes it easier for me, not looking after you too."

Miriael studied her closely. She was puffy around the eyes, and there was a drawn look to her normally plump features.

"Why are you looking after your father? What happened to him?"

"They broke his arms and legs."

"The Humen?"

"Yes, this one who was annoyed about Heaven attacking." Zonda scowled. "He took it out on my father. No reason, he just felt like breaking someone's arms and legs."

She sat down on a pile of bags and stared into empty space.

"But your father will recover, won't he?" Miriael suggested. "He won't die from broken bones?"

"I don't know." Zonda sniffed miserably. "He just lies in his corner like he's in a daze. He hasn't spoken since it happened. I think he's lost the will to live."

Miriael was at a loss what to say. "Give him time. With you looking after him—"

"What happens if he dies?"

"You shouldn't worry about—"

"What happens? Is it the end?"

Miriael could see that only a plain answer would do. "No, the body dies, but the soul lives on. You Residuals have souls."

"You said that before."

"Yes. And the soul is immortal."

"Where does it live on? In Heaven?"

"Not nowadays. Not with the war." Miriael knew that much, but little else.

"So where *does* it go?"

"I suppose it stays somewhere on the Earth."

"Huh!" Zonda snorted, not in the least consoled.

"I'm sure your father—"

But Zonda had finished with the subject. She jumped up again and began digging through various bags and baskets.

"What are you doing?"

Zonda's face had the look of someone trying hard not to cry. "I can't promise when I'll be back. If my father gets worse... I'm setting out food and drink in case you change your mind."

"I won't."

Zonda's ignored the denial. "This is all dried food. It'll keep better." She arranged two bags and two baskets within the angel's reach. "Dried peas, dried beans, dried tomatoes, dried mushrooms. You can't eat them without softening them first. Like this."

She dropped a dried mushroom into the drinking bowl. Miriael observed with curiosity.

"Wait a while," Zonda told her. "The longer you wait, the softer it gets."

"Thank you."

"Now I'll go and fill you a fresh bowl of water for drinking and another for softening food. Just in case."

"I—" Miriael bit back another denial as Zonda turned to go. "I hope you'll find time to visit some more. I appreciate your company, you know. Come and tell me how your father's doing."

8

Ferren slept most of the day, then lay on his back beneath the mechanical monster drinking syrup from the leaking tank. By nightfall, he was refreshed and ready to continue his search.

He intended to be more systematic about it this time. The camp was far bigger than he could ever have imagined. He decided on a new direction and headed across the tarmac compound between tarpaulin-covered monsters.

Beyond the compound were great piles of rusty metal scrap. He detoured around them and arrived at a high wire fence. On the other side, arc-lights on masts cast downward beams of light through the darkness. He couldn't see what they illuminated because the ground fell away in a wide, empty space.

Curious, he followed the fence around until he found a place where the wire was loose. He crept in underneath and advanced on all fours to the edge of the empty space.

It turned out to be an open pit like a quarry. Sheer rock walls dropped fifty feet to a level floor, which was starkly bright under the arc-lights.

Peering down over the edge, he saw that the floor was covered in shiny white tiles. A conveyor belt on rollers ran across at one end and various items of stainless steel equipment stood in the corners. The centre of the pit was occupied by three large rectangular depressions like enamel baths. The left-hand bath was hidden under a black plastic shroud, the other two baths were empty. Half a dozen Hypers in thigh-high boots stood idly around.

Nothing was going on, so far as Ferren could see. Curiosity satisfied, he headed back through the wire fence and continued on his way to the next area.

The next area was an area of huge glass vessels and retorts: chemical apparatus on a gigantic scale. Ferren jumped a ditch of scummy sludge, crossed a road of black cinders and slipped in among the apparatus.

Most of the vessels and retorts were empty, but some contained coloured liquids. Two or three times his own height, they were linked by an intricate network of hoses. He ducked under yellow tubes that looped through the air, stepped over corrugated black pipes that ran along the ground. It was like picking his way through an obstacle course.

He hadn't gone far when he became aware of a sound ahead: an excited murmur of many voices.

"Oooooooohhh!"

A sibilant hiss of breath indrawn…then silence for half a minute… then a slow shuddering gasp of breath released.

"Aaaaaaaahhh!"

The hairs stood up on the back of his neck. The voices were the voices of Hypers, not Residuals, and they seemed to be watching something.

He advanced with greater caution and found himself approaching a semi-transparent plastic screen. He could see vague silhouettes through the plastic—silhouettes in the shape of Hypers. Apparently they were lined up in a queue, but he couldn't see the cause of their excitement. He followed the screen around, moving parallel to the queue.

Thirty paces around, the line of Hypers came to an end. Whatever was happening was happening here. He brought his eye up against the screen, but still saw only shadows.

Then he heard someone say, *"One point five psycholitres."*

The voice sounded weird, like a whisper artificially amplified. Certainly not a Hyper voice or a Residual voice. Was it some other kind of Humen?

Although there was no break in the screen, a black corrugated pipe ran in under it at one point—just enough to lift the plastic. He lowered himself flat on his belly, wriggled forward, squeezed up against the pipe and peered in under the screen.

It was a strange perspective, looking up from ground level. The first thing he saw was a contraption like a stretcher on a trolley; then the queue of Hypers lined up behind it; then an attendant on one side of the stretcher carrying some sort of long-barrelled instrument. The attendant was clad in the same tight-fitting rubber as the other Hypers, but his costume was all white instead of all black. On the other side of the stretcher, a Humen who wasn't a Hyper sat hunched in a wheelchair.

"Aaaaaaaahhh!" came the slow shuddering gasp from the waiting queue.

In the next moment, a black-suited Hyper climbed down from the stretcher and sprang away. Then the artificially amplified whisper rang out again: "*Next dose.*"

The source of the whisper was the figure in the wheelchair. He might have been a very small Residual, if any Residual could have grown so incredibly old and shrunken. The back of his head was swathed in bandages, and his white medical coat hung down below his feet. His face was crumpled like a grey paper bag.

Meanwhile, another Hyper had climbed up onto the stretcher. The figure in the wheelchair inspected him.

"*One point three psycholitres.*" Several thin wires connected the bandaged head to a black box nearby, and display lights flickered on the box whenever the figure spoke or moved.

The attendant leaned over the Hyper on the stretcher and did something to his forehead. Then he applied his long-barrelled instrument to the same place.

"Ooooooooohhh!" The waiting queue craned forward and sucked in breath.

For the first time, Ferren noticed a long, thin tube that attached to the back of the instrument. The Hyper on the stretcher appeared to stiffen, while the attendant counted slowly.

143

"Nought point one, point two, point three…"

At "one point three", the long-barrelled instrument was withdrawn, and the watching Hypers let out their breath with a shuddering "Aaaaaaaahhh!" Then the attendant did something to the forehead of the man on the stretcher, who sat up, jumped down and went off flexing his limbs in a state of extreme animation.

"*Next dose,*" said the shrivelled figure in the wheelchair.

Ferren's neck was aching from his position on the ground looking up. He slid backwards and crept away. He had seen all he wanted to see.

He remembered that the angel had spoken of three types of Humen: Hypers, Doctors and Plasmatics. Presumably the figure in the wheelchair was a Doctor. Compared to the fearsome Hypers he had met, this first example of a Doctor seemed puny and almost pathetic.

He left the area of glass vessels and retorts by a different route and emerged onto a road of black cinders. Looking out right and left, he observed a vehicle that had just passed by: some sort of engine hauling a cage on wheels. Two Hypers marched alongside, and he was about to step back and wait.

Then he saw what the cage contained. *Residuals!*

9

Ferren stared in shock. He had almost stopped expecting to find Residuals inside the camp—and suddenly here they were! Not as workers, not even as slaves, but as prisoners! Where were the Hypers taking them?

He tracked after the cage at a distance. The road curved and hugged the edge of the area of chemical apparatus all the way around. Keeping close to the glass vessels and retorts, he was ready to vanish if either Hyper happened to turn.

He was visible to the Residuals in the cage, but they weren't looking. There were four males and four females, some with markings on their bodies, some with their hair tied up or braided. They wore loincloths and breast-bands similar to the People's, but dyed in the colours of other tribes. All held their heads in their hands and whimpered pitifully.

As the road continued to circle the chemical apparatus, Ferren realised he was returning to the area he'd visited before. There was the same ditch of scummy sludge and the same wire fence...and beyond the fence, the open space where the pit dropped down.

Then one Hyper shouted an order, and the vehicle halted in front of a gate in the fence. Another order, and the gate swung slowly open. The prisoners in the cage began to wail and plead, but the Hypers only laughed.

They laughed again when the vehicle lurched into forward motion, causing the Residuals to lose balance and tumble about in the bottom of the cage.

"Off to do your military service!" they jeered.

The vehicle crossed a bridge over the ditch and entered the gate. The Hypers followed it in. Ferren, watching, saw it tilt suddenly at the front and go down at a steep angle.

He was reckless and ready to take any chance. As the cage disappeared from view and the gate started to swing slowly shut, he crouched low and ran forward. Across the road, across the ditch, up to the fence— and in through the gate just before it closed.

Once in, he darted off to the side. The cage was descending by a ramp to the bottom of the pit, but he couldn't go down there himself. Still crouching, he stayed close to the fence and ran round until he was safely away from the gate. Then he lowered himself flat to the ground and crawled forward to look down and observe from above.

At the bottom of the pit, the illumination of the arc-lights seemed even brighter than before. All three baths now stood empty. High-booted Hypers waited on the white tiled floor as the cage completed its descent. When it arrived, they clustered around laughing and shouting.

"What've we got here?"

"Another load of crud!"

"Not much in this lot!"

Some carried long pointed rods, which they stuck in through the bars of the cage. When the escorting Hypers unlocked the cage door, the jabbing points drove the prisoners out onto the tiles.

"Make the most of 'em!" cried one escort.

"All needed for the new offensive!" cried the other.

The Residuals stood in a huddle like lost and helpless children. They were no longer wailing or whimpering, but mute with despair. Again the pointed rods jabbed, driving them towards the left-hand bath until all eight were lined up along the edge. Four high-booted Hypers climbed down the smooth enamel sides ahead of them.

Then more prodding and jabbing. The prisoners tried to fend off the points, but one by one they lost their balance and went slithering and sliding down into the bath. The four waiting Hypers seized hold of them, rolled them over on their backs and manoeuvred them into position. Soon a neat row of Residuals lay packed side by side like sardines.

In the next part of the procedure, the Hypers clambered over the eight bodies and inserted wads of something like cotton wool into their mouths. Then they unspooled electrical wires and attached small clips to fingers, toes and earlobes. Finally, while the four Hypers climbed out, the other Hypers brought forward a shroud of black plastic and spread it to cover the whole bath.

Ferren watched in horror. He didn't understand any of it, but he was sure it was wicked—and going to get worse.

The electrical wires connected to stainless steel equipment in one corner of the pit. One Hyper went across to the controls, and the equipment started up with a loud continuous hum. What was happening now under the shroud?

The engine hauling the empty cage chugged back up the slope, out of the pit and back to the gate. The high-booted Hypers wandered off, chatting among themselves. Clearly, whatever was happening would take time.

Ferren willed himself to stay watching. The truth about military service lay hidden under the black plastic shroud. He dreaded to find out what it was, yet he *had* to find out. He would wait all night if necessary.

10

An hour went by. Still Ferren hadn't moved from his position looking down at the pit; still there had been no further developments below. Then a loud beeping sounded out from the stainless steel equipment.

One Hyper went across to switch off the sound. Another lifted a corner of the black plastic to inspect what was beneath.

"Separation completed!" he called out. "Prepare for pumping!"

At once, Hypers converged from all sides. They rolled back the shroud to expose the bath and the eight bodies packed side by side. The Residuals still had wads of cotton wool in their mouths and electrical wires clipped to their fingers, toes and earlobes. But Ferren gasped in shock at the stuff that now covered them. They were submerged in jelly! Iridescent liquid jelly!

The Hypers gloated as they surveyed the contents of the bath. The faces and bodies of the Residuals were just inches below the surface of the jelly. They looked not exactly dead but waxy and lifeless.

"Hmm, not bad," one Hyper commented.

"Must've been a few okay ones in there," said a second.

They laughed together, an ugly humourless sound. Meanwhile, other Hypers had brought forward a long nozzle attached by a tube to a different piece of equipment. They plunged it into the jelly in the bath. Then someone rapped out a mathematical order, and the equipment kicked into action with a snuffling sound: *slupp-a-slupp-a-slupp-a-slupp*.

So this was "pumping", thought Ferren numbly. They were sucking up the jelly through the nozzle and tube. He was sure it had come out of the Residuals, though he didn't understand how. There was something very strange about the stuff…

When he stared straight at it, it appeared simply colourless. Yet when he turned his head and glimpsed it out of the corner of his eye, it came alive with every colour under the sun. He kept imagining he was seeing a million shifting shapes and images—but could never manage to focus on any of them. The effect was eerie and elusive.

For ten minutes the pumping continued, until every last drop of jelly had been drawn off. Then a couple of Hypers jumped down and clambered over the bodies, unclipping the clips and gathering up the wires. Another couple of Hypers went in after them to collect the mouth-wads of what looked like cotton wool. The Residuals remained utterly inert, eyes vacant and mouths open.

You killed them, thought Ferren. *Or something worse than killing.* This was what had happened to his sister Shanna and every other Residual ever selected for military service. He clenched his fists in impotent rage.

He was about to turn and leave when another gang of Hypers jumped down into the bath. There were eight of them, one for every Residual, and they wielded long shiny knives. Each straddled a body and began making deep incisions, cutting and slicing.

The bodies were still motionless, but their blood spurted in all directions. Soon the Hypers' black suits were red with gore. They went about their butchering with zest and practised efficiency.

Meanwhile, the Hypers above had set up a line of pails along the edge of the tiles. Every pail bore a number and a label. As the butchers below tossed up gobbets of flesh and innards, the Hypers above caught each specimen and dropped it into a particular pail.

Ferren couldn't watch a moment longer. He crawled away from the edge of the pit and vomited on the grass. He was sickened to the core.

His legs carried him along by the fence until he came to a spot where the wire was loose and he could wriggle underneath. All he wanted was to escape...to get back to his hiding place in the belly of the monster... to close out the horrors that his eyes had seen.

11

Of the four Seraphim who had visited Miriael before, it was Nathanael and Cedrion who returned to check on her progress. They descended into the Store with a great rushing noise in the middle of the night. Their eyes fell at once upon the bowls of water and dried food that Zonda had laid out for her.

"These are new." Nathanael's voice was very stern. "Have you been eating and drinking again?"

"I haven't touched a thing. No terrestrial food or water. I've kept my vow."

Cedrion examined her. "She *looks* a little less substantial," he agreed.

Nathanael remained focused on the bowls. "Explain these."

"A Residual filled them up for me. She thought I needed to keep eating and drinking, though I told her I didn't. But she meant well."

Nathanael merely curled his lip. Miriael turned to Cedrion. "You can see, the bags are still full and the water's still up to the brim. So I *can't* have touched them."

Cedrion nodded and conceded: "I believe you. And are you constantly striving to recover your true condition? With prayer and thoughts of Heaven?"

"All the time. I can't wait to return."

"Yes, well, the aspiration is good. Turn your thoughts to Heaven and away from Residuals."

"You have too much sympathy for them," Nathanael told her.

"I don't think we should—"

"Too much sympathy," he repeated. "Your spirit must transcend these sordid surroundings."

Miriael fell silent, while Nathanael and Cedrion continued to inspect her wings, hair and skin. She had the impression they noted an improvement.

"Can I make a request?" she asked at last.

"You may," answered Nathanael.

"Will you tell me the early history of the world?"

"Early history?" Nathanael frowned. "You don't need to know such things."

"It would help me transcend my surroundings," Miriael suggested. "I'd have something else to think about."

"Hmm. I suppose there is that."

Miriael pressed the point. "The history of the world before the Great Collapse."

"What? The Age of the Undead? The False Truce?"

"Yes! Please!"

The two Seraphs exchanged thoughtful glances.

"Not our role," said Cedrion. "Specialised knowledge."

"True." Nathanael nodded. "It would need the Cherubim to do it."

They weren't actually saying no. Miriael held her breath.

"Gethel's the expert on ancient lore and early times." Nathanael reflected aloud. "Even before the Trespass."

"And Asiel keeps the archives on the Far Past up to the Great Collapse," said Cedrion. "We could ask them."

They turned to Miriael.

"Very well. We shall pass on your request to Gethel and Asiel," said Nathanael.

"Two of the greatest scholars in Heaven," Cedrion explained.

"Thank you!" Miriael clapped her hands. "Thank you, thank you, thank you!"

The Seraphim frowned at her excessive enthusiasm. "*If* they can spare the time," said Nathanael.

"It may require higher authorisation," added Nathanael.

Miriael moderated her enthusiasm. "I'll be so grateful. I have some really important questions to ask."

But Nathanael and Cedrion were no longer listening. They raised their eyes to the night sky and willed themselves up through the air. With another great rushing sound, they ascended out of the Store and soared towards Heaven.

Probably lucky they cut me off, Miriael told herself. *If I'd told them the questions I want answered, they might have been less willing to help.*

12

Ferren was curled up in his hiding place in the belly of the monster. Hideous pictures kept playing through his mind: the Residuals packed side by side with cotton wool wads in their mouths; the iridescent jelly that had been extracted from them and covered them; the Hypers swinging their knives as they cut through joints and tissue. He couldn't sleep for the rest of the night and was still wide awake when daylight crept in under the bottom of the tarpaulin.

That was when he thought of the angel Miriael. She'd been right about Residuals not going out to fight on military service, though she could never have guessed what really happened. Her mind was too high and pure to imagine such horrors.

He unrolled the top of the cloth around his waist and drew out the two feathers. Even in the dim dark, they seemed to glow with a whiteness of their own. Better pictures came to his mind: her golden hair and yellow robe, her long pale limbs stretched out on the grass. What conversations they'd had! She'd liked talking to him, he was sure, and he'd more than liked talking to her.

You're so much better than the Humen, he thought. He didn't understand why his tribe—and other tribes—had chosen to be allies with the Humen instead of with Heaven. *It would be different if I had anything to do with it,* he thought.

Feeling more positive about the world, he threaded the feathers back into his cloth. Then he curled up again and fell into a deep and dreamless sleep.

Much later, he woke suddenly to light and sounds. The light wasn't bright, but it entered from a new direction—above and around him. Thin pencil rays angled in through chinks in the monster's metal plating. The sounds were above and around him too, sharp ringing sounds of boots on metal.

He took a moment to work out that the heavy tarpaulin covering the monster must have been pulled off. Now there were Hypers clambering around the outside. It was as though they were walking right over his head.

Then came a blare of sirens. Even deep inside the monster, the noise was like a blow to his ears. When the sirens died down, a booming, crackling voice cut in.

"ATTENTION ALL PERSONNEL! OFFENSIVE NOW UNDER WAY! BEGIN THE ADVANCE! EXIT THROUGH GATE NUMBER 5 ON THE SOUTH-WEST OVERBRIDGE!"

On all sides, machinery burst into life. Pistons heaved, cogs whirled, rods slid back and forth—and Ferren's monster lurched suddenly forward.

151

The jolt of movement caught him unawares, and he almost slipped and fell among the shafts and drivebelts.

He hung on and braced himself in his cavity above the wheel-arch. There was nothing he could do but get carried along.

13

Garrunng—unng—unng—unng! Garrunng—unng—unng—unng!

The walls of the cavity shook to the vibration, the noise of metal on metal was deafening. There were other noises too, like gasps and wheezes and grunts of exertion. The belly of the monster was a maelstrom of threshing machinery, all spinning and rotating at tremendous speed. Looking down through the shafts and drivebelts, Ferren could see the tarmac of the compound sliding past below.

He scanned the chinks in the metal plating. They were all tiny, so that nobody seeing them from outside could see *him*. But if he brought his eye up close, perhaps one would serve as a spyhole? His best chance was a chink, six feet to his left, which was a little less tiny than the rest.

He swung himself out of his hiding place and moved across handhold by handhold and foothold by foothold. Praying for no sudden jolts or jerks, he clung to perforations and projections, a vertical pipe, the rim of a flange and an inch-wide ledge.

At last he made it. He wedged himself into a niche, pressed his cheek against cold metal and applied his eye to the chink.

He was looking out over the back end of the monster. Following behind was another mechanical monster on wheels, then another, then another. They lumbered along like a procession of beasts—ugly, angular, brutal-looking beasts. The deep, dull thunder of their engines added to the reverberant din inside his own monster.

At present they were travelling through the camp on a concrete road. Hypers in military formation marched five abreast on either side, a sea of black rubbery skulls. Other Hypers rode on top of the monsters, some sitting, some standing.

But they can't see me, Ferren told himself.

In fact, they weren't even looking his way. Their eyes were all fixed forward and a little to the left. Something was happening up ahead. He heard martial music, then the amplified voice speaking again, then raucous cheers.

The Hypers marching along the road straightened their shoulders.

"Here we go!"

"Smarten up!"

"Ready for the Doctors!"

The road widened out into a parade ground. Ferren's monster changed direction, then changed direction again. Peering sideways through his spyhole, he saw a six-sided tower in the centre of the parade ground, topped by a huge dome of glass. At the base of the tower, the Doctors sat side by side on a platform surrounded by flags and banners. The platform was draped in red cloth with a guardrail all around.

There were ten of them, and they were observing the military march-past. Like the single Doctor Ferren had seen before, they sat in wheelchairs, wore white medical coats and had bandages wrapped around the backs of their skulls. So withered, so wizened, so shrunken!

As he watched, one of the ten leaned forward and spoke into a box on the arm of his wheelchair. An amplified roar boomed out across the parade ground.

"HUMEN SOLDIERS OF THE BANKSTOWN CAMP! WE GO FORTH ON A GREAT MISSION! OUR GOAL IS TO LEARN THE SECRET WORKINGS OF HEAVEN'S ANGELS! THEN SCIENCE CAN DESTROY THEM! PROGRESS WILL TRIUMPH! THE RATIONAL MIND WILL CONQUER MYSTERY AND SUPERSTITION! DEATH TO THE UNKNOWN!"

There were yells and cheers from the Hypers marching and the Hypers riding mechanical monsters. They raised their arms in a salute with clenched fists and middle fingers extended upwards. The speaker fell back exhausted in his wheelchair, while the amplifiers switched across to recorded martial music.

The line of monsters wheeled once more and left the parade ground by another road. The Hypers dropped their salutes, but their yelling grew louder and louder.

"Down with Heaven, rah-rah-rah!"

"We'll mangulate the suckers!"

"Pull down their angels!"

"Stuff their Blessed Souls!"

"Piss on their Patriarchs!"

"Give 'em the finger! Rah-rah-rah!"

A sudden banging of boots on metal made Ferren pull back and almost tumble down. Two Hypers seated right above his spyhole had started kicking with their heels in time to the rhythm. He retreated once more to the safety of his hiding place above the wheel-arch.

14

The two Cherubim scholars were very old and dignified, with fine silvery hair and long silvery beards. One carried a great book bound in leather and fastened with clasps. Their globes rocked and bobbed in the Store like bubbles of light.

"You've come to teach me!" Miriael cried. "It's been allowed!"

She didn't sit upright, but propped herself on one elbow. Her physical strength had declined since she'd stopped eating and drinking. The Cherubim looked down at her with furrowed brows.

"I am Gethel, Third Angel of Hidden Lore," said the one with the book. "I specialise in early history and the origins of the Millenary War."

"And I specialise in the Far Past up to the time of the Great Collapse." The other one raised his hand as if taking an oath. "I am Asiel, Tenth Angel of the Scripts."

"We are here to instruct you. As you requested, apparently."

"Yes, please. I want to know everything."

"Hmmm." Gethel unfastened the clasps of his book and started leafing through the pages. "Early history goes back a thousand years, to the start of the third millennium."

He found the page he wanted, and held the book open within the light of his aura. Miriael looked and saw a map tinted in many colours, with fine delicate lettering.

"Is that the Earth?"

"The Earth as it was in a period known as the Twenty-first Century. The different colours represent different nations. In those days the Earth had many separate governments, separate cultures, even separate languages."

"India. China." The angel read out the names printed across the patches of colour. "Brazil. Canada. U.S.A."

"Yes. The U.S.A. is where they carried out the Venables-Hirsch experiment. That's where it all began: at the Harvard Institute for Medical Research. Near one of their cities called Boston."

Gethel indicated a point on the map, and Miriael read the lettering. "Yes, I see it. That's a city, is it?"

Gethel ignored the question. "You see, by the start of the Twenty-first Century, the inhabitants of Earth had reached a very advanced state of material technology. But they didn't know when to stop. They ventured into forbidden areas."

"Medical science," Asiel put in.

"Medical science." Gethel nodded. "Their doctors weren't content just to cure diseases. They wanted to cure death itself. They kept on developing increasingly clever techniques and machines—transplants, implants, all sorts of life support systems. The gap between life and death became so narrow that it was hardly possible to say where one ended and the other began. Until the terrible Venables-Hirsch experiment."

Gethel slammed his book shut with a dramatic gesture. "They managed to create a discriminated electro-magnetic field in the brain that could substitute for the brain's own electro-chemistry. EBSS—the Electronic Brain Stimulation System. And in the Venables-Hirsch experiment, they finally reanimated the brain of a corpse."

"A life after death?" Miriael was shocked and amazed.

"A life after death on Earth instead of in Heaven," said Gethel. "Do you see what it means? When the brain was reanimated, the soul belonging to that particular brain was summoned back to its original owner. It vanished out of Heaven and returned to the body of the patient in the laboratory. And when the doctors interrogated the patient, they discovered that Heaven really existed after all."

"Why? I mean, why did they have to be told?"

"They'd stopped believing in our existence. Many people on Earth considered Heaven a fairy-tale, not only the medical scientists. They didn't want to accept it at first. But when the experiment was repeated, other post-mortem patients kept giving the same descriptions of the place where they'd dwelt after death. It became a sensation—the greatest scientific discovery of all time, they called it. The news spread to every country and city on Earth, and the millions and billions of ordinary human beings were even more excited than the medical scientists themselves. They read all about it in their newspapers, they saw it on their televisions and computers and smartphones. The entire population followed the latest reports on the Orders of Angels, the Great Patriarchs, the seven Altitudes of Heaven—"

"But I don't understand," Miriael broke in. "Why didn't we stop them? Didn't we know what was happening?"

"Yes, we knew, but we weren't sure what to think about it. After so much scepticism and atheism at the start of the Twenty-first Century, suddenly everyone was a believer again. In some ways it seemed like a very good thing. What we didn't realise was that they believed in Heaven, but they still didn't *respect* it. They only respected themselves for being so clever in discovering it."

Gethel re-opened his leather-bound book and turned to the same map as before. "Soon it turned into a competition between the different nations. The U.S.A., China, Japan, Russia"—he pointed to coloured areas on the map—" they all wanted to inaugurate the second phase of celestial exploration. It wasn't enough to hear secondhand descriptions from EBSS patients. They wanted to examine Heaven with their own scientific instruments."

He leafed through to another page of his book. "Here it is. March 13th, 2033 A.D. The date the Americans landed their first psychonauts on the First Altitude. Just five years after the original Venables-Hirsch experiment."

"What's a psychonaut?" Miriael asked.

"A human being in an artificial angel-like state. The scientists developed a technology to convert the atoms of the body into a form of transcendental energy. Similar to spiritual energy in some ways, though not really the same.

The psychonauts gave up their mortal bodies, yet still kept all their mortal goals and memories and desires. They were launched into the spiritual dimension by telekinesis, using bearings and information that the EBSS patients had revealed. It was the start of the Trespass upon Heaven."

"The Trespass upon Heaven." Miriael repeated the phrase in an awed whisper.

"That's our name for it. They named it Project Olympus. They landed on the Fields of Irin in the Province of Boriah, then marched along the Val Jehenna past the Tabernacle and the Seat of the Just, towards the New Jerusalem. Whatever they found they fed into their scientific analysing instruments. They took samples from our holy places, they broke into our shrines. Nothing was sacred to them. And everywhere they went, they planted flags and made speeches about Peace and Liberty."

"Peace!" exclaimed Asiel ironically. "They were starting a war but they called it peace!"

"They beamed images of their progress back to Earth for live broadcasting. The entire human population watched and thought it was wonderful. Of course, we knew something had to be done, but we wanted to do it without violence. When the psychonauts landed on the First Altitude, our angels simply withdrew to higher altitudes. We were in a state of confusion, debating and conferring for days on end. Meanwhile, more and more psychonauts were coming up by telekinesis. By the time they marched to Mount Horeb, there were forty of them trespassing on our dimension. Forty!"

For a moment Gethel couldn't go on. Then he heaved a heavy sigh and resumed.

"The Devastation at Mount Horeb! In those days, Mount Horeb was a resting-place for Blessed Souls. But the psychonauts were determined to capture some souls to feed into their instruments for analysis, and it turned into a massacre. A hundred and twenty souls annihilated forever."

"The barbarians!" cried Miriael. "We should've annihilated *them!*"

"Yes," said Gethel. "We did eventually. But then the days of mercy and gentleness were gone forever. Nothing could bring back the old way of thinking. And nothing could bring back those hundred and twenty souls we'd lost."

"The Devastation at Mount Horeb," murmured Asiel, shaking his head.

Looking into their faces, Miriael was surprised to see that they were both quietly weeping.

15

She waited in silence, moved by their grief. They said nothing for so long that she began to wonder if they'd abandoned their task of instruction. In the end, she broke the silence herself.

"May I ask a question?"

Gethel composed his features and cleared his throat. "You may."

"You spoke about a very advanced state of material technology on the Earth. In what ways 'advanced'?"

"Is it important?"

"I'm curious. Billions of people and cities, you said. Did they have tall white buildings made of metal, glass and stone?"

Gethel nodded. "Many of them would've been white, I expect."

"And moto-cars and electrics and shop-shops?"

"We believe they had shops and transport vehicles called motorcars. I'm not sure what you mean by electrics, but their computers and tele-visions worked by electricity."

"Where did you hear those terms?" Asiel asked.

"Oh, Residual myths," said Miriael vaguely.

Gethel frowned. "Myths are only myths, not history. As for Residuals, they didn't exist in those days."

"So who inhabited the Earth? Not the Humen."

"No, the Humen came later. The ordinary people were just ordinary people. Human beings rather than Humen. Very different."

"Because they had souls? They *did*, didn't they?"

"They did. Unluckily for them. Do you want me to continue the history?"

"Please."

"Very well. Where was I?"

It was Asiel who supplied the prompt. "The annihilation of the psychonauts."

"Ah, yes, the Battle of the Plenoma. Hardly a battle at all by later standards. They had no defence against our powers. An army under the Archangel Michael obliterated the psychonauts with a single coordinated blast of light."

"And then the punishment," said Asiel, still prompting.

"Indeed. Although it didn't begin as a punishment, simply a practical necessity. We couldn't tell how many brains might have been kept in laboratories ready for reanimation by EBSS. We only knew that any new soul from the time of the Venables-Hirsch experiment was a potential spy in Heaven. So we expelled them all. Countless innocent souls had to pay for what the scientists had done over the previous five years. It was the only way to make sure there was no further spying."

"How did that punish the scientists?" asked Miriael.

"Not directly. But it proved to be a punishment for the whole human race. When we expelled those souls, we forced them to return to their original bodies—and most of their bodies were in a state of decay. Rotting corpses rose out of their coffins, caskets and graves. And because those souls were trapped in their original bodies, it was impossible for them to die properly. They couldn't be shot or killed in any ordinary way. That was the start of the Age of the Undead."

Miriael had another question, but Gethel forestalled her with a raised hand.

"The Undead turned murderous and insane. They were filled with black hatred and a desire for revenge because they'd lost their place in Heaven. They became monsters, roaming the streets, battering down doors, slaying at random. For fifty years, human civilisation lapsed into chaos. Cities were deserted, law and order disintegrated. Every nation tried to drive the murderers across into other territories, spreading their depredations all over the Earth."

He paused for a moment, and Miriael seized the opportunity to ask her question. "We still don't allow souls back up into Heaven, do we?"

"No. The Blessed Souls in Heaven are all from before the start of the war."

159

"So where do they go? They don't go back into their own corpses."

"Of course not. That was only the ones we *forced* back. Nowadays they detach from their bodies and become Morphs."

"Morphs." Miriael knitted her brows. "I've heard of Morphs."

Asiel joined in. "Morphs haunt the Earth. They float around for a while after the death of their bodies, then congregate and settle down in lonely spots. There are hundreds and thousands of them living where no one can see them."

"They hide away?"

"They're invisible to the eyes of terrestrial beings. But we can still see them with our angelic sight."

Miriael fell silent. Her question was Zonda's question, and she now had her answer. Gethel resumed his instruction.

"No new souls are allowed up into Heaven nowadays, but it was a hotly argued issue at the time. It almost caused fighting in Heaven, and led to the withdrawal of the Supreme Trinity."

"What withdrawal?" Miriael didn't understand.

"Ah, you don't know the background to the current system in Heaven, I suppose. Things weren't always as they are now. When the war began, the Supreme Trinity ruled unchallenged. The challenges arose during the Age of the Undead—in the first place, over the issue of the Fallen Angels. You know they were once exiled in Gehenna? Also called Hell?"

"I knew they were once exiled, yes."

"It was when the inhabitants of Earth were suffering their punishment, and the Supreme Trinity deemed that the punishment of Fallen Angels had lasted long enough. But the four great archangels weren't so forgiving, and they had the support of most angels among the other Orders."

"Everyone who'd learned the new way of thinking," Asiel put in. "Less gentle, less merciful."

Gethel went on. "In the end, a compromise was reached. All of the Gregori were allowed to return, the Watchers who'd fallen in love with terrestrial men and women. And those of Lucifer's rebel angels who were judged to have been followers rather than leaders. But not the Satan himself, nor any of his chief lieutenants."

Miriael was still trying to adjust to the idea that there were two types of Fallen Angel. No one had ever told her that before.

"However, the divisions remained and came to a head soon after the end of the Age of the Undead. The Supreme Trinity wanted to allow all souls back up into Heaven again—and this time there was no compromise. Michael, Gabriel, Raphael and Uriel refused outright, and the Angelic Orders united behind them. It would have been a terrible conflict, except that the Supreme Trinity chose to withdraw onto the Seventh Altitude."

"So the Seventh Altitude…it wasn't always closed off?"

"That's right. It was the seat of Godhead and the Eternal Thrones, but it wasn't closed off. No curtaining clouds."

"And the War Council that runs Heaven now—"

"Is actually the Provisional War Council." Gethel nodded. "But it's been running things for so long that most angels forget about the 'Provisional'."

And I was never told in the first place, thought Miriael. Her head was spinning with so many revelations. She'd wanted to learn about early times and the Far Past for a specific reason, but she'd never guessed the extent of her ignorance.

"And with the reorganisation of Heaven, we come to *my* period of expertise," said Asiel. His globe bobbed a little closer to Miriael, while Gethel's retreated by the same distance. "From the withdrawal of the Supreme Trinity through to the Great Collapse."

16

"The Age of the Undead ended with the rise of the United Earth Movement," Asiel began. "Governments of all nations realised that only international cooperation could solve the crisis. And when the scientists also pooled resources, they came up with a way to kill the Undead so that they stayed dead."

"How?" asked Miriael.

But Ariel shook his head and looked stern. "Please don't interrupt. This is complicated history. You'll understand it better without interruptions, and I'll be able to tell it better too."

Miriael resigned herself to listening in silence. Clearly, Asiel was less tolerant than his colleague.

"So the old national governments dissolved themselves. No more Americans or Russians or British or Chinese. The First United Earth Congress took over and sued for peace with Heaven. They seemed to have learned their lesson, and we thought they were repentant. But we were the ones who hadn't learned our lesson. Even without the Supreme Trinity, even with the Provisional War Council in power, we were still too trusting. The rulers on Earth had changed their name, but they hadn't changed their nature.

"So we entered into negotiations with the United Earth Congress and prepared to draw up conditions for peace. We allowed them to send their ambassadors to Heaven, using their telekinesis and psychonaut technology. We even let them set up their technology in Heaven so that they could return their ambassadors more easily to Earth. Such fools we were! We allowed their scientists up onto the First Altitude to build and operate the technology—those scientists who were our deepest, most abiding enemies. They hated our very existence.

"Exactly how it was done, we still don't know, but it was the scientists who did it. We envisage it as a hook secretly attached to the underside of Heaven, some kind of connection grappling our world to theirs. Like a transcendental cable between the different dimensions! In the meanwhile, their ambassadors must have been told to spin out the negotiations. There were more and more problems over the peace treaty, debating tinier and tinier issues. Five years it went on. And all those years, they were secretly dragging us into their own dimension, hauling Heaven slowly down into terrestrial space and time."

"The deceit!" Gethel couldn't hold back. "The treachery!"

Asiel's voice was a little unsteady as he went on. "We didn't notice until it was too late. They dragged Heaven so low that the underside of the First Altitude was almost grazing the tops of their highest mountains. So low that people on Earth could look up and see the silver clouds and radiant walls of the Celestial Realm right above them in the sky. Of course, they were ecstatic. All the masses of ordinary people wanted to enjoy the bliss of Heaven—and thought they could experience it the easy way, without having to die.

"The politicians of the United Earth Congress encouraged the popular folly. They broadcast announcements as though it was something that government and scientists had done for the happiness of humanity. They had brought Paradise to Earth, according to their boasts. So countless aeroplanes carried passengers up to the First Altitude. By the time we realised how we'd been tricked, there were thousands of terrestrial beings already swarming around in our fair fields and gardens. Great crowds of them enjoying themselves and taking holiday photos! Even up to the Second Altitude!"

"Horrible!" breathed Gethel. "Obscene!"

"Then the catastrophe occurred," said Asiel. "So many physical bodies were more than the fabric of Heaven could support. Resulting in—"

Miriael had already guessed. "The Great Collapse!"

This time Asiel allowed the interruption. "Yes, the Great Collapse. Whole portions of Heaven gave way under the intruders' gravitational weight. We lost whole provinces out of the First and Second Altitudes. Vast radiant blocks of ether broke off and fell down to the Earth below. The most terrible disaster in all of history."

"And a disaster for human beings too," Gethel put in.

"Yes. When the blocks of ether crashed onto the surface of the Earth, they released tremendous amounts of incandescent light and heat. Raging fires devastated the Earth, especially in Europe and Asia where the largest blocks of ether came down. The fires on those continents were so intense they've never been put out."

"The Burning Continents," Miriael murmured to herself.

"The population died in their millions upon millions. Naturally all those who'd climbed into Heaven were killed by the fall back to Earth. Then the inhabitants of Europe and Asia were incinerated in the fires. The famines that followed wiped out millions more on other continents. The whole Earth became one vast charnel house."

Asiel stopped and fell silent, but it didn't sound like a conclusion. Miriael waited for him to go on. When he didn't, she prompted him. "What happened next?"

"That's the limit of my expertise," Asiel replied. "The Far Past up to the time of the Great Collapse."

Gethel frowned. "Isn't that what you wanted to know? Early history and the Far Past?"

"Yes, but… What came after the Great Collapse? There must've been more before the start of the Weather Wars. That's where I was taught history from."

"The Weather Wars were three hundred years later," said Gethel. He sounded stiff and haughty, as though the importance of his own area of expertise was under challenge.

Asiel was equally dismissive. "What we know of the period in between is mere common knowledge."

"But I don't even know that!" cried Miriael. "When did the Humen come in? You haven't mentioned them yet."

"They didn't exist in the Far Past," said Asiel. "They emerged only after the Great Collapse."

"Emerged how? From where?"

"Who knows?" Asiel shrugged. "Hypers and Plasmatics are new types of beings. Quasi-immortals. Maybe the Doctors descended somehow from the old medical scientists."

"What about Residuals?"

"Tribes like this?" Asiel surveyed the Store with a look of distaste. "We don't concern ourselves with Residuals."

"They probably emerged around the same time as the Humen," added Gethel.

"Maybe they descend from—"

Asiel cut her off. "You're only speculating. And we'd be speculating too. Our factual knowledge is in the areas of our expertise. So if that's all…"

"We hope we've done you some good," said Gethel. "It was our task to set your mind at rest about the questions we'd been told you were asking."

"We're sorry if our answers don't live up to your wishes," added Asiel.

The tone was unmistakably peevish now. Miriael realised she'd offended them and tried to make amends.

"You've been very, very helpful. I really appreciate it. When I asked about the Far Past, I was thinking of all the—"

"Good." Asiel's tone remained unchanged. "Our task is finished, then."

Two minutes later, their globes of light were dwindling dots in the night sky, and Miriael was left alone in the darkness of the Store. But her mind was definitely *not* at rest. She'd had the glimmer of an idea before, and now it was coming clearer and clearer. An idea about the history of Residuals…

17

Ferren's mechanical monster travelled for hours and days along the overbridge, carrying him with it. Closed up in metal walls, he lived with a din of engines, wheels, shafts and drivebelts all around him. But at least the din was constant, and eventually sank to the back of his consciousness. He even managed to sleep—or a half-sleeping sort of drowse.

He'd expected to escape when the Humen army halted at sunset, but instead it kept moving all through the night. It stopped only for short breaks at random intervals, never longer than half an hour. He climbed down briefly then, but when he looked out, the Hyper foot-soldiers who'd been marching alongside were still there on both sides of the monster. They sat talking in small groups as though they had no need of ordinary sleep.

He couldn't escape, but he could lie on his back hidden by the wheels and drink syrup from the leaking tank. In fact, he discovered how to loosen the plastic hose and increase the flow from the leak. Naturally he tightened the hose again afterwards.

Still, the leak must have registered somewhere. On the second day when the army stopped for a break, he climbed down to take a drink—then paused at the sound of approaching voices and footsteps. Voices and footsteps weren't unusual, but the footsteps came right up to the side of the monster and the voices were talking about a "leak" and a "fuel tank". He realised that a pair of Hypers were about to duck down between the wheels.

What saved him was a momentary delay while they sorted out tools. He didn't have time to make for his hiding place above the wheel-arch, he just launched upwards through the nearest space between shafts and drivebelts. He was in luck: his hand closed on a rung that turned out to be the bottom rung of a ladder.

He hoisted himself up rung by rung as the first Hyper slithered in under the belly of the monster. The second Hyper went down on one knee at the side, ready to offer advice and carrying the spare tools. Ferren moved more quietly, but he kept climbing.

The air grew very warm, and smelled rank and sweaty. Compared to his hiding place, he was more in the middle of the monster here, right up inside the engines. At present the engines were quietly idling with a murmurous pulsing sound: in-out, in-out, in-out.

There was something oddly wet and squishy about the sound, but so far as he could see, the engines were all cold, hard metal. His eyes took in a baffling intricacy of rods, gears, cylinders, springs and ratchets. Here and there were small movements as a cogged wheel ticked over or a valve opened or closed. The metal was shiny with grease and gleamed in the darkness.

"Found it!" a harsh voice called out below. "Leakin' right here!"

Ferren realised with a start that the first Hyper had now rolled over onto his back and was gazing upwards. But he was gazing up at the join between the hose and tank, not in the direction of the engines. Still, Ferren squeezed further out of sight, pressing himself flat against the ladder and a box-like shape to the side. The pulsing sound came louder to his ears, and the metal felt hot against his cheek.

"Yeah, I can fix it." The Hyper under the tank responded to a question from the Hyper crouching outside. "Chuck me the tape and one of them small clips."

For five long minutes, Ferren stayed frozen in position while the repair went on below. A plastic hose hung close by his hip, a hose very similar to the hose that joined onto the tank. When he traced the line of it down through several branchings, yes, it did start with the hose from the tank; when he traced it back up, it led to the box-like shape he was leaning against.

So what was in the box-like shape that needed syrupy liquid? It made no sense at all.

His muscles were aching by the time the leak was fixed.

"Okay, that'll do it." The Hyper below addressed his colleague. "It's a bodgy job, but it'll hold up for now."

Except I'll undo it again, thought Ferren grimly.

The first Hyper rolled over onto his front, collected his tape and tools, and crawled towards the side of the monster.

"It better hold up," said the second Hyper. "We gotta keep our Plasmatics fed. There'll be big trouble if the engines stop working."

Plasmatics?

18

Ferren was more puzzled than ever. He remembered that the angel had named Plasmatics as one type of Humen along with Hypers and Doctors. He'd now seen the Doctors and plenty of Hypers—but, so far, not a single Plasmatic. On the other hand, he *had* seen a great many machines... Perhaps he'd had the wrong idea about Plasmatics.

He resolved to find out. The box-like shape next to him was about two feet high by two feet wide, with rounded edges and an inspection panel at the front. As well as the plastic hose at the side, metal pipes connected to it at the top, and more pipes at the bottom. But it was the inspection panel that interested him.

Four wing nuts held the panel in place. One by one, he gripped them between thumb and forefinger, and turned. Three came undone after a struggle, but the fourth refused to budge. In desperation, he brought his face up against the panel, opened his mouth and clamped onto the wing nut with his teeth. The harsh metallic contact made him wince, but the smallest start of a turn would be enough. He twisted his head—and success! The nut yielded.

He finished the job with thumb and forefinger, then yanked the panel open. What was inside made him gasp. The pipes went through from top to bottom, and on each pipe was a valve. Controlling the valves were glistening straps of living muscle, strung between the pipes and the walls of the box. He could tell they were living by the way they dilated and shrank in tiny regular movements as he watched.

So these were Plasmatics! This was the grisly secret! Organic tissue locked inside a mechanism! Warm living muscle attached to cold hard metal!

Were all Humen machines the same? He looked around for more examples, and saw a gleaming cylinder over his head. He climbed a few more rungs of the ladder, and yes, the cylinder had an inspection panel too.

In fact, the cylinder was one of four parallel cylinders. All had plastic hoses feeding in at the back and piston rods emerging at the bottom. The piston rods connected to cranks, flywheels and further rods. He attacked the nuts that fastened the panel, and this time undid them all with his fingers.

He was prepared for a shock when the panel swung open, but he wasn't prepared for the shock he received. Suddenly he found himself face to face with a mass of fatty flesh packed tight inside the cylinder. Purple veins ran through it, and it was suffused with a redness of blood. When it bulged out suddenly, he jerked away before it could slop all over him.

But although it bulged, it stayed inside the cylinder. His mind clicked into gear as his shock and revulsion passed. If the plastic hoses piped syrup into these cylinders, then the fatty flesh must be thriving on the same nourishment that *he* consumed. Was that a coincidence or what?

He stared at the blood-suffused flesh, and a dreadful image flashed into his mind. The Residuals in the bath! When the Hypers jumped down after the jelly had been drawn off, when they began butchering the bodies…and they'd tossed gobbets of flesh to their colleagues… who had caught and dropped different lumps of tissue and organs into different numbered pails…

No sooner had the connection come to him than he knew it was true. The butchery wasn't random hacking, but carried out for a purpose. The Hypers had been extracting body parts to use in their machines!

His gorge rose, and he swung the inspection panel shut in a hurry. In the next moment, there was a shouted order from somewhere outside— and the engines burst into action all around.

Ussh-gaah! Ussh-gaah! Ussh-gaah! Ussh-gaah!
Ussh-gaah! Ussh-gaah! Ussh-gaah! Ussh-gaah!

More than ever, it sounded to him now like trapped human voices struggling to speak. Valves rose and fell, flywheels rotated, piston-rods moved back and forth—but so far the shafts and drivebelts hadn't been engaged.

He half-slid down the ladder and dropped to the ground, then climbed back up above the wheel-arch. Just in time! Following another shouted order outside, the shafts and drivebelts all began spinning and whizzing around at tremendous speed.

Curled up in his hiding place again, he wished he could forget what he'd seen. But every sound from the engines brought pictures into his mind: Residual flesh expanding and contracting in the cylinders, Residual muscles twanging and tightening as they worked the valves…

19

It was Bethor and Adonael who next descended to the Store, the other two of the original four Seraphim. Miriael had been eagerly awaiting a visit from Heaven so that she could try out her new idea of Residual history.

She held her tongue while the two Seraphs examined her. Finally they announced that she *had* improved, but not as much as they'd hoped.

"Keep meditating on your true condition," Bethor advised. "All the time. It's becoming urgent."

Miriael wondered about the urgency, but didn't want to admit how little meditating she'd done lately. "I'll try my very best," she promised. "Can I tell you something and see what you think?"

Neither Seraph showed any enthusiasm. "What?"

"It could be important. It's an idea from all the history I've been learning. You know how we live in an age with Humen but no humans?"

The Seraphim said nothing. They were obviously familiar with the facts.

"I believe the Residuals are descended from the original humans. They *are* human, but degraded from how they were in the past."

"It's possible," Bethor agreed without surprise.

"But hardly important," added Adonael. "A species in decline."

"Not a *natural* decline, though." Miriael came to the real of her new idea. "It's because of the Humen and their Selectors. Does anyone in Heaven know how the selecting works?"

"Selectors?" Adonael raised an eyebrow.

"Ah, you *don't* know! The Residual tribes think they're allies with the Humen, and contribute someone every year for military service."

"Military service?" Adonael's lip curled scornfully. "I don't think so."

"No, that's only what they call it. But the important thing is how the Selectors select the ones for military service. Always the smartest and cleverest. Anyone who can think a bit for themselves."

"So?"

"Don't you see? They're reducing the intelligence of the tribes. How long ago was the Great Collapse? Nearly a thousand years?"

"Nearly."

"So what happens if you cull intelligence and initiative over hundreds and hundreds of years? Residuals *have* to evolve backwards. They probably don't even *want* intelligence or initiative if it means getting taken away by Selectors."

Bethor nodded. "Yes, that would explain a decline, if what you say is true. Unfortunate for them, but hardly relevant to us."

The Seraphim were still unimpressed. Miriael intensified her appeal.

"It *is* relevant. I can see sparks of intelligence and initiative in them even now. Here in this tribe! It hasn't been bred out of them yet. We should form an alliance with them."

"What!?" Bethor and Adonael exclaimed together in surprise.

Miriael hadn't intended to introduce the suggestion so suddenly. "I mean, we should win them over to our side. I'm sure they could help us in small ways. They don't like the Humen, they're only afraid of them. I believe—"

"And *I* believe you've been living too close to Residuals for too long," Bethor said coldly. "Eating their food is what made you like this in the first place. No wonder your improvement is so slow when you keep thinking about them."

"The original humans were no friends of ours either," said Adonael. "If modern Residuals descend from them, they descend from the fools who caused the Great Collapse."

"Yes, I know about that," Miriael agreed. "They *were* fools. But not evil or vicious, not like the Humen."

"Enough!" Bethor raised his voice. "Focus on yourself and your own spiritual recovery!"

"But will you report my idea back in Heaven? You could tell the War Council or someone—"

"We shall not."

"I wouldn't need to think about Residuals if I knew the War Council was thinking about them."

It was a kind of threat—and the Seraphim understood it as such.

"We shall report your attitude." Bethor glared at her. "That's what we shall be reporting."

"And there will be consequences," added Adonael.

I was only trying to help, thought Miriael, as they soared off into the sky.

20

The consequences came later the same night. Miriael trembled in awe as a mighty angel descended towards her. At first he seemed like a moving star, then growing larger and larger like a great vessel of light. Finally he entered the Store in a rush of snowy whiteness.

It was Uriel, commander of the South, lord of thunder and lightning, wielder of the Sword of Judgement. Along with Michael, Gabriel and Raphael, he was one of the four highest archangels. Miriael, who had never seen him close up before, shielded her eyes against his dazzling aura.

He was tall and old with long flowing hair, and his aquiline face was etched as sharp as a granite crag. His sixfold wings spread out within his globe, and his very presence was charged with power. Every time he moved he gave off crackles of light.

"You are Miriael the Fourteenth Angel of Observance?"

"I am," she replied, heart racing. She must be in very grave trouble to receive such a visit as this.

"I have heard disturbing reports about you. It appears you are not fully committed to recovering your true condition as an angel."

Miriael unshielded her eyes and gazed at his sandalled feet, blinking. "I want to. I was just thinking about the Residuals at the same time."

"A distraction."

"But such an opportunity for us. I mean, no one from Heaven has ever made contact with Residuals before, have they? I'm the first. And I know things about them that could aid us against the Humen. I'm serving our cause too."

"It is *not* for you to choose how to serve. You serve by recovering your true condition. That is all."

"But—"

"*Desist!* You have only one duty to Heaven, and nothing else matters. Time is running out."

"Bethor and Adonael said it was urgent."

"You may as well know. An immense Humen army is on its way here at this very moment. They seek to capture you and extract information. That must not happen."

"Oh. Umm. What will you do if I'm still here by the time they arrive?"

"Heaven can not allow you to fall into enemy hands."

"Will you annihilate me?" Miriael looked into his radiance, then dropped her eyes again. "You ought to annihilate me."

"Just do your duty as Heaven requires."

"I've been trying. I can't seem to help myself. I want to return to Heaven more than anything in the world."

There was an odd silence. When Miriael looked up again, Uriel's silvery-white brows were creased in perplexity.

"Return to Heaven?" he said at last. "You expect to return to Heaven?"

Now Miriael was equally confused. "I thought… Isn't that what I'm trying to do?"

"You seem to be under a misapprehension. You are trying to recover your true condition as an angel."

"So that I can come back up to Heaven."

"No. So that you can become like any other angel on Earth without an aura."

Miriael gulped. "You mean…extinction?"

"Our spiritual essence cannot survive unprotected in the terrestrial atmosphere."

"You want me to *die?*"

"Earthly creatures die. Angels are extinguished."

Miriael didn't know how to protest. The Seraphim *must* have realised she expected to return to Heaven, and they'd never contradicted her. But she couldn't remember anything they'd actually said.

"Choose it and strive for it," Uriel went on. "Will you do that?"

"I don't know," Miriael answered in a very small voice.

He raised a hand, and crackling light played around his fingers. "I can allow you one more day before the Humen army arrives. You have until tomorrow nightfall. Then I return. Decide your fate."

Miriael looked down at the ground as his globe lifted off with a great roaring *WHOOSH!* The turbulence of his wake was like a tremendous rushing wind.

21

All morning, the Residual tribe had been moaning and groaning and praying to their totems. The dismal sounds echoed Miriael's own wretched mood. Then Zonda appeared.

She stood just inside the curtain, rubbing her nose and looking miserable. "I think he's going to die," she announced.

Miriael understood that she was talking about her father. "No, don't give up," she said.

"*He's* given up. He doesn't care about living anymore. How is that possible? How can anyone not care about living?"

How indeed, thought Miriael, applying the words to herself. For Uriel and all the proper angels in Heaven, she ought to embrace extinction after falling to Earth. But she couldn't. Something in her was desperate to live, no matter what duty might command.

Zonda came closer and squatted in front of her. "What did you say happens when someone dies? The body dies but the soul lives on?"

Miriael shook off her own troubles for a moment. "Ah, I can tell you more about that. I've found out where human souls go nowadays after death."

"Not up to Heaven, you said."

"No. They become Morphs and drift around in the air until they attach themselves to things. They like to congregate together in quiet places where nobody comes."

"What do they look like?"

"They're invisible to humans."

"What about you? Can you see them?"

"I suppose so. They're visible to angels." Miriael wasn't sure about the capacities of an angel not in her true spiritual condition.

Zonda remained silent for a while. Moans and groans from the Residuals in the Dwelling Place came louder, then softer, then louder again.

Miriael pointed to the curtain. "Are they upset about your father?"

Zonda shrugged. "We'll be left leaderless if he dies. There's no older male suitable to take his place." She paused. "*And* they're upset about your visitors coming down in the night. They're scared of strange lights through the blanket."

"Hmm. And they're praying to their totems for protection?"

"Yes." Zonda rose to her feet again. "Now I'd better go back and see to my father. You're all right for food? Still not eating?"

"No-o. Not yet, anyway."

Zonda went off through the curtain, and Miriael caught a glimpse of hunched, woebegone figures sitting around outside.

They're fearful now, but they'd be a hundred times more fearful if they knew there's a great Humen army approaching, she thought. *Praying to their totems won't help them then.*

22

Immediately after nightfall, Uriel descended once more into the Store. His radiance was so intense that Miriael had to cover her face with both hands. Peeking out between her fingers, she saw that he now carried the terrible Sword of Judgement.

For me, she thought, and quailed inwardly. But she couldn't back down.

"Miriael the Fourteenth Angel of Observance." He addressed her formally. "I have returned for your decision. Will you or will you not fulfill your duty to Heaven?"

Miriael could hardly manage to speak, but she gestured towards one of her water bowls. Uriel's brows descended in a stern frown.

"What? What is this?"

"Dried peas and beans soaking in the water. I'm going to eat them when they're soft."

"Eat Residual food!" His voice was an ominous whisper, far worse than an angry roar.

"I've already drunk some water."

"*Perditus es!*" he murmured. "*O crimen maiestatis!*"

"I...I can't recover my spiritual essence. I think I've become a sort of hybrid."

"Weakness of will. No self-control."

She shook her head. "I've seen too much on the Earth. I've had experiences I can't undo. This is me now. I choose it."

"Then *this* is what you choose!" Uriel raised the Sword of Judgement high in the air.

The blade burned like a thousand suns as he poured his spiritual power into it. Miriael couldn't look, not even between her fingers. When the blade came down, it would shoot forth a bolt of energy to annihilate her. She bowed her head in helpless submission.

"I pronounce you recreant! Renegade! Apostate! *Proditor!*" His voice rose to a thunderous roar. "Do you have anything to say for yourself?

Any shred of justification? *Do you?*"

She was sure that her last moment had come. "No. I am what I am."

"Without justification there can be no forgiveness. The War Council of Heaven endorses my judgement."

Only a provisional War Council in place of the Supreme Trinity, Miriael thought to herself. *There might have been more forgiveness otherwise...*

She could almost feel the blast of energy that would consume her utterly. Yet still nothing happened.

"Finish me, then," she said aloud. "Get it over with."

"We follow our ethical principles in Heaven. Absolute unbreakable ethical principles."

"So do it!" she cried in fear and frustration.

"One of our principles is that we only destroy the guilty. Never the innocent. Have you forgotten your ethical teachings too?"

Miriael didn't understand. Why did he have to draw out the torture? And *still* he kept talking.

"Believe me, I have good practical reasons for destroying you. I would do it if I could. But that one ethical principle prevents me."

Doubtfully, Miriael looked up. The Sword of Judgement still hovered above her.

"Aren't you going to do it?"

"We may not be as merciful as we might wish, but there are certain things we will never do. We are not like the Humen, you know."

"You don't destroy the innocent," she murmured.

"I can't persuade myself that you are guilty." He shook his head, and his eyes were troubled. "I have seen many strange things, but this is the strangest of all. I don't understand the change in you, but you're not responsible for the way you are."

"Am I forgiven?"

"No, not forgiven. Never. But I can't judge you."

Slowly he lowered the sword. Miriael breathed a sigh of relief.

"Thank you," she said.

But Uriel wasn't interested in her thanks. "Do you realise what this means? We shall have to defend you. We shall have to confront the Humen army with all our forces."

"I'm sorry."

He wasn't interested in her contrition either. "Our war in the Southern Hemisphere will move into a new phase of violent confrontation. Many angels will be extinguished."

"What about the Residuals?"

"What about them? We don't wage war on Residuals, but we don't protect them. If their territory becomes a battleground…"

"I was thinking about *this* tribe of Residuals."

"Yes, there will be a great battle in this area here."

"Because of me. Because of this." She shook her ankle, shaking the chain. "I could go somewhere else if you freed me."

"No, that would only postpone the inevitable. And since you seem to have an affinity with this tribe, you may share your fate with them too."

It's true, I'm really not forgiven, thought Miriael. *And nor are the Residuals.*

Uriel's globe pulsed radiance as he prepared to depart.

"You are on your own," he told her. "Whether or not you survive, we don't want you up in Heaven in any form. This will be our last contact with you."

Then, with a *WHOOSH!* and a rush of wind, he was gone.

23

The Humen army had come to a stop in the middle of the night. Ferren sensed at once that it was a different kind of stop. Instead of flopping down and relaxing for a brief break, the Hypers who had been marching alongside remained on their feet. When they talked, their voices sounded keyed-up with excitement. As for the Hypers on his mechanical monster, the scrape of boots on metal told him they were descending to the ground. Had the army reached its destination?

He descended to the ground himself, beneath the belly of the monster. Looking out right and left, he saw light and movement—more light and movement than on any previous nighttime stop. There was even less chance of slipping out and escaping over the side of the overbridge.

When he looked to the front and back, though, he noted a more promising difference. This time, the mechanical monsters ahead and behind had parked almost touching nose to tail. And if all the monsters were equally close…

He crawled to the rear of his own monster. The monster behind was less than an arm's length away, while the Hypers to the sides were mere glimpses in the gap. Easy! He scuttled across in the dark.

The next monster was lower to the ground, with metal plates filling the gaps between the ribs of its chassis. No doubt it had Plasmatics and a fuel tank higher up. But his aim right now was to continue crawling from monster to monster in search of a spot where there were fewer Hypers on the overbridge.

Five monsters later, he was beginning to think he'd made a bad plan. The monsters were still parked nose to tail, and he always managed to slip across in the dark. But the Hypers on either side seemed more numerous than ever.

He saw only their boots and their black rubbery costumes to the height of their calves. Gradually, though, he became aware of a contrast. Those on his right were all heading the same way he was heading, and moved as if shuffling along in a queue. Those on his left came from the opposite direction, and moved with a strut and swagger, almost skipping.

Crawling under the sixth monster, he decided he needed a vantage point from which to survey the whole Humen army. Then he could see whether there *were* any quieter spots for escaping. Was it possible to climb up high on one of the monsters? Although Hypers occupied both sides of the overbridge, the monsters themselves seemed unusually deserted. Perhaps all the drivers and riders had come down to join the queue?

He arrived at the next narrow gap and looked for signs of life or movement on the monster ahead and the monster behind. No, nobody around. He rose to his feet in the gap and began climbing.

He hauled himself rapidly up over the massive bars and wire shield that protected the front end of the seventh monster. Then came a metal surface, smooth in itself but well furnished with projections, turrets and attached items of equipment. It was simple climbing. The light seemed brighter to the right of the monster, so he stayed more to the left.

Nobody called out, nobody caught sight of him. He kept going until he was high above the overbridge and hidden from view by the sides of

‑

the monster. When he peered over to the left, he gazed down on the Hypers' heads below.

Although there were no signs of life inside the monster, he took care not to pass in front of any window-slots. He climbed to the topmost turret, which was surmounted by an antenna, then scanned the wider scene all around.

The landscape was flat and grassy, the same in every direction. It reminded him of the Plain, with scattered pale patches that could have been ruins. He turned his attention to the Humen army—and his heart sank.

The line of monsters stretched endlessly along the overbridge both ahead and behind. Everywhere he looked he saw lights and Hypers... nowhere a quiet spot where he might make his escape...

There were ramps too, sloping down from the overbridge to the ground below. The nearest ramp was only fifty yards away, and a large illuminated sign announced its number: **D223**. He remembered how all the ramps he'd seen on his journey to the Humen camp had been similarly numbered. In fact...

In fact, when he thought back, wasn't **D223** the actual number of the very first ramp he'd seen? Right at the very start of his journey? The more he considered, the more he was sure of it.

In which case, he must be very close to the Home Ground! Right back in the same place where he'd started!

What could it mean? Why would the Humen army have travelled to this particular district of all districts? And if this *was* their destination, what was their purpose?

He was still puzzling over it when he became aware of sounds from the other side of the monster. He hadn't consciously registered them before, but he registered them now—and knew them for what they were as well.

"Ooooooohhh!" A multitude of throats sucked in breath.

He waited, and a minute later heard the long shuddering exhalation: "Aaaaaaaahhh!"

So that's why the Hypers were all in a queue! They were getting their doses!

24

When Ferren made his way around to the other side of the turret, he discovered that the brighter illumination to the right of the monsters came from a set of three arc-lights. They had been rigged up next to the monster in front and shone down on the activity taking place below.

It was the same activity he'd observed in the Humen camp. But then he'd been squinting up from ground level; whereas now he had a much clearer view from above. A Doctor in a wheelchair directed operations, and this time there were two attendants in white rubber suits, two stretchers on either side of the wheelchair. As Ferren watched, a pair of Hypers who'd just sprung up from the stretchers strode away, while a new pair came forward to take their place.

He was too far away to hear what was said, although he remembered the previous Doctor speaking about "doses" and "psycholitres". As the new Hypers lay down on the stretchers, the attendants stood over them cradling the same long-barrelled instruments. When they reached towards the Hypers' foreheads, Ferren could see exactly what they were doing. Each forehead was fitted with a black plug, which they unscrewed to expose a small round hole.

"Ooooooooohhh!"

The attendants inserted the nozzles of their instruments into the holes and began to count. The Hypers on the stretchers stiffened as something was pumped into them. Ferren shuddered and turned his gaze away.

But he looked again when the nozzles were withdrawn—just in time to glimpse an eerie light shining from the two foreheads. Whatever had been pumped in glittered with an unstable shimmering brightness. Then the attendants closed the holes with the plugs and stepped back.

"Aaaaaaaahhh!"

The two Hypers jumped down from their stretchers and flexed their limbs. When they moved away, they were almost dancing.

The brightness had reminded Ferren of something—he was afraid to think what. A fearful premonition hovered on the margins of his mind.

He focused on the long-barrelled instruments under the attendants' arms and saw thin tubes attached at the back, the same as he'd seen before. The tubes ran across the ground to the monster in front of the monster he was on. But the monster in front was of a different kind, more like a transport vehicle, with some huge covered shape on a flat-topped trolley.

He studied the shape under its dark green canvas cover. It appeared more or less spherical—which *also* reminded him of something. But he couldn't pin down the memory until he noticed an opening where the cover wasn't properly fastened. The shape was a huge glass vessel like the ones in the chemical apparatus area of the Humen camp. And inside the glass was some kind of stuff that gave off elusive iridescent colours, full of glimpses that never quite turned into pictures...

He gaped in shock. It was the same jelly he'd seen in the bath in the pit! The shimmering liquid jelly that had been drawn off from Residuals after they'd been packed side by side with wires clipped on and cotton wool wads in their mouths!

And this was the stuff he'd just seen glittering inside the Hypers' foreheads! The stuff that was pumped into them! Their doses! Their psycholitres!

His head spun, his stomach churned, he clenched his fists and dug his fingernails into his palms.

All he wanted was to get away. He forgot about self-preservation, he felt nothing except horror and hatred. He half-slid and half-scrambled down from the turret, back over the sloping surface of the monster. He didn't care about avoiding window-slots, he didn't care about scraping his skin on sharp metal edges. Plunging past the wire shield and bars, he landed back on the overbridge.

Away! *Now!* He sprang to his feet in the gap between monsters. He was about to rush straight out without even looking. Another three paces, and he would have crashed right into a pair of Hypers going past outside. But he came to his senses just in time.

181

"What a blast!'"

"What a surge!'"

"What a buzz!'"

The Hypers' voices were harsh as Hypers' voices were always harsh, yet they also sounded oddly wet or lubricated. Ferren guessed these were the very two who'd received their doses a minute ago. He held himself motionless until they'd gone past.

Then he stuck out his head to observe them from behind. They walked with uncontrollable vitality, twitching and quivering at every step. One let out a rippling wet snarl from the back of his throat.

"Yaraaaghh! I'm burning it up!'"

"I'm living a million miles an hour!'"

"I got two and a half psycholitres in me!'"

"Doing so much experience!'"

"Doing so many memories!'"

Their silhouettes diminished into the darkness. Ferren couldn't wait until they were out of sight. He made a dash for the side of the overbridge, flung himself under the cordon of cables, twisted around and dived in among the struts and braces of the underframe.

Finally he understood the whole appalling truth about psycholitres.

25

Sitting with his head in his hands underneath the overbridge, Ferren couldn't stop the chaos of thoughts that whirled through his brain. He had shinned down the nearest pylon to the ground, fully intending to run off and leave the Humen far behind. But an urge for revenge had taken over from the urge to get away. He wanted to inflict the most terrible revenge on the whole Humen army—but he had no idea how to inflict it.

Then a sudden blare of sirens shook him out of his inertia. He raised his head and listened to an amplified voice booming out above.

"ATTENTION ALL PERSONNEL! COMMENCE DESCENT

TO THE PLAIN AND TAKE UP BATTLE FORMATION! WE EXPECT ENEMY FORCES TO CHALLENGE AS WE ADVANCE TO OUR DESTINATION! COMMENCE DESCENT! TAKE UP BATTLE FORMATION!"

He realised then that the darkness under the overbridge was no longer absolute. Not far away, ramp **D223** was lit up by a string of lights. Of course, the Humen army would have to make their descent by way of the ramps. At the bottom of ramp **D223**, a group of Hypers stood around chatting.

Forgetting for a moment about psycholitres and Hypers and the bath, his thoughts went back to the mystery of ramp **D223**. If it really was the ramp closest to the Home Ground, why would the Humen army be coming down here? What *was* their destination? Surely not the Home Ground itself!

Perhaps he could learn something from this group of Hypers. They had probably been responsible for stringing up the lights on the ramp; now they stood waiting for the first vehicles and troops to descend. He crept stealthily towards them, keeping always in the shadow of the pylons.

Their words carried to him clearly as he came up to the last pylon before the ramp. He ducked out of sight as one turned suddenly and pointed out over the darkened landscape.

"Somewhere over there, I reckon."

"Can't see nothing," said another.

"What's to see? You know the dumps Residuals live in. Just a few old ruins. Probably a bit over the horizon anyway."

They were talking about the very thing he wanted to hear! He followed the direction of the Hyper's pointing finger. "A bit over the horizon," he'd said. Could that be the direction of the Home Ground?

A different voice chimed in. "I heard Celestials attacked us when we sent a squad to collect her before."

"Who told you that?"

"You ain't heard the rumours? It was a squad from Combat Group 84, and they got just about wiped out."

"A squad? A single squad?"

"They weren't expecting an attack. We're going out with *everything* this time."

"Hope it's a big bash-up! We'll flatten 'em!"

"The Doctors expect a battle, but they're not after a big bash-up. Just so long as they can get their hands on this angel. Take her apart and see what makes her tick."

"A junior warrior angel, ain't she?"

"Yeah, but her rank don't matter. What matters is she's still alive on the Earth. We've never found a live one before."

"'Cos they shrivel up and vanish, right?"

"Somethin' like that. But this one's still in good nick, except she can't fly. She's chained up in some ruins with a bunch of Residuals."

"We'll get her this time."

"You betcha."

Ferren felt as though a bomb had gone off inside his head. It *had* to be his angel! The angel Miriael! She hadn't gone back up to Heaven after all! He'd got everything wrong!

A fierce joy coursed through him. He didn't understand about her being chained up in the Home Ground, but if she was still on the Earth he'd be able to see her again. All of a sudden, he discovered how very much he wanted to see her again.

Instinctively, his hand moved to touch the rolled-over top of the cloth around his waist, where the two white feathers nestled. Whatever they were meant to mean, they *weren't* tokens of farewell!

But he had to warn her that the Humen army was coming for her. All thoughts of revenge could wait. He had to reach her before the Humen did.

Even as he decided, a great rumbling clanking noise came from the top of the ramp. The group at the bottom cheered and raised their fists with middle fingers extended. The first mechanical monster was starting to descend.

Ferren backed away in the shadow of the pylons, then crouched down low and ran for the open grass. He tried to follow the direction the Hyper had pointed.

PART FOUR

THE BUNKER

1

Miriael had been eating in the night. After Uriel's departure, she hadn't waited long before scooping up softened peas and beans, then popping them in her mouth. They tasted delicious!

It was what her body had been telling her to do all along. Whatever was proper for a proper angel, this was *natural* for the kind of angel she had become. She didn't feel the least bit guilty. At last she was truly living in her own body.

"Beautiful," she murmured. The peas and beans were beautiful, eating was beautiful, and *she* was beautiful. She cupped her face in her hands and felt the shape of her cheeks and cheekbones; she shook her head and felt the soft silken fall of her hair across her shoulders; she ran her fingers along one arm and felt the sleek smoothness of her skin. This was something different to moral beauty—and it was all *her*. Unfamiliar sensations came alive in her mind.

Could she stand upright? Of course she could! She slid herself up against the wall of the Store, pushed away and stood balancing on both legs. No spiritual will, just muscles and tendons! She gloried in her newfound physical strength.

She ate all the food she'd softened, then stretched out on her chain to other stacked bags and baskets. Opening a bag here or the cover of a basket there, she inhaled smells that were wonderfully rich and appetising. She started off with dried fruit, then moved on to try every kind of food within reach.

The more she ate, the stronger she felt. An energy surged through her such as she'd never known before. She swung her arms and flexed her wings; she wanted to grip hard with her hands and kick out with her legs.

I could do incredible things, she thought. *I could if I wasn't chained to the wall.*

She waited for the first faint light of dawn, then took another look at her chain. As she'd expected, the chain and padlock were of indestructible metal, which no physical strength could have broken. The bolt in the wall was of the same metal, but the brick in which the bolt had been anchored was relatively old and crumbly. Definitely the weakest point.

She tugged the chain this way and that, struggling to work the bolt loose. She felt strong and full of energy—but she wasn't strong enough. Perhaps the bolt moved a fraction, but it refused to come free. By the time dawn spread across the sky, she was ready to give up.

Suddenly there was a great wailing cry from another part of the Dwelling Place.

"WAAAIIIIIIIIIIII!"

It could only be Zonda. She had been caring for her father in his counting-corner, struggling to keep him alive. From the sound of the cry, she had just lost the struggle.

"WAAA-AAA-AAAHHHHHH!"

Longer and longer the wail drew out, until it became an ululation. The rest of the tribe made echoing sounds, still muffled under the thickness of their blanket. No doubt they too understood the cause of Zonda's grief.

Then Zonda's ululation ceased all at once, turned off like a tap. While the People continued their wails and moans, only a strange silence came from Neath's counting-corner. Miriael wondered and waited.

She didn't have to wait long. A few minutes later, the curtain drew back, and Zonda burst into the Store.

"Help me," she blurted, her face all wet and blubbered with tears. "Please, you have to help me."

2

"Your father?" Miriael prompted gently. "He's gone?"

Zonda snuffled and wiped her nose with the back of her hand.

"He died in his sleep. But he's not gone."

"Not gone?"

"His—whatever you call it—his soul. It's still there."

"So he's a Morph."

"Yes, but he's scared. I can hear him."

"You can talk to him?"

"Not talking. He just sounds lost."

"He's probably not used to being a Morph. He'll soon float off when he adjusts."

"I don't think he *wants* to float off. And he's been dead for hours. His body was stone cold when I woke up. What do I have to do?"

Miriael shrugged helplessly. "I don't know."

"But you're supposed to know!" Zonda was on edge, her voice quavering. "Maybe you could talk to him. I can't even see him."

"I could try. I would, except for this." Miriael shook her chain.

"Oh." For the first time, Zonda seemed to register that the angel was standing on her own two feet.

"I could try to talk to him and explain what's happened," Miriael went on. "But I can't help from here."

Zonda frowned at Miriael's chain, and appeared to be considering the possibilities.

"How strong are you?" Miriael asked.

"I couldn't break that chain."

"No, but there's the bolt in the wall." Miriael pointed. "It's not so secure in the brick. I don't have the strength, but you might be able to pull it out."

"Though at least you're strong enough to stand," Zonda commented, before turning her attention to the bolt in the wall.

She took hold of the chain very close to the bolthead and tugged it this way and that, as Miriael had done. Then she inspected to see if she'd loosened it.

"Hnuh!" She wasn't pleased with the result so far.

She took a different grip on the chain, braced one foot against the wall and attempted to yank the bolt straight out. For a while she heaved and strained, and Miriael stood behind her and pulled on the chain too. But the bolt stayed fixed.

"Stupid thing!" Zonda broke off. "Stupid, stupid, stupid, *stupid!*"

She dropped the chain and backed off three paces. Then, with all her pent-up fury and frustration, she threw herself forward and shoulder-charged the wall. There was a loud crack—and the brickwork disintegrated and toppled to the ground. Zonda crashed down with it, and Miriael lost her balance as the chain pulled her over.

When the angel sat up a moment later, her eyes went wide with amazement. Instead of solid wall, a gaping hole had opened up on one side of the Store. Now there was only a rubble of bricks and a view out over the Swimming Pool.

On the other side of the curtain, cries of fear and alarm came from the People in the Dwelling Place. Zonda picked herself up as the dust settled, grimacing and rubbing her shoulder.

"You did it!" Miriael told her with a grin.

In fact, Zonda had done more than knock the wall over. When Miriael drew the chain towards her, she discovered that the only weight was the weight of the bolt itself. The brick in which it had been fixed had broken apart in the fall.

"I'm free!" Miriael held up the end of the chain so that the bolt dropped out. "Look!"

Zonda was still grimacing and rubbing her shoulder.

"Good," she said. "Now come and talk to my father's Morph."

3

Neath's body lay to one side of the counting-corner. Zonda had drawn down his eyelids and folded his arms over his chest. Miriael couldn't help looking, but the girl called her attention elsewhere.

"That's where his sounds were coming from," she said, and pointed to the angle between the walls of the corner.

Miriael turned. One end of her chain was still padlocked to her ankle, but she now carried the other end over her arm.

"Where?" She stared in vain. She hoped she'd retained an angel's power to see Morphs, but it was only a hope. She saw the rough brick of the walls and rows of counting-marks scratched on the brick—but nothing that might have been a disembodied soul.

She was aware of Zonda watching her expectantly, but could only shake her head. Then Zonda raised a hand.

"Wait! Listen!"

They stood very still. A tiny plaintive cheep sounded behind their backs.

Zonda whirled around. "He's moved!"

Miriael turned and caught a glimpse of something against the curtain over the entrance. But it was gone before she could focus on it.

"Can you see him? Can you?" Zonda demanded.

"I did, but he blew away." Miriael felt more confident now. "Try to avoid sudden movements. I think it frightens him off."

"All right. Let's shush again."

They stood straining their ears. After a while, a plaintive fluting sounded from somewhere near the floor.

Miriael signalled to Zonda—*Be quiet, be careful*—and rotated to face the source of the sound.

He was there between a collection of items left lying on the floor: a small blanket, a pillow, a drinking bowl. As Miriael's vision came clearer, she saw him as a pattern of faint lines attached to the corner of the pillow, the lip of the bowl and several projecting folds of the blanket. One point of his pattern was actually attached to the foot of his own corpse. The Morph was frail and delicate as a snowflake.

Miriael knelt and leaned forward, wondering how to communicate. There were no words in the fluting, but the cadence rose and fell in a kind of singsong.

"I can see you," she said softly. "You're the Morph of Neath, who used to be the father of Zonda. Now you've become pure soul. You don't need your body anymore."

He responded with a sad, wavering, uncertain sound. Did he understand? The Blessed Souls in Heaven communicated through language, so he surely had the *capacity* to understand.

"It's all very new, isn't it?" she went on. "New and confusing and a bit frightening? I know I'd be frightened. You're like a baby just come into the world. But don't worry, you'll soon get used to it."

She made her voice calm and soothing, but the Morph wasn't soothed. The lines of his pattern trembled as if shivering.

"You can let go now," she encouraged him. "No need to cling to old familiar things. Trust me, your old body isn't you anymore."

She reached towards the foot of his corpse—and the Morph reacted as though she meant to part him from it by force. There was an explosion of furious chittering. She heard the blind terror in it, and drew back at once.

Zonda crouched to whisper in her ear. "Don't hurt him."

"I won't, I promise. He's afraid of losing control. He doesn't know what's happened, so he feels unsafe and insecure."

"He always liked to feel safe," Zonda agreed.

"But he'll do so much better floating free. He'll find out when he tries."

Gradually the chittering faded and changed to another sound. Now the Morph seemed to be fluting a kind of lament. Miriael suspected there were words in it, but muddled together and all at once. Still, she thought she recognised one repeated sound as "lone" or "alone".

She leaned forward again. "You're lonely, aren't you? But you're not the only Morph, you know. There are many more like you. You only have to find them."

Was there a kind of question in the fluting now?

"You can find them by letting go and floating free. Let the wind carry you. You'll drift to one of the places where the other Morphs gather. You want to be with them, don't you? The sooner you start looking, the sooner you'll find them."

The response came in a high piping voice, and this time Miriael was sure she heard a repeating word in it.

"Can't, can't, can't!

Can't, can't, can't!"

He was full of panic and despair, but there was also an element of self-pity. Miriael wondered how to persuade him.

"You can, you can, I know you can," she told him.

Almost unconsciously, she echoed the singsong cadence of his own piping voice…and the cadence seemed to communicate better than language alone. Seeing his agitation decrease, she crooned the same phrase like a lullaby.

"You can, you can, I know you can
You can, you can, I know you can."

The effect was magical. His piping quietened to a soft chirrup that echoed the lilt of her lullaby back to her. A kind of acceptance? She tried putting new words to the tunes she'd once sung in the choirs of Heaven.

"All's right, all's well, as it should be
You're now a Morph, you're floating free
All Morphs are like you, every one
They all start off as you have done."

Calmer and calmer... It was working! She changed tunes and sang about being brave and adventurous, then about finding new companions and a better place to stay. When she was sure he was responding to her influence, she reached out to the foot of the corpse and moved it little by little away.

"You can fly like a bird
Give yourself to the wind
You don't need this body
Your new life begins."

For one moment, the Morph parted from the dead foot, hovering unattached. Then panic returned, and he clung on to the nearest solid object—which was Miriael's finger. She felt his touch like the touch of a snowflake, a tiny pinprick of cold.

She held her finger very still while continuing to sing. She sang about having taken the first step and how easy it was and not being afraid. Then she reached out with her other hand and edged the pillow further away.

This time he didn't panic, but stayed with one point of his pattern floating free. Miriael crooned praise of his success. Very carefully, she went on to dislodge him from the drinking bowl and the folds of the blanket. In the end, his only remaining attachment was to her fingertip.

Then she rose and stood upright, holding her finger steadily before her. The Morph rose with her, poised in mid-air.

"Make ready, you're ready
You feel the wind blow
Your moment has come
And you're eager to go."

She breathed out gently, and her breath fluttered his snowflake-form. But it was no longer the agitation of fear. He parted from his last attachment and floated upwards. He was infinitely light and insubstantial.

"Let the wind take you and carry you high
Blessings upon you, goodbye, goodbye."

Slowly he passed above the walls of the counting-corner and wafted away out of sight.

"Has he gone?" Zonda asked.

Tears hung on her eyelashes, but not the same tears as before. Now there was a relief that showed through her sadness, while a tremulous smile came and went on her mouth.

"Yes, he's gone to find a home with others of his kind." Miriael smiled back at her.

"Will he be happy now?"

"Happier," Miriael answered. She didn't believe he could be truly happy until he was allowed into his true Heavenly home. But although she wouldn't tell a lie, she didn't have to make a point of telling the *whole* truth.

"How did you know what to say to him?"

Miriael couldn't answer; she was still surprised at herself. She had been sure of exactly what to say, yet she had no idea where the assurance had come from.

Zonda pointed to the loose end of chain that the angel held over her arm. "You can go anywhere now," she said. "I'll stay with my father a while, but you should go."

Miriael nodded. A new life was beginning for her too...a life with, not without, her own body.

4

Ferren had been running non-stop. He had hoped that the Home Ground would appear suddenly out of the dark if he kept running in the right direction. But the Plain by night looked everywhere the same. Although he'd come across two creeks, one seemed too big for the People's Creek, the other too small.

When dawn crept into the sky, he could see clumps of ruins in the grass, but none that he recognised. Was he too far to the left? Or too far to the right? Or perhaps he'd overshot entirely? He changed course several times, but feared he was only running further off track.

The sun was lighting up the whole Plain when he looked back and saw the ruins he sought in the distance. He *had* overshot the Home Ground, and by a long way. At once he turned and headed towards it.

A moving brightness drew his attention as he approached, a spot of gold against the green of the grass. Not far from the ruins, it seemed to flash and fly out, almost as if dancing. Nothing he knew was that kind of gold—except her hair! It had to be her hair!

He had no time for wonder. He gulped in air and accelerated to a sprint. Soon he could see the whiteness of her wings and the yellow of her robes. She *was* dancing, or at least spinning around with outspread arms. Her movements seemed vague and unbalanced, yet graceful even in their awkwardness.

Absorbed in her dancing, she didn't notice him. He was thirty paces away when she lost her balance and fell over completely. Her laugh was a pure, joyous sound. A moment later, he burst through the grass in front of her.

Her eyes went wide with surprise, her expression changed to a different sort of joy. "Ferren!"

He was panting so hard, he could barely manage one word at a time. "Came...to...save...you!"

Her face and form were even more beautiful than he remembered. In one hand she carried a chain, the other end of which was fastened around her ankle. A million questions whirled in his head, but he couldn't focus on any of them.

"I'm already saved," she answered with a smile. "As you see."

"Thought...you...went...back to Heaven," he brought out.

"No, I was captured by the Selectors. Where did—"

"You were here...the whole time?"

"Heaven doesn't want me." She shrugged. "Where did you go?"

"The Humen camp."

"*Really?* Inside the camp?"

"I saw horrible things. And then—"

"What things?"

"And then more on the way back. I came with their army."

"Their army?" She stiffened in sudden alarm. "Where is it?"

"On the overbridge." He jerked a thumb in the direction.

"No! So close!" She struggled to her feet. "I never guessed they were so close!" She stood head and shoulders above him.

"They were coming down a ramp when I escaped. Probably in battle formation now."

"Already! This is the worst news! There'll be a great battle with the forces of Heaven—"

"I heard that too."

"—and your tribe will be in the middle of it. We have to warn them."

"I thought we—"

"What?"

"Why do *you* care?"

"Don't you?"

"Yes, but—"

"Of course you do. You *have* to. Your tribe, your home. They'll be wiped out if they don't get away quick."

Ferren was confused. This wasn't what he'd expected. He hadn't come back to save anyone except the angel, he'd never thought of returning home. After they'd beaten him unconscious and tied him up and planned to hand him to the Selectors...

Yet the angel was right. Of course he had to try and save them. Of course. But would they take a warning?

"I don't think—" he began, then stopped.

Already the angel had turned away, already she was heading towards the Home Ground. He set off after her.

5

The Dwelling Place looked as it had always looked, but the People seemed lost in a new kind of apathy. Although it was now an hour after sunrise, they remained cowering under their nighttime blanket. They didn't want to come out to face the day.

Ferren and Miriael surveyed the scene from the Back Door. "We'll never get them to do anything," he whispered. "You see what they're like."

Miriael remained determined. "I'll talk to Zonda. She'll wake them up."

She went off to Neath's counting-corner and vanished behind the curtain. Ferren waited, not understanding the situation. Several familiar faces peeped out from under the blanket: Shuff, Jollis, Urlish, Meggen... They didn't seem hostile, but they weren't interested in him either. They gazed at him blank-eyed for a moment, then disappeared once more under the blanket.

He spoke to Meggen before she could disappear. "Where's Neath? We have urgent news for him."

Meggen only groaned. "He's dead. No leader now."

Other moans and groans echoed her from under the blanket. "No leader." ... "We don't know what to do." ... "No one to tell us any-more."

"*We'll* tell you what to do," said Ferren. But he wasn't optimistic.

Then Miriael and Zonda emerged from the counting-corner. Zonda looked puffy around the eyes, as though she'd been crying. Still, she clapped her hands and yelled at the top of her voice.

"Everybody up! Get up now!"

When they didn't immediately throw back the blanket, she began pulling it off them. They murmured and protested as they found them-selves uncovered.

Miriael crossed back to Ferren. "You speak to them first," she said. "You can persuade them as one of their kind. They won't believe a Celestial."

"Persuade them to run off across the Plain?" He grimaced. "They'll never leave the Home Ground. They're terrified of the open Plain."

"Mmm, yes, they are, aren't they? Maybe there's an alternative." She compressed her lips and thought for a moment.

Ferren waited to hear her alternative, but she only snapped her fingers. "Start without me. I have to check on something."

She spun away and headed for the other curtained corner of the Dwelling Place. The Store? Why the Store? Ferren understood less and less. For a second time the angel vanished.

Meanwhile, Zonda had chivvied the People into sitting up and paying attention. She prodded, pushed and even kicked them until they were ready to listen. They still didn't *want* to listen—but Ferren was aware that every face had now turned towards him.

He cleared his throat just as Miriael reappeared through the curtain of the Store. She caught his eye and nodded to him to begin. Whatever she'd been checking, she seemed satisfied with the result.

"You all know me," he began. "I never expected to be back, but I'm here with a warning. A great Humen army is coming this way. Right now, this morning! Hundreds of mechanical monsters, thousands and thousands of soldiers—I've seen them. The Home Ground is in terrible danger."

The People responded with whimpering sounds. Some closed their eyes, a few wrapped their arms over their heads.

"Nothing we can do."

"Stay low, stay quiet, stay out of sight."

"No, listen." Ferren spread his hands in appeal. "I haven't finished. The forces of Heaven are going to fight the Humen. We'll be right in the middle of it."

"The Humen will protect us," said Shuff. "They're our allies."

"Allies!" The word filled Ferren's mouth with bile. "They're not our allies."

"They are. Neath always told us—"

"He didn't know what I know."

"What?" asked Zonda.

"They're parasites who live off us. I was in the Humen camp—I saw it all. You want to know what happens when they take us away for military service? They separate out our muscles and organs and use them to power their machines. Our body parts for their Plasmatics! It's a fact! And that's not the worst..."

He sucked in breath as the image of Residuals packed side by side in the bath flashed before his mind. "The worst is what they do with our minds. They have a science to extract all our memories and thoughts and feelings—all of it, like a sort of jelly. They suck it out and store it in huge glass jars and then inject it into their Hypers. The ones like Selectors—

that's what they live off. *Our* experiences!"

The People understood enough to be horrified. "Why us?" "Why us?"

"We die so that their machines and Hypers can live! Everyone who was ever taken for military service got used for body parts and memories! Yes! Your granddaughter, Shuff!" He swung an arm and pointed. "Your brother, Tunks! Your mother, Moya! And my sister—they did it to my sister!" A red mist rose before his eyes. "How can you not want revenge? They deserve to die! We ought to fight them and kill them and...and..."

He was beside himself, unable to continue. He wanted to inspire the People with his own rage and spur them into action. But there was no answering rage from them.

6

You're going off-track, thought Miriael. *You're doing it the wrong way.*
Positioned in front of the Store, behind the People, she had been as shocked as anyone by Ferren's revelation. It made sense and explained many things about Hypers and Plasmatics, which she would need to think through later. She could never have imagined such evil, even from the Humen.

But the effect of Ferren's revelation on the People was the *wrong* effect. Instead of turning against the Humen, they were becoming more helpless and beaten down than ever. They rocked themselves back and forth in a state of mute despair. It was all too much for them. As for actually fighting the Humen...of course, such an idea was completely beyond them.

Why did you have to bring it up? she thought. Irrational anger had blinded him—anger over the memory of his sister. What mattered at present wasn't fighting the Humen but simply avoiding annihilation.

And she had something to propose that wasn't beyond the People. Better than fleeing over the open Plain—they wouldn't even have to leave their Home Ground. She had hoped to explain after Ferren had won them over, but now she would need to do the winning over too.

"Can I speak?" she called out. "I have a suggestion."

The People swivelled to look at her. Immediately they began

muttering among themselves.

"It's that Celestial."

"She was chained up in the Store."

"How did she get free?"

Zonda raised her voice. "She's free 'cos I freed her. We ought to listen to her."

The People continued to mutter.

"Don't want to hear."

"Our allies wouldn't like it."

"She'll make trouble for us."

"Shut up and listen to her!" cried Zonda.

Miriael began. "You're already in trouble, you just don't understand how much. What he said about the battle"—she gestured towards Ferren—"is all true. Tremendous destructive energies will be released. The whole landscape around here will be flattened. And you with it. I know *because* I'm a Celestial."

The People moaned and put their hands over their ears.

"You don't need to fight the Humen," Miriael insisted. "You don't need to be on anyone's side except your own. You can protect yourselves right here in the Home Ground. I can show you how to build defences to keep out the energies."

Old Shuff shook his head and started to chant.

> "O we are little, weak and small
> We do not matter much at all
> O grant that we may not offend…"

"No! Don't think like that!" Miriael tried to drown him out. "You have the perfect place for building a bunker! See! There!"

She stepped back and pulled aside the curtain over the Store. The People gasped as they saw the hole in the wall brought down by Zonda's shoulder-charge. But Miriael was pointing to something further beyond, now visible through the hole.

"The Swimming Pool!" cried Ferren. "You mean the Swimming Pool?"

"Yes, if that's what you call it. It just needs covering over and a few other things."

"We can't do that," Urlish objected.

"Why not?"

"Too much change. Too different."

"Keep to the Old Ways," said Dugg.

"We can't build new things," said Hodd.

Miriael couldn't believe them. "Why not? What about your Ancestors? Didn't they build great cities and towers of glass and stone?"

The People snuffled and whacked their foreheads with the flat of their hands.

"They were mighty, but we are small."

"We are humble and unworthy."

"All lost, all gone."

Miriael hadn't anticipated such an attitude. "Believe me, you're still the same original human beings. You have the same brains, you can have the same skills. You only need to start developing them. You can do it."

"*I* can," said Zonda.

"So can I," said Ferren.

But they were the only two. The rest of the tribe remained unconvinced. Though proud of their Ancestors, they had no pride in themselves. Miriael couldn't think how to motivate them, unless…

It was a desperate last chance, based on nothing more than guesswork. However, it was now the only chance.

She turned to Zonda. "Can you fetch your totems?"

Zonda's jaw dropped. "Our totems?"

"Bring them here. Quickly."

The People murmured with shock and disapproval as Zonda went off to the Sanctuary to fetch the totems.

7

The four totems stood lined up in a row: the fly spray can, the plastic cigarette lighter, the alarm clock and the Baby Jane Ma-ma doll in her basket. Zonda made everyone sit in a half-circle facing them.

The People still disapproved of what was happening. "Only Neath ever touched the totems," old Urlish objected.

"No, I did too," Zonda shot back. "I helped him clean and polish them."

"Hnnh!" Urlish sniffed and pointed to the angel. "He'd never have let *her* touch them."

Miriael had been crouched over the totems, inspecting for clues. She wished she'd tested her guesses when she'd examined them before; now she had to be right first time. She straightened and stepped back.

"And I won't touch them," she said. "Zonda will do it. She'll do it on your behalf."

"What do I do?" Zonda came forward for her starring role.

"I'm going to prove that your Ancestors' powers aren't lost." Miriael addressed the People, then turned to Zonda. "Pick up that one."

"Our Guardian Fly Spray?" Zonda picked up the can and held it gingerly in both hands.

"You see the button on top where it says PRESS?"

"I can't read writing."

"All right, the button on top. Put your finger on it. Raise the can high in the air."

"Like this?"

"Now press down with your finger."

Zonda pressed, but nothing happened.

"Harder."

And then the miracle! A *hisssss!* came forth from the nozzle of the can.

The People were overwhelmed with wonder. "Sssssssssss!" they repeated, in imitation of the sound. In the next moment, Zonda discovered something even more extraordinary.

"There's a smell!" she cried.

"Yes, the smell of the spray from the can," said Miriael. "Go and do it over the People."

Zonda marched across, held the can over the heads of the People and pressed the button again. Another *hisssss!* When the spray drifted down, it was like a mystic revelation.

"Oh, perfume!"

"The perfume of the Ancestors!"

"So sweet! So sweet!"

One by one they sat up, snuffing and inhaling with rapturous expressions. Zonda directed the can from side to side, as Neath had done in the
traditional ritual.

Then Miriael called her back and pointed to the plastic cigarette
lighter. "Now this one. I suspect it makes a flame."

Zonda replaced the fly spray can and took up the cigarette lighter.

"I think you have to squeeze there on the side." Miriael indicated the
spot.

Zonda was enjoying herself. She swung to face the People and held out
the lighter for them to see. "Our Light in the Darkness!" she proclaimed.

Then she squeezed. A jet of flame leapt up from the nozzle, almost
singeing her eyebrows.

"Yiieeee!" she cried in alarm.

"Ahhhhh!" cried the People in ecstasy. They stared as if hypnotised
at the long yellow flame. It was like a dream come true. The things
inherited from the Ancestors were working again! For them!

Zonda kept the lighter going until suddenly it grew too hot to hold.
Releasing the trigger, she juggled it smartly from hand to hand.

"The powers of the Ancestors!" Ferren yelled at the top of his voice.
"They're coming back to us!"

The People were beginning to believe it. They looked across to the
row of totems, eager for the next miracle.

This time it was the alarm clock. Zonda held it by the carrying
handle, as Neath had always done.

"Wait, let me see the back," said Miriael.

She re-inspected the tiny knobs and levers on the back, and decided
on the largest key, which had an arrow above it.

"Try turning that," she said, and demonstrated the direction for
turning.

Zonda did as instructed. She kept on turning and turning.

"Nothing happening," she said, then jumped in surprise. "Oh! It's
making a noise! It's doing a tick-tock! I'll show them!"

"No, wait." Miriael pointed to another key, not quite as large as the
first. "Try that one."

Zonda turned the smaller key. "Still only a tick-tock," she said after
a while. "Can I show them now?"

"Push some of the knobs and levers."

"Which way?"

"Any way."

Zonda shrugged, and pushed and pulled at random. Until suddenly—
RRRINNNGGGINNNGGGINNNGGGINNNGGG!!

The People cheered and clapped like excited children. Ewling and Moya jumped to their feet and started leaping about in the ritual dance. Zonda paraded around the Dwelling Place with the alarm clock still ring-ringing. Soon a line of dancers formed behind her, all whirling and jigging and singing to the sound.

"Rrrring rrring! Rrrring rrring!

"Rrrring rrring! Rrrring rrring!"

Then the alarm ran down, and the ringing died away. Zonda replaced the clock in the row of totems and lifted the Ma-ma doll from her basket.

"What about our Baby Jane?" she asked. "How does she work?"

Miriael could only shake her head. "I don't know. Does she have any controls anywhere? Or words printed on her?"

Zonda rolled up the doll's woollen baby clothes and searched for buttons, knobs, levers or printed words. But there was only smooth pink plastic. The People, who had remained on their feet, now came clustering around.

"There must be something to push or turn," said Ferren.

Zonda experimented with every part of the doll that would move. She raised and lowered her eyelids, twisted her arms and legs in circles, rotated her head. Nothing made any difference.

Meanwhile, the People had started up a chant:

"Baby Jane! O Baby Jane!

O Jane of Janes and Baby of babies!"

Miriael was at a loss. They were all awaiting a final proof, but she couldn't supply it.

"Let me have a look," said Ferren, reaching out.

"No. Don't touch. I'm the one—"

Backing away from him, Zonda trod down on the fly spray can. She skidded as the hard metal cylinder rolled under her foot, then lost her balance completely. But she clasped the doll protectively to her chest as she went over backwards. With a bruising thump she landed flat on her back.

"MAMAAA! MAMAAAAAAAA!!!"

There was absolute silence. Everyone stared at the Baby Jane in utter amazement. Then Zonda stood up, clasped the doll to her chest and fell down backwards again.

"MAMAAA! MAAAMAAAAAAAA!!!"

Ferren broke the silence with a great whoop of triumph. "We have the powers!"

The People whooped too. "We have the powers! We have the powers!"

"We are the People! Descended from the Ancestors!"

"We can do anything!"

Miriael raised her voice above the clamour. "Let's build this bunker. I'll tell you how to do it."

8

Ferren could hardly believe the change. The People were like a new race of beings. No more slumping or cowering or hanging their heads—now they were attentive and alert and eager to act. They sat in a circle and listened as Miriael told them what they would need to do.

She didn't minimise the danger. The energies released in Terra-Celestial warfare were truly terrifying. But nobody panicked. Quietly and thoughtfully, they listened to her descriptions of force-fields and spectral energy, electrostatic emissions and psychic radiation. And when she explained the construction of a bunker, they started calling out with suggestions of their own.

"We've got some long metal poles!"

"Can we use the blanket?"

"How about the wire of the Fence?"

One valuable suggestion came from Shuff, when Ferren told Miriael about the fermenting water at the bottom of the Swimming Pool.

"We can get rid of it," he said. "There's a hole to let the water run out. We blocked it up ages ago, but we can unblock it again."

"Excellent. Then we won't be standing in water." Miriael clapped her hands. "Can you do it?"

"Me and Urlish will."

The planning went on until every aspect of the construction was covered.

"How much time have we got?" asked Zonda.

"Not long." Miriael stood listening for a moment, and the People listened too. Far off in the distance were faint sounds like a low mutter of thunder. As they strained their ears, the sounds grew clearer: a rumble and grumble of machinery, a clang of metal on metal. But still nobody panicked.

"Those are their mechanical monsters," said Ferren. "Huge things on wheels."

"And they're starting their advance." Miriael nodded.

Another sound started up, which Ferren recognised as a siren. Further strange booms and whistles followed.

"No time at all!" he cried. "Let's get started!"

"Wait!" Miriael held up a hand. "We need a lookout. One person up high to give us a warning."

"I'll do it," Zonda volunteered at once. "I know a place. I'll watch from on top of Number Forty-two."

"Call when they're getting close." Miriael turned from Zonda to the People. "All right, everyone to their tasks!"

The People scrambled to their feet and dispersed. While Shuff and Urlish went off to drain the Swimming Pool, the others set about collecting the necessary building materials. The women carried loose sheets of corrugated iron from the Shed; the older children scavenged for loose bricks in every part of the Home Ground; the younger children gathered up the blanket, woven bags from the Store and every other scrap of cloth available.

Ferren went with the adult males to the Garage and the four rusted poles at the corners of the platform. Lumb, Tunks and Burge threw their combined weight against each pole in turn; once the poles had bent, the others heaved them this way and that to weaken the metal. Eventually they broke them all off at the base.

When the groups regathered around the Swimming Pool, the fermented water had emptied out, and only a sludge of sunflower petals remained. Under Miriael's supervision, half the tribe climbed down and erected a pier of bricks six feet high in the middle of the tiled floor. Then the four poles were laid across from the sides of the Pool to the pier. The poles were the beams for supporting the roof.

Next came the sheets of corrugated iron, then the blanket, bags and scraps of cloth spread out over top. But the real protection for the roof was a covering of earth. Men, women and children ran back and forth, transporting and depositing soil from the fields in double handfuls. Then someone had the idea of using bowls and baskets to transport soil in larger quantities. Soon the bunker looked from the outside like a low mound of the ground itself.

Now there was only one more defence to construct. Everyone hurried to the old wire Fence near the side of the Garage. They uprooted the wooden posts and marched back in procession bearing a full thirty yards of fencing. Hammering the posts into the ground, they surrounded their bunker with a circle of protection.

"Perfect!" cried the angel. "The metal wire conducts electrical forces away before they can reach us. All we need is a place to earth the wire." Her eyes lit on the Creek at the bottom of the Back Garden. "All right. We'll pull off one strand and run it down there to the water."

They had just begun loosening one strand when Zonda called out from her lookout post. "Hurry! They're coming close!"

"Quick now!" Miriael urged everyone on. "Last thing! Let's get it done!"

9

Zonda stood with her feet braced across a corner of the ruined walls of Number Forty-two. She felt horribly exposed, but she could see far and wide across the Plain.

At first, the advance of the Humen army had been visible only as a cloud of dust against the sky. Then a line of mechanical monsters had appeared above the horizon: ugly lumpish machines, painted either black or in camouflage colours. Zonda shivered. They were like a tidal wave surging towards her.

As they continued to approach, she saw that their lumpishness took different forms. Some were slab-sided like great boats, some bristled with masts and antennae, some sprouted white ceramic discs like shallow saucers. Then there were the ones carrying long cylindrical tubes and the ones carrying huge spherical shapes hidden under dark green canvas. Strangest of all was a mobile platform draped in red cloth and flying flags and banners.

Soon she could make out several white-coated figures on the platform, along with many black-costumed figures riding on the mechanical monsters. The black-costumed figures reminded her of Selectors in their rubbery suits…and she could see thousands more of them advancing to the rear of the monsters.

She hoped they weren't focused on her as she was focused on them. She called down a warning to the People and kept watching as the army came nearer and nearer. No more than two hundred yards away now…

Focused entirely upon the Humen threat, she hardly paid attention to a different kind of threat from above. Dense white clouds had materialised out of nowhere, rolling and boiling with an unnatural turbulence. But she wasn't aware of the faces until—

"ABI MALEDICTE!"

A thunderous voice spoke from the sky—followed by a mighty rushing sound—followed by a loud explosion out on the Plain.

Zonda swivelled, looked up and almost lost her balance. Giant faces were outlined upon the clouds. There were at least a dozen of them, and all had stern mouths, heavy brows and long white beards.

As Zonda stared, another mouth opened to utter a second curse: "TERROREM PRONUNCIO!"

For a moment, the words actually showed forth in visible letters of gold. Then the curse hurtled through the air to land with a second explosion. When Zonda lowered her gaze, she saw that it had struck in the middle of the Humen army.

"EXSECRETUR!"

"INTERDICTIO!"

"IGNE DIRUE!"

The battle had begun, and the bombardment flew thick and fast. Every explosion produced a burst of golden vapour; when the vapour cleared, Humen soldiers lay scattered like dead black ants. The curses had no impact on the mechanical monsters, but wrought havoc among those who rode upon them or marched behind.

Then orders rang out in a crackling amplified voice. The Humen army ceased to advance and began to form itself into a square. The mobile platform with flags and banners went into the middle, along with the vehicles carrying huge spherical shapes. Around the outside went the vehicles equipped with ceramic saucers.

Zonda cupped her hands around her mouth and shouted down to the People below. "They've stopped! The Humen army's stopped!"

The People had finished whatever it was they'd been doing. Now she saw them going into the bunker, where a single sheet of corrugated iron had been left open for an entrance.

The angel paused and looked up at her. "Time to shelter! Come down!"

"They're still two hundred yards away!"

"Not safe! Two hundred yards is nothing!"

"Another minute! Want to see what happens next!"

Glancing back over the Plain, Zonda saw that something *was* happening. As the Humen army reorganised into a square, the vehicles on the outside activated their ceramic saucers. The white discs now spun around at tremendous speed.

Zonda stared—and stared again. It wasn't her eyes: the Humen army was starting to blur. A kind of obscurity spread out from the spinning saucers like a haze in the air.

"Humen are doing something weird! Like a haze!" she shouted down. When she turned, she saw that the People had all disappeared into the bunker, and only Miriael and Ferren remained outside.

"It's a force-field!" cried Miriael. "You can't stay up there!"

"Come *down!* Come *inside!*" Ferren added his voice to the angel's—and both sounded frantic.

"Coming," Zonda replied. Already the haze extended over the entire Humen army—and a curse hurtling down bounced harmlessly off it.

She jumped straight down, landed on all fours, sprang to her feet and headed for the Swimming Pool. There were no more curses from the voices overhead; instead she heard a loud, dull hum rising steadily in pitch. She pictured the ceramic saucers spinning faster and faster.

Ferren stood outside the bunker, holding up the wire of the Fence for her to crawl under. Miriael was half in and half out of the entrance.

Then Zonda skidded to a halt. "I've just remembered! Did anyone—"

"Come *on!*"

But Zonda was thinking of the totems. The People didn't believe in touching them, so they would still be in the Dwelling Place. But she *couldn't* abandon them there! They meant more than ever now!

"Back in a second!" she cried, and raced off to the Dwelling Place.

She took a short cut, leaping over fallen rubble and in through the hole in the wall. The curtain over the counting-corner had been removed, the blanket in the main area had gone—but there stood the four totems, exactly as she'd left them. She swooped and gathered them up, then turned and raced back to the Pool.

It seemed no more than a minute since she'd jumped down from her lookout post, yet the haze had already spread across the Plain and was invading the Home Ground. The Rushfield was starting to go blurry—and the sunflowers of the Sunflower Field—

Ferren still stood holding up the wire of the Fence. Zonda scrambled underneath, then dived into the bunker through the entrance hole. She heard the *twang!* as Ferren released the wire behind her.

10

Jumping down beside Zonda, Ferren slid the sheet of corrugated iron over their heads and closed the entrance hole. It was dark and dim inside the bunker, with only small chinks and crannies of light at the sides. As his eyes adjusted, he saw that some of the People sat on the floor around the central pier, while others stood by the chinks and crannies, peering out. The atmosphere was tense, yet nobody cried or whimpered.

"What's a force-field, then?" Zonda asked him.

"I don't know. That haze." He looked around for Miriael. "She said the faces in the clouds were the Great Patriarchs, raining down curses from Heaven."

"I saw. And the force-field blocked them off."

Miriael stood nearby, peering out through a cranny. Because of her height, she had to stoop until she was almost kneeling.

"Let's go and ask her," he suggested.

They crossed to Miriael, but Zonda claimed her attention first. Ferren found a chink under the roof through which to look out, while he listened with one ear to the angel explaining force-fields. Outside, the haze had now enveloped their bunker, and great throbbing waves pulsed through the air. The entire world seemed to shudder under a tremendous wind—yet nothing got blown away.

"Force-fields?" Miriael clicked her tongue. "The Humen have invented machines for weaving them. They can generate psycho-affective forces to mimic hate, pain, jealousy—all the most intense emotional vibrations."

"They're feelings?" Zonda sounded puzzled. "Is that what you're saying?"

"*Like* feelings. Every emotion has its own special frequency, and the Humen create those frequencies artificially. They only use the most violent ones."

Then someone else called out a different question. "What's happening now?"

"Where?"

"The Sunflower Field. Look!"

Squinting sideways through his peephole, Ferren could see a part of the Sunflower Field. The great golden heads of the plants were turning black, shrivelling and falling to the ground.

"Is it the haze?"

"Yes," Miriael responded. "Psycho-affective forces are a kind of hotness without heat. They can vibrate things until they self-combust and burn."

Even as she spoke, a sheet of red-and-orange flame shot up behind the Sunflower Field. Everyone who was watching gasped.

"That's the Rushfield!"

"On fire!"

"The dry reeds!"

Ferren turned to Miriael with a question of his own. "Are we going to lose our vegetables and crops and everything?"

Miriael nodded, and her beautiful eyes were sad. "Probably. Everything that can be made to vibrate to the frequencies of the force-field."

Another voice called out from another side of the bunker. "What's this? Why all the birds?"

Ferren returned to his peephole, and Miriael to hers. He twisted his neck to look as far as possible upwards, but saw nothing at first. Then suddenly they came into view: a thousand thousand beating wings. The sky was alive with them, all white as the purest snow.

Miriael had seen them too. "Not birds," she said. "Those are the Blessed Souls from Heaven."

Lower and lower they came, fluttering and wheeling and spiralling downwards.

"What are they trying to do?" asked Ferren.

Miriael answered without turning her head. "They'll try to break through the force-field and attack the Plasmatics inside the machines."

The sound of the wings was a vast soft clamour. At the same time, the hum of the force-field rose to a whine. The waves in the air took on a baleful purple glare.

"They're weaving sheer homicidal mania," Miriael muttered. "I never heard of such intensity."

The leading flight of Blessed Souls fluttered down into the force-field. For a moment they seemed to twinkle in the haze. Then small tips of fire broke out along their wings, small glowing patches smouldered upon their breasts. They twisted and turned in desperate aerial manoeuvres. But in vain. One by one their bodies were engulfed in flames. They plummeted earthwards trailing smoke and sparks.

"They don't stand a chance!" Miriael was beside herself now. "Nothing can pass through those vibrations!"

But the fluttering white wings continued to descend, flight after flight. Every time the same thing happened. Every time the same tips of fire and patches of smouldering, the same twisting, turning manoeuvres, the same final trails of smoke and sparks.

"Stop it!" Miriael cried. "Call off the attack!"

Yet the sacrifice went on and on. Most Blessed Souls were incinerated as soon as they entered the force-field, a few penetrated deeper down. But none reached the machines of the Humen army.

While Miriael turned away with a sob, Ferren stayed watching in horrified fascination. He watched until every single one of the Blessed Souls had plummeted to the ground in flames.

Finally the sky was empty, except for a pall of smoke rising up from the Plain. Heaven's attack had failed. The whine of the force-field diminished once more to a hum .

Inside the bunker there was a stunned silence. Miriael was quietly weeping. Then sudden shouts broke the silence.

"Hey! Our Fence! Over here!"

"Our Fence has fallen down!"

11

Miriael hurried to look, with Ferren right behind her. It was Mell and Jossock who had called out from their peepholes. On their side of the Swimming Pool, a section of the Fence had collapsed. One post lay flat on the ground, while two others tilted at precarious angles.

"Our protective barrier," said Miriael grimly. "We have to have it."

"The post in the middle caught fire," Mell explained.

"But it could still be propped up," added Jossock. "It's stopped burning."

"If there was something to prop it up with," said Ferren.

Miriael turned to him. "It has to be done."

"What, go outside now?"

"The force-field's winding down. Listen."

Ferren listened. It was true, the hum of the weaving machines was diminishing all the time. "Okay. You want me to do it?"

"We'll do it together."

He glowed inwardly at the sound of that *together*.

They crossed to the entrance hole, and Ferren slid back the sheet of corrugated iron. When he stuck out his head, there was a smell of smoke and small flakes of soot drifting in the air. But the pulsing psycho-affective vibrations had gone. He climbed out, and Miriael followed.

"The force-field's done its job," she commented. "The Humen will be starting a new phase of the battle now."

Ferren surveyed the Plain. There was a clear view over the Humen army where the Rushfield and Sunflower Field had been burnt to the ground. Behind the vehicles with ceramic saucers, the vehicles carrying long cylindrical tubes had come into play. Slowly the tubes reared up at one end, higher and higher until they were pointing like guns at the sky.

"I think they've already started," he said.

"Boost-beams," said Miriael. "Let's fix the Fence first."

Ferren didn't need to re-examine the fallen section of fence to know the kind of prop required. It would need to come from somewhere in the Home Ground. Though he shivered at the thought of going out to beyond their protective barrier, he had an idea for something suitable.

"I know what to get," he said. He dropped to the ground and wriggled under the bottom strand of wire. The soil felt warm with a strange kind of heat.

"Wait!" Miriael called after him. "Let me come with—"

"Be back in a moment!" he called over his shoulder, and raced off to the Dwelling Place.

He headed straight for the rubble where the wall of the Store had been knocked over. He was hoping to find several bricks still joined together. He dug into the pile and struck lucky at once: half a dozen bricks in a single solid chunk.

It was a struggle to unearth the chunk, then pick it up and carry it. The bricks weighed a ton. He staggered back to the bunker, where Miriael had already taken up position beside the fallen section of fence.

"Just what we need!" she exclaimed.

When he lowered the chunk to the ground, he was breathless and shaking from physical exertion. But it wasn't only the exertion—he also buzzed with a kind of inner excitement. The force-field must have left a lingering influence...

But there was no time to think about it. Out on the Plain, the raised tubes on the Humen vehicles were now aiming beams of light up at the clouds.

"We need to prop the Fence from the inside," Miriael said

So Ferren lay on the ground and pushed the chunk of brickwork through with his feet. The angel wasn't strong, but she had strength enough to hold the post vertical while he leaned the weight of the bricks against it. When they both let go, the post and section of fence stayed upright.

"We did it!" cried Ferren.

"*You* did it!" laughed Miriael.

But their sense of triumph didn't last long. When they turned to observe the progress of the battle, a dozen beams of light now played over the boiling clouds.

"What are boost-beams?" Ferren asked. "What do they boost?"

His question was answered before Miriael could explain. Inside each beam, a single black-clad Hyper appeared. They began to ascend as if swimming upwards in the light.

12

"Why doesn't Heaven act?" Miriael muttered between clenched teeth. "Beat them back now! Don't we know what's happening?"

"What are the Humen trying to do?" asked Ferren.

"Break into the First Altitude. That's the underside of it there."

Ferren didn't really understand, though he could see that the clouds weren't like ordinary clouds. He continued to watch as the Hypers rose higher and higher inside the beams.

"Maybe we ought to get back in the bunker," he suggested. But Miriael wasn't listening.

From this distance, the Hypers looked as tiny as insects. Each ascended to the top of his beam, then attached himself to the underside of the First Altitude. Ferren couldn't tell exactly how they did it—and seemingly many of them didn't do it very well. When the beams retracted a moment later, nine lost their hold and fell down out of the sky.

Still three remained. Hanging upside down, they uncoiled and lowered something to the Humen far, far below. Ferren couldn't see what they were lowering—but no doubt some sort of cord. It must have been incredibly fine and strong to span the distance from Heaven to Earth.

Miriael groaned. "Stop them! It'll be ladders next!" She turned to Ferren. "How can I send a warning?"

He shook his head. "You can't. What ladders?"

She didn't answer, but he saw for himself a minute later. The cords must have reached the ground because suddenly the three Hypers were reeling them back up. The Humen army cheered. When the cords went up, they rose with rope ladders attached.

Miriael let out another groan. "It's only a matter of time! More and more Hypers will climb up and attack! If they can cut through the floor of the First Altitude, they'll infest everywhere! They'll defile everything!"

Ferren gestured towards the entrance of the bunker. "We ought to go back inside."

But he couldn't make the angel listen. She was in a state of despair and hardly seemed to care what happened to her. The three Hypers had already reeled the rope ladders halfway up to the clouds.

"Oh, the filth, the filth, the filth! I don't understand! Why aren't we—"

She broke off as a tremendous flourish of trumpets rang out. Then came a mighty rumble, and the clouds parted. Like a screen rolling away, the floor of the First Altitude opened up. Ferren gasped as he caught a glimpse of the green hills and flowery fields of Heaven. So remote and serene, such ethereal beauty...

He gasped again as a host of angels appeared in the opening. They wore breastplates of burnished gold and robes of yellow and red. In their hands they carried short swords and circular shields. Their auras shone around them as they descended through the gap in the clouds and stayed hovering in mid-air.

> *"Hosanna!*
> *Hosanna!*
> *Hosanna in Excelsis!"*

It wasn't only the visible angels who sang, but a vast invisible choir in the higher Altitudes of Heaven.

"Hosanna!" Miriael sang out in response and spread her wings. They

might have been purely ceremonial, but they were magnificent—much larger than Ferren had ever guessed.

He didn't see what happened to the three Hypers. Perhaps they panicked and lost their grip, perhaps they were dislodged by a movement of the clouds. When he looked again, the rope ladders had fallen and the Hypers were no longer there.

While the first host of angels stayed hovering, a new brightness showed through the opening in the sky. It was shaped like a great ball, so dazzling that Ferren had to shield his face and narrow his eyes. A smaller host of purple-robed angels guided it downward with the tips of their swords.

"It's the Fourth Celestial Sun!" cried Miriael. 'They've taken the Celestial Sun from the Fourth Altitude! It's pure electrostatic energy!"

There were shouts of alarm and cries of dismay from the army out of the Plain.

The angels in yellow-and-red robes had arranged themselves in concentric circles, tier upon tier. The ball passed through the middle, accompanied by the angels in purple robes. An even greater angel with sixfold wings followed them down, bearing a prodigious sword. Watching through slitted eyes, Ferren had a sense of overwhelming power and majesty.

"Uriel!" Miriael breathed. "Uriel with the Sword of Judgement! We must be using the Sun as a weapon!"

A tremendous reverberation of organ music filled the air. The angels lifted their voices and sang:

> *"Cordis nostra mundamus*
> *Et labiae nostrae*
> *Ut puris mentibus introire*
> *Mereamur as sancta sanctorum!"*

Ferren felt awe—and also terror. He could see that the Fourth Celestial Sun was going to drop at any minute.

"Let's go! *Please!*" Desperately, he pulled on Miriael's sleeve.

She came out of her trance and furled her wings. "All right. Let's go."

Together they ran to the entrance of the bunker.

13

The Fourth Celestial Sun hit the Earth with a stupendous ringing sound. Ferren dived into the bunker without looking back, but he had the impression that it had landed right on top of the Humen army, and that a pool of dazzling light had exploded across the Plain. He could hear Hypers cursing and screaming in agony.

He was ready to close over the entrance hole, but Miriael stopped him. She still stood full height with her head, wings and shoulders out above the ground.

"Wait a minute," she said.

Ferren paused, then rose to look out too. The Humen army was now in total disarray. The electrostatic energy of the Sun had fanned out horizontally in rivers of sizzling lightning. Everywhere it touched, it carved swathes of destruction, crisping and crumpling the Hypers, sluicing them away like dead black leaves.

Even untouched parts of the army were frenzied with fear. Small groups of Hypers rushed madly in all directions, seeking escape but not knowing where to run. The mechanical monsters seemed to have gone equally berserk, lumbering about at random, colliding and crushing foot-soldiers in their path.

"It's the Plasmatics out of control," said Miriael, half to Ferren and half to herself. "Flying sparks of energy must have penetrated inside the machines."

Ferren was already aware of flying sparks coming dangerously close to the bunker. Only the Fence protected them. Spark after spark struck the wire, flickered and flashed, then shot away in a ribbon of light. He flinched at the flashes, which seemed right in front of his face.

Miriael was triumphant. She laughed at Hypers and mechanical monsters even when they seemed to be charging straight towards the Home Ground.

"Watch!" she cried, as one slab-sided monster mowed down a group of three Hypers on the other side of the Creek. Massive wheels ran over their black-clad bodies and cracked them open with a dry splitting sound. Then a shimmering iridescent vapour burst forth from the cracks and erupted in an explosion of colours and images. It was like seeing a million dreams…someone else's dreams…

"Psychic reserves volatilising," said Miriael.

Ferren continued to watch after the explosion had dissipated. The Hypers' bodies lay wide open, but he saw no flesh or bones or any internal organs. There was nothing inside but a dry porous stuff like pumice or honeycomb—the same all the way through.

Meanwhile, the mechanical monsters were also breaking apart. As they blundered this way and that, their engines came loose from their mounts, their wheels detached, their chassis separated from their superstructures. Cylinders, gears, pumps and pistons hopped and flapped on the ground, individually driven by their own flailing bits of muscle.

Watching it all through the Fence, Ferren had to keep blinking and closing his eyes. The flashes on the wires were almost constant now, as more and more sparks of energy flew their way.

Still, he stared wide-eyed when one very distinctive vehicle emerged from the chaos. It was a platform on wheels with a surrounding guardrail, draped in red cloth, trailing fallen flags and banners…

"The Doctors!" he cried. "The Humen Doctors!"

Hauled by a demented engine, the platform careered from side to side as it surged towards them. The Doctors still sat in their chairs, but their chairs bumped and slid about behind the guardrail.

"So that's what Doctors look like," Miriael murmured.

Then the engine veered away and passed out of sight behind the ruins of Number Forty-two. A minute later it was back on the *other* side of the Home Ground, having made a complete circuit. By this time, most of the chairs had toppled over, yet the Doctors remained fixed in them. It was impossible to tell if they were shouting or crying, their faces were so grey and wizened. Around their heads where the wires went in, the bandages were red with blood.

Ferren felt no pity. "Good riddance to *them!*" he cried.

But now a new development was taking place in the sky. Miriael was looking up, and Ferren followed the line of her gaze. The great

218

archangel she'd called Uriel hovered directly above the Humen army—or what was left of it. He raised his sword and spoke in a voice of thunder.

"Humen of the Bankstown Camp! I find you in violation of all ethical principles! Unworthy of existence! I destroy you as I destroy your psychic reserves! *Ad nihilum! Judicavi!*"

Ferren didn't understand what was happening, but he heard Miriael's gasp of indrawn breath.

"What?" he asked.

But the angel had already dropped down below the level of the bunker's roof, stooping low and turning to the People within.

"Seal up our shelter!" she shouted. "This will be the worst! Block every crack and cranny!"

The globe of the great archangel descended lower over the centre of the Humen army. Some particular target on the ground? But Ferren couldn't see what it was.

"Shut the entrance!" Miriael shouted back up at him.

He ducked down and slid the sheet of corrugated iron closed.

14

Inside, everyone was already at work sealing up the bunker. There were many cracks and crannies under the roof, but all of them small. Ferren saw how the People were scooping up sunflower-petal sludge from the floor, then pressing and squashing it into the gaps.

"Help needed here!" Zonda called out in the dim light.

Miriael swept across in response, and Ferren followed. Zonda pointed to all the cracks in the space alongside her. Miriael and Ferren took up position and began filling in cracks.

"What's this worst going to happen?" Zonda asked, without pausing for a moment in her work.

Miriael also kept working as she answered. "Uriel will detonate the Humen psychic reserves. They store them in great glass vessels."

Ferren had been listening. "Sphere-shape things?" he asked.

"Yes. You saw them in the camp?"

"And travelling with the army."

"I think I saw them too," Zonda put in. "In the middle of their army."

"Normally we'd never get close to them," said Miriael. "Too well protected."

With the cracks filled in, the bunker was in near-total darkness. The last remaining light came from a crack in front of Ferren. He plugged it shut with a final handful of sludge—

KRRRUMMMFFF!!!

The floor under their feet shuddered with the force of a dull explosion. An ear-splitting roar passed overhead, and bits of soil and grit cascaded from the roof. Many of the People cried out in the darkness. Ferren staggered and clutched at the side wall before him.

"Into the middle!" Miriael shouted. "Safest place! More to come!"

KRRRUMMMFFF!!! KRRRUMMMFFF!!!

Ferren joined the huddle of bodies around the central pier. As explosion followed explosion, they held on to one another for balance and comfort. The whole bunker seemed to heave and pitch like a boat on the sea. Creaking and scraping noises came from the roof.

KRRRUMMMFFF!!! KRRRUMMMFFF!!! KRRRUMMMFFF!!!

Coloured light flashed in where one plug in a crack had been shaken loose. Strange violent whirling light—but only for a moment. Then someone dashed across and squashed the sludge back in again.

KRRRUMMFF-UMMFF-UMMFF!!!

Children were wailing, mothers trying to soothe them. How many more explosions still to survive? Ferren thought back to the Humen army stretching out along the overbridge. There must have been many glass vessels in that endless line...

KRRRUMMMFFF!!!

KRRRUMMMFFF!!!

FARRRROOOMMMMM!!!

The bunker was pummelled on all sides as if by giant fists. The wailing of the children intensified, the adults were at breaking point. Then a voice called out—Zonda's voice.

"Wait! I know! I'll show you! Let me find... Here it is!"

There was a loud click. Three yards to Ferren's right, a jet of flame shot vertically in the air. Zonda had ignited the cigarette lighter.

"Our Light in the Darkness!" she cried. "See our Light in the Darkness!"

Everyone hushed and gazed in awe. The lighter flame meant much more than illumination; it meant the Ancestors, it meant the Good Times, and now it meant the powers they'd inherited in themselves.

Zonda kept the flame burning for a while—then the lighter grew too hot to handle. She dropped it with an "Ow!" and rubbed her fingers. But there had been no more explosions while she held it aloft, and there were no more explosions afterwards. The roof hadn't blown off, the central pier hadn't collapsed, the tiled floor hadn't disintegrated.

"I think we've survived," said Miriael.

15

The People could hardly believe it was over. They waited for the next explosion, but none came. Instead, they heard a soft swishing sound like rain pattering down upon the roof of the bunker.

"What's that sound?" asked Ferren. "Can we look out now?"

"Not yet," Miriael answered. "Give it time to settle."

"What?"

"Everything. Everything for miles and miles around. Let's all sit, and I'll explain."

The People rearranged themselves on the floor. They couldn't see the angel in the dark, but they turned their faces to her voice.

"The world as you knew it has gone," she told them. "Those explosions pulverised every solid thing into particles. Tiny particles of matter all mixed together in the air. What you're hearing is the sound as the particles condense and drift back down again."

Nobody really understood. "What about the Home Ground?" Zonda asked.

"It's not there anymore."

"Where's it gone?"

"Pulverised by the explosions, as I told you. All your walls and bits of ruin have been destroyed. When the silt settles, it'll cover what used to be your Home Ground under a layer of sediment."

The People were stunned. There were moans and groans and grizzles.

"No more Dwelling Place!"

"No more lizard pens!"

"No High Hedge! No Front Gardens! No Mushroom Beds!"

"Why did we want to survive?"

The old cringing tone was returning. Ferren recognised some of the grizzlers by their voices.

"Shut up Tuller!" he shouted. "Shut up Jossock! Shut up Lumb!"

Zonda weighed in too. "You great lugs! We oughter think ourselves lucky!"

"Very lucky," said Miriael. "And you've become new people, not like the way you were. Now you have the chance to make a new Home Ground, better than the old. You're makers and builders, remember."

The People considered. Their mood was still uncertain: not enthusiastic, but not hopeless either.

For a long while they sat waiting and thinking. The interior of the bunker grew hot and stuffy, and the smell of fermented sunflower petals grew more and more potent until they were almost dizzy with the fumes.

At last Miriael spoke up again. "It should be safe to open some of the cracks now. Though I doubt you'll see anything much."

The People jumped up at once, Ferren included. He went across to the cracks he'd previously blocked, and unpicked one of the plugs. Outside the bunker, the world had turned to a dim browny-grey miasma. It might have been murk or mud or anything—but it blanked out his view completely.

There were similar disappointed reactions from all sides. As the People unblocked more and more cracks, a hint of light filtered into the interior, yet no one could see through the miasma. They turned to Miriael.

"Yes, you'll have to wait till it clears," she told them. "It'll take several hours yet."

"Hours!"

She nodded. "I suggest we all get some rest. It'll be dark before it clears. Let's sleep through the night, then go outside tomorrow morning."

The mention of sleep reminded the People of how tired they were.

The yawns spread like wildfire. In a matter of minutes, everyone had settled down for sleep.

16

A s soon as daylight arrived, the People crowded around the entrance of the bunker. Ferren attempted to slide back the sheet of corrugated iron on his own, but it was weighed down with sediment. It took half a dozen pairs of hands pushing together to heave it open.

They came forth then and stood blinking in the light. The sun shone, yet there was also a fine mist in the air. Ferren felt a tingle of moisture on the skin of his face, mild and fresh and invigorating. He filled his lungs and surveyed the new landscape spread out before him.

It might have been the very first morning of the Earth. Over the Home Ground and the Plain lay a soft brown cover of soil. Where the battle had been, there were no visible wrecked machines, charred bodies or burnt grass. Instead, he saw a great many mounds and small moulded hills, everything smoothed over and made gentle. Scattered clumps of ruins such as Beaumont Street had also gone, flattened and buried like the Home Ground itself.

The Creek remained, but not as it had been before. Now it flowed in a very different course through pools and tiny waterfalls. Ferren traced its meanders far across the Plain to where it joined up with other streams.

"Yip-a-dooley!" he yelled. "It's a whole new world!"

But nobody responded—and when he turned around he saw why. They were all staring in the opposite direction, and there was wonder and delight on every face. Pure prismatic bands of colour soared in a great arc across the sky—a rainbow! Red, orange, yellow, green, blue, violet!

He felt like crying; no sight had ever seemed so glorious. After all the terrible burning lights of the battle, this seemed like a message of peace. He gazed and gazed, lost in a dream.

He didn't move to join Miriael's audience when she began to address the People, but he could hear her words from a distance.

"Look at this new soil," she told them. "So fertile! So easy to dig and sow! You'll be able to grow every kind of plant when you create fresh fields. Bigger and better fields than ever before."

"What will we grow them from?" somebody asked.

"From seeds and roots. Your old plants are right here under the soil, you just have to dig them out. In a way, this is the best thing that could have happened. You can make a complete new start."

"We still have to eat in the meanwhile," one grumbling voice objected. "What are we supposed to—"

Another voice cut in over the objection. "Our provisions in the Store, of course! Didn't you hear her? Everything's here, we just have to dig it out."

"Let's begin!" cried someone else.

They set to work with a will, delving into the loose soil with their bare hands. Ferren grinned as he watched, but didn't join in. Somehow he knew this wasn't his future...

He wandered off, still thinking. He was glad to be accepted once more by his tribe, yet he couldn't go back to being the boy who'd worked with Shuff in the Blackberry Patch. He had seen too much and done too much to live that life again. Whatever turn his future took, it would have to be *new*—even newer than creating a new Home Ground.

His wandering brought him to a bend of the Creek's changed course. He sat by the water and let the memories drift through his mind. The Humen camp...the mechanical monster...the overbridge...his sister Shanna...

"*Here* you are!" cried Zonda, breaking in on his reverie. She came down the slope of soft brown earth behind him. "What're you doing?"

"Nothing."

"You're weird." She sniffed. "The angel wants to talk to you about something. She was wondering where you'd got to."

"Right." Ferren rose at once to his feet.

Zonda folded her arms and watched him. "You really think you have a connection with her, don't you?"

He didn't answer. He was sure Zonda's notion of "a connection" didn't match the way he felt about Miriael.

Zonda shrugged. "Maybe you do. She's all right."

Ferren passed her by as he walked up the mound heading back.

"You're all right too," Zonda added. "Except you have weird ideas about who's beautiful."

17

Miriael wanted to hear the full detail of Ferren's experiences in the Humen camp and with the Humen army. Then she called the People together for an important announcement.

"Makers and builders!" she addressed them. "Yesterday you built a bunker so strong it protected us through a battle between Heaven and Earth. Today you're starting to build yourselves a new Home Ground. You're not little, weak and small anymore!"

She gestured towards Ferren. "I've been talking to your tribe member here about what he saw in the Humen camp. You heard him say it before—how they use your body parts for their Plasmatics and your minds and memories for their Hypers. In their eyes, you're nothing more than raw material.

"But there's another way of looking at it. You see, the only life they have is what they steal from you. In themselves, they're nothing more than parasitical imitations. Artificial bodies, no minds or memories of their own! They depend on you for their existence. And that makes you very very very important!"

She paused to let the idea sink in, then went on. "Yes, you are the real original human beings, like the beings you call your Ancestors. The Earth belongs to you, not the Humen. And you can take it back by not letting them steal your bodies and minds."

"No more military service!" Meggen called out.

"No more Selectors!" cried somebody else.

"But..." Miriael raised a hand. "But you can't stop them on your own. There are many other Residual tribes also giving up victims for military service. And what if the Humen sent a great army to collect *all* of the People for military service?"

"They've been defeated," said Zonda.

"Temporarily. They've lost one huge army and some of their Doctors.

Maybe all of the Bankstown Doctors. But they still have the Bankstown Camp with its impregnable defences. And there are plenty of other camps on this continent, and other Doctors ready to step in. More camps and Doctors on other continents too. They *will* rebuild their forces, so you have to be ready for them."

"All the tribes together!" Ferren pumped his fist in the air. "Unite against the Humen!"

"That's the way to do it," Miriael agreed. "The only way to do it. Send a representative from the People to go round from tribe to tribe. They probably know as little about each other as you used to know about them. I'm sure they all think they're allies with the Humen too. You'll need a representative who can explain about military service and how the Humen only exist because of what they steal from you."

"I'll do it," said Ferren at once.

"Good." Miriael smiled. "You *are* the most suitable, since you can describe it by your own experience."

"And I'll tell them the Humen can be beaten because I've just seen their army annihilated."

"Exactly. Persuade them to drop the idea of the Humen as allies. Inspire them to join up with all the other tribes instead."

"A Residual alliance." Ferren couldn't quite meet the angel's eyes. "Will you come with me?"

Miriael smiled again. "Yes, I can come with you. As long as you need my help, anyway. I've seen other Residual settlements from the air, so I'll be able to locate some of them for a start." She turned to the People at large. "That is, if everyone approves?"

They not only approved, but whooped and cheered. Then Shuff started up a new version of their old chant—

"We are *not* little, weak and small"

—and Zonda produced a new second line—

"Because we matter *most of all!*"

Everyone laughed and joined in, repeating the new lines over and over.

"Amen!" they cried. "Amen! Amen! Amen!"

18

All day, the People dug and excavated different parts of the Home Ground. They unearthed the Store, the Blackberry Patch, the Mushroom Beds and the buried vegetables in the Driveway and Front Garden. It was like finding buried treasure.

Naturally, Urlish's fire had been smothered under the sediment, but they used twigs and stems recovered from the Blackberry Patch as material for a new one. Then Zonda showed Urlish how to hold the cigarette lighter, press her finger on the trigger and shoot out a jet of flame. The old woman was wildly excited when she applied the flame and started a new fire burning.

"We'll have a real feast cooked up tonight!" said Zonda, clapping her hands.

One buried item was less a cause for celebration. When they dug down into Neath's counting-corner, they uncovered the body of their old leader, laid out exactly as Zonda had left him. She sniffled and rubbed at her eyes.

"No, don't dig him out," she said. "We'll bury him here. He'd like to lie in his favourite place."

It was an unusual burial, and the burial service that Zonda conducted was even more unusual. She brought out the Fly Spray Can, brushed loose dirt from the body and sprayed him from head to toe with a fine mist.

"For my father, our leader!" she proclaimed. "The perfume of the Ancestors!"

The People prayed the traditional prayers, then piled earth on top of the body. A low rounded hummock marked the site of Neath's grave.

"Who's going to tell us what to do now?" Cress wondered.

"Yes, we'll need a new leader," said Hodd.

"Let it be decided tonight," Miriacl proposed. "Before the feast."

The cooks began preparations for the feast soon afterwards, and the cooking went on all afternoon. It was a magnificent spread, with two different kinds of soup, four different kinds of stew and an assortment of special delicacies. Everyone's mouth watered, and they could hardly wait to begin eating.

But Miriael held up a hand. "First you have to choose your new leader."

The People tore their eyes away from the bowls of food.

"Neath never named anyone to follow him," said Unce, knitting his brows.

"It was going to be his daughter's mate," said Stessa. "But he never told us who."

Zonda snorted in disgust. "Phuh! *Mate!*"

"It has to be a male, does it?" asked Miriael.

"Always has been," said Jossock.

Ferren caught Miriael's eye. "Doesn't *have* to be, though," he said. "And we're making a new start, aren't we? We're not like the way we were."

The People thought it over. "I suppose…" "Could be…" "She's the obvious choice…"

Zonda jumped up. "Of course I'm the obvious choice! *I'll* tell you what to do!"

The idea caught on in a flash. "Yes!" "Zonda!" "She can lead!" "She'll tell us what to do!"

"Settled!" cried Zonda. "I'll be the new leader! And right now, the first thing to do is…start eating!"

She dived into the feast, and everyone dived in after her.

19

Two days later, Ferren and Miriael set off to look for other tribes. Ferren carried a pack of dried food on his back for the first part of the journey. With her wings, Miriael couldn't fit anything on her back, and she still had to carry her chain. But she was growing stronger every day.

Zonda and the People accompanied them as far as the Creek in its new watercourse. Urlish held the cigarette lighter aloft, Tunks the fly spray can, Shuff the alarm clock and Zonda the Baby Jane doll. They exchanged final farewells before Ferren and Miriael went on alone.

"Good luck!" they shouted.

"Find many tribes!"

"The Residual alliance!"

Then Zonda lifted the Baby Jane high in the air and tilted her sharply backwards.

"MAMAAA! MAMAAAAAAAA!!!"

Ferren and Miriael waved over their shoulders, and the shouts continued until they passed over a rise in the ground. Then the People and Home Ground vanished from view.

"This could be the beginning of a whole new chapter in the history of the world," Miriael reflected aloud.

"What we're about? Or what they're about?"

"Both."

For a long time they walked on in silence, each lost in their own thoughts. Ferren was pondering a particular obligation…something he ought to do, though he didn't want to do it…

"Ah," said Miriael suddenly, pointing ahead. "Do you see greenery there? I believe we're coming out beyond the battlefield. Back to the ordinary landscape."

Ferren followed her finger and saw what looked like a tree-covered hill in the distance. He stopped abruptly.

"I have to tell you something," he began.

"Oh?"

"I thought you'd left them for me. I mean, as reminders. Because you'd gone back up to Heaven. Except you hadn't. But I didn't know, I *couldn't* know…"

His tongue was tying itself in knots, and his explanation ground to a a halt. He gave up, and instead unrolled the top of the cloth around his waist and drew forth the two white feathers. He held them out to her, but she only studied them.

"They're mine, are they?"

He nodded. "I'm giving them back."

"Where did you find them?"

"In the grass. You know, where you were lying…where we used to talk."

"I must've lost them when a Selector trampled on my wing."

"I thought they were reminders. You know, so I'd think of you when you were gone. But you never *meant* to leave them."

"No, I didn't." The angel smiled. "I'd still like you to have them, though."

"But…but…they can't be reminders. You're still here."

"Not reminders, no. They can be a token."

"A token?"

"Of the bond between us. The first angel and first Residual ever to be friends."

She strode forward again, and Ferren went with her. His heart was too full to speak.

Forever and ever, he vowed. *I'll be your true loyal friend as long as I live.*

AND THE STORY CONTINUES ...

What kind of being will gain control of the Bankstown Camp now that the ten Doctors have been annihilated?

How will Ferren react when Miriael has the chance to go back up into Heaven?

What's been happening to Ferren's sister Shanna since she was taken for military service?

Follow the further adventures of Ferren and Miriael as other tribes join up to the Residual Alliance—and a terrible force assumes leadership of the Humen, with a new strategy and secret weapons to destroy Heaven forever. A great confrontation approaches, and the stakes are rising. Ferren will have to play a crucial role and take part in the war himself...

Stunning shocks and developments in FERREN AND THE DOOMS-DAY MISSION, the second book of The Ferren Trilogy, appearing soon from IFWG Publishing!

Read a sample chapter at www.ferren.com.au under Ferren and the Angel > Sequels or at www.richardharland.au, under Ferren books > Ferren and the Doomsday Mission.

APPENDIX 1
TIMELINE OF THE WAR

1961	USSR sends first human into space
1969	US lands first human on the moon
2028	The Venables-Hirsch experiment
2031	Inauguration of Project Olympus
2033	The Trespass upon Heaven
	The Devastation at Mount Horeb
	Battle of the Plenoma
2034	Start of the Age of the Undead
2038	The Depopulation of New York
2075	Fallen Angels allowed back into Heaven
2079	Withdrawal of the Supreme Trinity
2086	Formation of the United Earth Movement
2088	The First United Earth Congress
2089–94	The False Truce
2094	The Great Collapse
2094–2112	Period of the Long Famine
2223	First appearance of Plasmatics
2228	First appearance of Hypers
2262–91	Construction of the Endless Wall
2305	The Declaration of Material Being
2436–40	The Weather Wars
2440–2543	The Hundred Years' Blizzard
2742	Humen colonies set up in the Burning Continents
2755	Extinction of the colonies
2904	Foundation of the South American Empire
2912	First appearance of force-fields and boost-beams
2927–45	The Wars of Doctor Mengis and Doctor Genelle
2943–45	The Campaign of the Five Zones
3003–3022	Rise of the Bankstown Doctors

APPENDIX 2
ANGELOLOGY: TRADITIONAL FACTS ABOUT THE FIGURES IN THIS BOOK

There are seven distinct Heavens in the standard concept of Heaven; in this book, seven distinct Altitudes of the one Heaven. Angels are divided into nine Orders, from Seraphim on the highest level, through Cherubim, Ofanim, Dominions, Virtues, Powers, Principlaities down to (mere) Archangels, then (mere) Angels on the lowest level. But 'archangels' can also apply to the very highest rulers in Heaven, while 'angels' can also apply to beings of all Orders. In this book, angels of the lowest level have been renamed Junior Angels.

Adonael: an archangel who has a particular power to counteract disease.

Asiel: a transcriber of books; therefore suited to the role of Angel of the Scripts.

Bethor: one of seven high angels who share in ruling the 196 provinces of Heaven.

Cedrion: an important angel who rules in the south.

Chrymos: a minor angel of the fifth hour of night.

Eiael: an angel with a reputation as a teacher, especially of esoteric arts and sciences.

Gethel: an angel set over hidden things; therefore suited to the role of Angel of Hidden Lore.

Harahel: according to the cabbala, Harahel is an angel in charge of libraries.

Metatron: among other roles, Metatron is the Heavenly scribe and keeper of records. It is often said that he is the tallest of all angels.

Miriael: in traditional angelology, Miriael is a minor angel who is also a warrior.

Nathanael: a lord of the element of fire, and one of the twelve Angels of Vengeance.

Neriah: a minor angel whose name signifies 'lamp of God'.

Propator: a powerful Aeon in charge of myriads of lesser angels.

Uriel: an Angel of the Presence who is one of the four greatest arch-angels along with Michael, Gabriel and Raphael. He is also commonly included among the Angels of Destruction. When serving as an agent of divine punishment, he carries the fiery Sword of God (here re-christened as the Sword of Judgement). He controls the south and is associated with thunder and lightning.

Caveat: there are endless variations in Christian sources (especially the Apocrypha), Jewish sources (especially the Kabbalah) and Islamic sources (especially Sufi texts). The facts I've given are traditional but not absolute! Other versions also exist ...

ABOUT THE AUTHOR

Richard was born in Yorkshire, England, then migrated to Australia at the age of twenty-one. He was always trying to write, but could never finish any of the stories he began. Instead he drifted around as a singer, songwriter and poet, then became a university tutor and finally a university lecturer. But after twenty-five years of writer's block, he finally finished his cult novel, *The Vicar of Morbing Vyle*, and resigned a seniour lectureship to follow his original dream.

Since then, he's produced seventeen books of fantasy, SF and horror/supernatural, ranging from Children's to Young Adult to Adult. Best known internationally for *Worldshaker* and its sequels, he has won many awards in France and Australia.

He lives with partner Aileen near Wollongong, south of Sydney, between golden beaches and a green escarpment. His favourite relaxation is walking Yogi the Labrador while listening to music—when he's not writing like a mad workaholic, catching up on those wasted twenty-five years…

His author website is at www.richardharland.au and his Ferren Trilogy website is at www.ferren.com.au.

For all aspiring writers, he's put up a comprehensive 145-page guide to all aspects of writing fantasy fiction at www.writingtips.com.au.

OTHER BOOKS BY RICHARD HARLAND

For YA Readers

Worldshaker
Liberator
Song of the Slums

For Younger Readers

the Wolf Kingdom quartet:
      Escape!
      Under Siege
      Race to the Ruins
      The Heavy Crown
Sassycat
Walter Wants to Be a Werewolf

For Adult Readers

The Vicar of Morbing Vyle
The Black Crusade
the Eddon and Vail series:
      The Dark Edge
      Taken By Force
      Hidden From View